The Hermits

Charles Kingsley

INTRODUCTION

St. Paphnutius used to tell a story which may serve as a fit introduction to this book. It contains a miniature sketch, not only of the social state of Egypt, but of the whole Roman Empire, and of the causes which led to the famous monastic movement in the beginning of the fifth century after Christ.

Now Paphnutius was a wise and holy hermit, the Father, Abba, or Abbot of many monks; and after he had trained himself in the desert with all severity for many years, he besought God to show him which of His saints he was like.

And it was said to him, "Thou art like a certain flute-player in the city."

Then Paphnutius took his staff, and went into the city, and found that flute-player. But he confessed that he was a drunkard and a profligate, and had till lately got his living by robbery, and recollected not having ever done one good deed. Nevertheless, when Paphnutius questioned him more closely, he said that he recollected once having found a holy maiden beset by robbers, and having delivered her, and brought her safe to town. And when Paphnutius questioned him more closely still, he said he recollected having done another deed. When he was a robber, he met once in the desert a beautiful woman; and she prayed him to do her no harm, but to take her away with him as a slave, whither he would; for, said she, "I am fleeing from the apparitors and the Governor's curials for the last two years. My husband has been imprisoned for 300 pieces of gold, which he owes as arrears of taxes; and has been often hung up, and often scourged; and my three dear boys have been taken from me; and I am wandering from place to place, and have been often caught myself and continually scourged; and now I have been in the desert three days without food."

And when the robber heard that, he took pity on her, and took her to his cave, and gave her 300 pieces of gold, and went with her to the city, and set her husband and her boys free.

Then Paphnutius said, "I never did a deed like that: and yet I have not passed my life in ease and idleness. But now, my son, since God hath had such care of thee, have a care for thine own self."

And when the musician heard that, he threw away the flutes which he held in his hand, and went with Paphnutius into the desert, and passed his life in hymns and prayer, changing his earthly music into heavenly; and after three years he went to heaven, and was at rest among the choirs of angels, and the ranks of the just.

This story, as I said, is a miniature sketch of the state of the whole Roman Empire, and of the causes why men fled from it into the desert. Christianity had reformed the morals of individuals; it had not reformed the Empire itself. That had sunk into a state only to be compared with the worst despotisms of the East. The Emperors, whether or not they called themselves Christian, like Constantine, knew no law save the basest maxims of the heathen world. Several of them were barbarians who had risen from the lowest rank merely by military prowess; and who, half maddened by their sudden elevation, added to their native ignorance and brutality the pride, cunning, and cruelty of an Eastern Sultan. Rival Emperors, or Generals who aspired to be Emperors, devastated the world from Egypt to Britain by sanguinary civil wars. The government of the provinces had become altogether military. Torture was employed, not merely, as of old, against slaves, but against all ranks, without distinction. The people were exhausted by compulsory taxes, to be spent in wars which did not concern them, or in Court luxury in which they had no share. In the municipal towns, liberty and justice were dead. The curials, who answered somewhat to our aldermen, and who were responsible for the payment of the public moneys, tried their best to escape the unpopular office, and, when compelled to serve, wrung the money in self-defence out of the poorer inhabitants by every kind of tyranny. The land was tilled either by oppressed and miserable peasants, or by gangs of slaves, in comparison with whose lot that even of the American negro was light. The great were served in their own households by crowds of slaves, better fed, doubtless, but even more miserable and degraded, than those who tilled the estates. Private profligacy among all ranks was such as cannot be described in these or in any modern pages. The regular clergy of the cities, though not of profligate lives, and for the most part, in accordance with public opinion, unmarried, were able to make no stand against the general corruption of the age, because- -at least if we are to trust such writers as Jerome and Chrysostom— they were giving themselves up to ambition and avarice, vanity and luxury, intrigue and party spirit, and had become the flatterers of fine ladies, "silly women laden with sins, ever learning, and never coming to the knowledge of the truth." Such a state of things not only drove poor creatures into the desert, like that fair woman whom the robber met, but it raised up bands of robbers over the whole of Europe, Africa, and the East,—men who, like Robin Hood and the outlaws of the Middle Age, getting no justice from man, broke loose from society, and while they plundered their oppressors, kept up some sort of rude justice and humanity among themselves. Many, too, fled, and became robbers, to escape the merciless conscription which carried off from every province the flower of the young men, to shed their blood on foreign battle-fields. In time, too, many of these conscripts became monks, and the great monasteries of Scetis and Nitria were hunted over again and again by officers and soldiers from the neighbouring city of Alexandria in search of young men who had entered the "spiritual warfare" to escape the earthly one. And as a background to all this seething heap of decay, misrule, and misery, hung the black cloud of the barbarians, the Teutonic tribes from whom we derive the best part of our blood, ever coming nearer and nearer, waxing stronger and stronger, learning discipline and civilization by serving in the Roman armies, alternately the allies and the enemies of the Emperors, rising, some of them, to the highest offices of State, and destined, so the wisest Romans saw all the more clearly as the years rolled on, to be soon the conquerors of the Caesars, and the masters of the Western world.

No wonder if that, in such a state of things, there arose such violent contrasts to the general weakness, such eccentric protests against the general wickedness, as may be seen in the figure of Abbot Paphnutius, when compared either with the poor man tortured in prison for his arrears of taxes, or with the Governor and the officials who tortured him. No wonder if, in such a state of things, the minds of men were stirred by a passion akin to despair, which ended in a new and grand form of suicide. It would have ended often, but for Christianity, in such an actual despair as that which had led in past ages more than one noble Roman to slay himself, when he lost all hope for the Republic. Christianity taught those who despaired of society, of the world—in one word, of the Roman Empire, and all that it had done for men—to hope at least for a kingdom of God after death. It taught those who, had they been heathens and brave enough, would have slain themselves to escape out of a world which was no place for honest men, that the body must be kept alive, if for no other reason, at least for the sake of the immortal soul, doomed, according to its works, to endless bliss or endless torment.

But that the world—such, at least, as they saw it then—was doomed, Scripture and their own reason taught them. They did not merely believe, but see, in the misery and confusion, the desolation and degradation around them, that all that was in the world, the lust of the flesh, the lust of the eye, and the pride of life, was not of the Father, but of the world; that the world was passing away, and the lust thereof, and that only he who did the will of God could abide for ever. They did not merely believe, but saw, that the wrath of God was revealed from heaven against all unrighteousness of men; and that the world in general—above all, its kings and rulers, the rich and luxurious—were treasuring up for themselves wrath, tribulation, and anguish, against a day of wrath and revelation of the righteous judgment of God, who would render to every man according to his works.

That they were correct in their judgment of the world about them, contemporary history proves abundantly. That they were correct, likewise, in believing that some fearful judgment was about to fall on man, is proved by the fact that it did fall; that the first half of the fifth century saw, not only the sack of Rome, but the conquest and desolation of the greater part of the civilized world, amid bloodshed, misery, and misrule, which seemed to turn Europe into a chaos,—which would have turned it into a chaos, had there not been a few men left who still felt it possible and necessary to believe in God and to work righteousness.

Under these terrible forebodings, men began to flee from a doomed world, and try to be alone with God, if by any means they might save each man his own soul in that dread day.

Others, not Christians, had done the same before them. Among all the Eastern nations men had appeared, from time to time, to whom the things seen were but a passing phantom, the things unseen the only true and eternal realities; who, tormented alike by the awfulness of the infinite unknown, and by the petty cares and low passions of the finite mortal life which they knew but too well, had determined to renounce the latter, that they might give themselves up to solving the riddle of the former; and be at peace; and free, at least, from the tyranny of their own selves. Eight hundred years before St. Antony fled into the desert, that young Hindoo rajah, whom men call Buddha now, had fled into the forest, leaving wives and kingdom, to find rest for his soul. He denounced caste; he preached poverty, asceticism, self-annihilation. He founded a

4

religion, like that of the old hermits, democratic and ascetic, with its convents, saint- worships, pilgrimages, miraculous relics, rosaries, and much more, which strangely anticipates the monastic religion; and his followers, to this day, are more numerous than those of any other creed.

Brahmins, too, had given themselves up to penance and mortification till they believed themselves able, like Kehama, to have gained by self-torture the right to command, not nature merely, but the gods themselves. Among the Jews the Essenes by the Dead Sea, and the Therapeutae in Egypt, had formed ascetic communities, the former more "practical," the latter more "contemplative:" but both alike agreed in the purpose of escaping from the world into a life of poverty and simplicity, piety and virtue; and among the countless philosophic sects of Asia, known to ecclesiastical writers as "heretics," more than one had professed, and doubtless often practised, the same abstraction from the world, the same contempt of the flesh. The very Neo-Platonists of Alexandria, while they derided the Christian asceticism, found themselves forced to affect, like the hapless Hypatia, a sentimental and pharisaic asceticism of their own. This phase of sight and feeling, so strange to us now, was common, nay, primaeval, among the Easterns. The day was come when it should pass from the East into the West. And Egypt, "the mother of wonders;" the parent of so much civilization and philosophy both Greek and Roman; the half-way resting-place through which not merely the merchandise, but the wisdom of the East had for centuries passed into the Roman Empire; a land more ill-governed, too, and more miserable, in spite of its fertility, because more defenceless and effeminate, than most other Roman possessions— was the country in which naturally, and as it were of hereditary right, such a movement would first appear.

Accordingly it was discovered, about the end of the fourth century, that the mountains and deserts of Egypt were full of Christian men who had fled out of the dying world, in the hope of attaining everlasting life. Wonderful things were told of their courage, their abstinence, their miracles: and of their virtues also; of their purity, their humility, their helpfulness, and charity to each other and to all. They called each other, it was said, brothers; and they lived up to that sacred name, forgotten, if ever known, by the rest of the Roman Empire. Like the Apostolic Christians in the first fervour of their conversion, they had all things in common; they lived at peace with each other, under a mild and charitable rule; and kept literally those commands of Christ which all the rest of the world explained away to nothing.

The news spread. It chimed in with all that was best, as well as with much that was questionable, in the public mind. That men could be brothers; that they could live without the tawdry luxury, the tasteless and often brutal amusements, the low sensuality, the base intrigue, the bloody warfare, which was the accepted lot of the many; that they could find time to look stedfastly at heaven and hell as awful realities, which must be faced some day, which had best be faced at once; this, just as much as curiosity about their alleged miracles, and the selfish longing to rival them in superhuman powers, led many of the most virtuous and the most learned men of the time to visit them, and ascertain the truth. Jerome, Ruffinus, Evagrius, Sulpicius Severus, went to see them, undergoing on the way the severest toils and dangers, and brought back reports of mingled truth and falsehood, specimens of which will be seen in these pages. Travelling in those days was a labour, if not of necessity, then surely of love. Palladius, for instance, found it impossible to visit the Upper Thebaid, and Syene, and that "infinite multitude of monks, whose fashions of life no one would believe, for they surpass human life; who to this day raise the dead, and walk upon the waters, like Peter; and whatsoever the Saviour did by the holy Apostles, He does now by them. But because it would be very dangerous if we went beyond Lyco" (Lycopolis?), on account of the inroad of robbers, he "could not see those saints."

The holy men and women of whom he wrote, he says, he did not see without extreme toil; and seven times he and his companions were nearly lost. Once they walked through the desert five days and nights, and were almost worn out by hunger and thirst. Again, they fell on rough marshes, where the sedge pierced their feet, and caused intolerable pain, while they were almost killed with the cold. Another time, they stuck in the mud up to their waists, and cried with David, "I am come into deep mire, where no ground is." Another time, they waded for four days through the flood of the Nile by paths almost swept away. Another time they met robbers on the seashore, coming to Diolcos, and were chased by them for ten miles. Another time they were all but upset and drowned in crossing the Nile. Another time, in the marshes of Mareotis, "where paper grows," they were cast on a little desert island, and remained three days and nights in the open air, amid great cold and showers, for it was the season of Epiphany. The eighth peril, he says, is hardly worth mentioning—but once, when they went to Nitria, they came on a great hollow, in which many crocodiles had remained, when the waters retired from the fields. Three of them lay along the bank; and the monks went up to them, thinking them dead, whereon the crocodiles rushed at them. But when they called loudly on the Lord, "the monsters, as if turned away by an angel," shot themselves into the water; while they ran on to Nitria, meditating on the words of Job, "Seven times shall He deliver thee from trouble; and in the eighth there shall no evil touch thee."

The great St. Athanasius, fleeing from persecution, had taken refuge among these monks. He carried the report of their virtues to Treves in Gaul, and wrote a life of St. Antony, the perusal of which was a main agent in the conversion of St. Augustine. Hilarion (a remarkable personage, whose history will be told hereafter) carried their report and their example likewise into Palestine; and from that time Judaea, desolate and seemingly accursed by the sin of the Jewish people, became once more the Holy Land; the place of pilgrimage; whose ruins, whose very soil, were kept sacred by hermits, the guardians of the footsteps of Christ.

In Rome itself the news produced an effect which, to the thoughtful mind, is altogether tragical in its nobleness. The Roman aristocracy was deprived of all political power; it had been decimated, too, with horrible cruelty only one generation before, {12} by Valentinian and his satellites, on the charges of profligacy, treason, and magic. Mere rich men, they still lingered on, in idleness and luxury, without art, science, true civilization of any kind; followed by long trains of slaves; punishing a servant with three hundred stripes if he were too long in bringing hot water; weighing the fish, or birds, or dormice put on their tables, while secretaries stood by, with tablets to record all; hating learning as they hated poison; indulging at the baths in conduct which had best be left undescribed; and "complaining that they were not born among the Cimmerians, if amid their golden fans a fly should perch upon the silken fringes, or a slender ray of the sun should pierce through the awning;" while, if they "go any distance to see their estates in the country, or to hunt at a meeting collected for their amusement by others, they think that they have equalled the marches of Alexander or of Caesar."

On the wives, widows, and daughters of men of this stamp—and not half their effeminacy and baseness, as the honest rough old soldier

Ammianus Marcellinus describes it, has been told here—the news brought from Egypt worked with wondrous potency.

Women of the highest rank awoke suddenly to the discovery that life was given them for nobler purposes than that of frivolous enjoyment and tawdry vanity. Despising themselves; despising the husbands to whom they had been wedded in loveless marriages de convenance, whose infidelities they had too often to endure: they, too, fled from a world which had sated and sickened them. They freed their slaves; they gave away their wealth to found hospitals and to feed the poor; and in voluntary poverty and mean garments they followed such men as Jerome and Ruffinus across the seas, to visit the new found saints of the Egyptian desert, and to end their days, in some cases, in doleful monasteries in Palestine. The lives of such women as those of the Anician house; the lives of Marcella and Furia, of Paula, of the Melanias, and the rest, it is not my task to write. They must be told by a woman, not by a man. We may blame those ladies, if we will, for neglecting their duties. We may sneer, if we will, at the weaknesses—the aristocratic pride, the spiritual vanity—which we fancy that we discover. We may lament—and in that we shall not be wrong—the influence which such men as Jerome obtained over them— the example and precursor of so much which has since then been ruinous to family and social life: but we must confess that the fault lay not with the themselves, but with their fathers, husbands, and brothers; we must confess that in these women the spirit of the old Roman matrons, which seemed to have been so long dead, flashed up for one splendid moment, ere it sunk into the darkness of the Middle Age; that in them woman asserted (however strangely and fantastically) her moral equality with man; and that at the very moment when monasticism was consigning her to contempt, almost to abhorrence, as "the noxious animal," the "fragile vessel," the cause of man's fall at first, and of his sin and misery ever since, woman showed the monk (to his naively-confessed surprise), that she could dare, and suffer, and adore as well as he.

But the movement, having once seized the Roman Empire, grew and spread irresistibly. It was accepted, supported, preached, practised, by every great man of the time. Athanasius, Basil, Chrysostom, Gregory of Nazianzen in the East, Jerome, Augustine, Ruffinus, Evagrius, Fulgentius, Sulpicius Severus, Vincent of Lerins, John Cassian, Martin of Tours, Salvian, Caesarius of Arles, were all monks, or as much of monks as their duties would allow them to be. Ambrose of Milan, though no monk himself, was the fervent preacher of, the careful legislator for, monasticism male and female. Throughout the whole Roman Empire, in the course of a century, had spread hermits (or dwellers in the desert), anchorites (retired from the world), or monks (dwellers alone). The three names grew afterwards to designate three different orders of ascetics. The hermits remained through the Middle Ages those who dwelt in deserts; the anchorites, or "ankers" of the English Middle Age, seem generally to have inhabited cells built in, or near, the church walls; the name of "monks" was transferred from those who dwelt alone to those who dwelt in regular communities, under a fixed government. But the three names at first were interchangeable; the three modes of life alternated, often in the same man. The life of all three was the same,—celibacy, poverty, good deeds towards their fellow-men; self-restraint, and sometimes self-torture of every kind, to atone (as far as might be) for the sins committed after baptism: and the mental food of all three was the same likewise; continued meditation upon the vanity of the world, the sinfulness of the flesh, the glories of heaven, and the horrors of hell: but with these the old hermits combined—to do them justice—a personal faith in God, and a personal love for Christ, which those who sneer at them would do well to copy.

Over all Europe, even to Ireland, {15} the same pattern of Christian excellence repeated itself with strange regularity, till it became the only received pattern; and to "enter religion," or "be converted," meant simply to become a monk.

Of the authentic biographies of certain of these men, a few specimens are given in this volume. If they shall seem to any reader uncouth, or even absurd, he must remember that they are the only existing and the generally contemporaneous histories of men who exercised for 1,300 years an enormous influence over the whole of Christendom; who exercise a vast influence over the greater part of it to this day. They are the biographies of men who were regarded, during their lives and after their deaths, as divine and inspired prophets; and who were worshipped with boundless trust and admiration by millions of human beings. Their fame and power were not created by the priesthood. The priesthood rather leant on them, than they on it. They occupied a post analogous to that of the old Jewish prophets; always independent of, sometimes opposed to, the regular clergy; and dependent altogether on public opinion and the suffrage of the multitude. When Christianity, after three centuries of repression and persecution, emerged triumphant as the creed of the whole civilized world, it had become what their lives describe. The model of religious life for the fifth century, it remained a model for succeeding centuries; on the lives of St. Antony and his compeers were founded the whole literature of saintly biographies; the whole popular conception of the universe, and of man's relation to it; the whole science of daemonology, with its peculiar literature, its peculiar system of criminal jurisprudence. And their influence did not cease at the Reformation among Protestant divines. The influence of these Lives of the Hermit Fathers is as much traceable, even to style and language, in "The Pilgrim's Progress" as in the last Papal Allocution. The great hermits of Egypt were not merely the founders of that vast monastic system which influenced the whole politics, and wars, and social life, as well as the whole religion, of the Middle Age; they were a school of philosophers (as they rightly called themselves) who altered the whole current of human thought.

Those who wish for a general notion of the men, and of their time, will find all that they require (set forth from different points of view, though with the same honesty and learning) in Gibbon; in M. de Montalembert's "Moines d'Occident," in Dean Milman's "History of Christianity" and "Latin Christianity," and in Ozanam's "Etudes Germaniques." {17a} But the truest notion of the men is to be got, after all, from the original documents; and especially from that curious collection of them by the Jesuit Rosweyde, commonly known as the "Lives of the Hermit Fathers." {17b}

After an acquaintance of now five-and-twenty years with this wonderful treasury of early Christian mythology, to which all fairy tales are dull and meagre, I am almost inclined to sympathise with M. de Montalembert's questions, — "Who is so ignorant, or so unfortunate, as not to have devoured these tales of the heroic age of monachism? Who has not contemplated, if not with the eyes of faith, at least with the admiration inspired by an incontrollable greatness of soul, the struggles of these athletes of penitence? . . . . Everything is to be found there — variety, pathos, the sublime and simple epic of a race of men, naifs as children, and strong as giants." In whatever else one may differ from M. de Montalembert — and it is always painful to differ from one whose pen has been always the faithful servant of virtue and piety, purity and chivalry, loyalty and liberty, and whose generous appreciation of England and the English is the more honourable to him, by reason of an utter divergence in opinion, which in less wide and noble spirits produces only antipathy — one must at least agree with him in his estimate of the importance of these "Lives of the Fathers," not only to the ecclesiologist, but to the psychologist and the historian. Their influence, subtle, often transformed and modified again and again, but still potent from its very subtleness, is being felt around us in many a puzzle— educational, social, political; and promises to be felt still more during the coming generation; and to have studied thoroughly one of them—say the life of St. Antony by St. Athanasius—is to have had in our hands (whether we knew it or not) the key to many a lock, which just now refuses either to be tampered with or burst open.

I have determined, therefore, to give a few of these lives, translated as literally as possible. Thus the reader will then have no reason to fear a garbled or partial account of personages so difficult to conceive or understand. He will be able to see the men as wholes; to judge (according to his light) of their merits and their defects. The very style of their biographers (which is copied as literally as is compatible with the English tongue) will teach him, if he be wise, somewhat of the temper and habits of thought of the age in which they lived; and one of these original documents, with its honesty, its vivid touches of contemporary manners, its intense earnestness, will give, perhaps, a more true picture of the whole hermit movement than (with all respect, be it said) the most brilliant general panorama.

It is impossible to give in this series all the lives of the early hermits—even of those contained in Rosweyde. This volume will contain, therefore, only the most important and most famous lives of the Egyptian, Syrian, and Persian hermits, followed, perhaps, by a few later biographies from Western Europe, as proofs that the hermit-type, as it spread toward the Atlantic, remained still the same as in the Egyptian desert.

Against one modern mistake the reader must be warned; the theory, namely, that these biographies were written as religious romances; edifying, but not historical; to be admired, but not believed. There is not the slightest evidence that such was the case. The lives of these, and most other saints (certainly those in this volume), were written by men who believed the stories themselves, after such inquiry into the facts as they deemed necessary; who knew that others would believe them; and who intended that they should do so; and the stones were believed accordingly, and taken as matter of fact for the most practical purposes by the whole of Christendom. The forging of miracles, like the forging of charters, for the honour of a particular shrine, or the advantage of a particular monastery, belongs to a much later and much worse age; and, whatsoever we may think of the taste of the authors of these lives, or of their faculty for judging of evidence, we must at least give them credit for being earnest men, incapable of what would have been in their eyes, and ought to be in ours, not merely falsehood, but impiety. Let the reader be sure of this—that these documents would not have exercised their enormous influence on the human mind, had there not been in them, under whatever accidents of credulity, and even absurdity, an element of sincerity, virtue, and nobility.

The Hermits

SAINT ANTONY

The life of Antony, by Athanasius, is perhaps the most important of all these biographies; because first, Antony was generally held to be the first great example and preacher of the hermit life; because next, Athanasius, his biographer, having by his controversial writings established the orthodox faith as it is now held alike by Romanists, Greeks, and Protestants, did, by his publication of the life of Antony, establish the hermit life as the ideal (in his opinion) of Christian excellence; and lastly, because that biography exercised a most potent influence on the conversion of St. Augustine, the greatest thinker (always excepting St. Paul) whom the world had seen since Plato, whom the world was to see again till Lord Bacon; the theologian and philosopher (for he was the latter, as well as the former, in the strictest sense) to whom the world owes, not only the formulizing of the whole scheme of the universe for a thousand years after his death, but Calvinism (wrongly so called) in all its forms, whether held by the Augustinian party in the Church of Rome, or the "Reformed" Churches of Geneva, France, and Scotland.

Whether we have the exact text of the document as Athanasius wrote it to the "Foreign Brethren" — probably the religious folk of Treves- - in the Greek version published by Heschelius in 1611, and in certain earlier Greek texts; whether the Latin translation attributed to Evagrius, which has been well known for centuries past in the Latin Church, be actually his; whether it be exactly that of which St. Jerome speaks, and whether it be exactly that which St. Augustine saw, are questions which it is now impossible to decide. But of the genuineness of the life in its entirety we have no right to doubt, contrary to the verdicts of the most distinguished scholars, whether Protestant or Catholic; and there is fair reason to suppose that the document (allowing for errors and variations of transcribers) which I have tried to translate, is that of which the great St. Augustine speaks in the eighth book of his Confessions.

He tells us that he was reclaimed at last from a profligate life (the thought of honourable marriage seems never to have entered his mind), by meeting, while practising as a rhetorician at Treves, an old African acquaintance, named Potitanius, an officer of rank. What followed no words can express so well as those of the great genius himself.

"When I told him that I was giving much attention to those writings (the Epistles of Paul), we began to talk, and he to tell, of Antony, the monk of Egypt, whose name was then very famous among thy servants: {23} but was unknown to us till that moment. When he discovered that, he spent some time over the subject, detailing his virtues, and wondering at our ignorance. We were astounded at hearing such well-attested marvels of him, so recent and almost contemporaneous, wrought in the right faith of the Catholic Church. We all wondered: we, that they were so great; and he, that we had not heard of them. Thence his discourse ran on to those flocks of hermit-cells, and the morals of thy sweetness, and the fruitful deserts of the wilderness, of which we knew nought. There was a monastery, too, at Milan, full of good brethren, outside the city walls, under the tutelage of Ambrosius, and we knew nothing of it. He went on still speaking, and we listened intently; and it befell that he told us how, I know not when, he and three of his mess companions at Treves, while the emperor was engaged in an afternoon spectacle in the circus, went out for a walk in the gardens round the walls; and as they walked there in pairs, one with him alone, and the two others by themselves, they parted. And those two, straying about, burst into a cottage, where dwelt certain servants of thine, poor in spirit, of such as is the kingdom of heaven; and there found a book, in which was written the life of Antony. One of them began to read it, and to wonder, and to be warned; and, as he read, to think of taking up such a life, and leaving the warfare of this world to serve thee. Now, he was one of those whom they call Managers of Affairs. {24} Then, suddenly filled with holy love and sober shame, angered at himself, he cast his eyes on his friend, and said, 'Tell me, prithee, with all these labours of ours, whither are we trying to get? What are we seeking? For what are we soldiering? Can we have a higher hope in the palace, than to become friends of the emperor? And when there, what is not frail and full of dangers? And through how many dangers we do not arrive at a greater danger still? And how long will that last? But if I choose to become a friend of God, I can do it here and now.' He spoke thus, and, swelling in the labour-pangs of a new life, he fixed his eyes again on the pages and read, and was changed inwardly as thou lookedst on him, and his mind was stripped of the world, as soon appeared. For while he read, and rolled over the billows of his soul, he shuddered and hesitated from time to time, and resolved better things; and already thine, he said to his friend, 'I have already torn myself from that hope of ours, and have settled to serve God; and this I begin from this hour, in this very place. If you do not like to imitate me, do not oppose me.' He replied that he would cling to his companion in such a great service and so great a warfare. And both, now thine, began building, at their own cost, the tower of leaving all things and following thee. Then Potitianus, and the man who was talking with him elsewhere in the garden, seeking them, came to the same place, and warned them to return, as the sun was getting low. They, however, told their resolution, and how it had sprung up and taken strong hold in them, and entreated the others not to give them pain. They, not altered from their former mode of life, yet wept (as he told us) for themselves; and congratulated them piously, and commended themselves to their prayers; and then dragging their hearts along the earth, went back to the palace. But the others, fixing their hearts on heaven, remained in the cottage. And both of them had affianced brides, who, when they heard this, dedicated their virginity to thee."

The part which this incident played in St. Augustine's own conversion must be told hereafter in his life. But the scene which his master-hand has drawn is not merely the drama of his own soul or of these two young officers, but of a whole empire. It is, as I said at first, the tragedy and suicide of the old empire; and the birth-agony of which he speaks was not that of an individual soul here or there, but of a whole new world, for good and evil. The old Roman soul was dead within, the body of it dead without. Patriotism, duty, purpose of life, save pleasure, money, and intrigue, had perished. The young Roman officer had nothing left for which to fight; the young Roman gentleman nothing left for which to be a citizen and an owner of lands. Even the old Roman longing (which was also a sacred duty) of leaving an heir to perpetuate his name, and serve the state as his fathers had before him—even that was gone. Nothing was left, with the many, but selfishness, which could rise at best into the desire of saving every man his own soul, and so transform worldliness into other-worldliness. The old empire could do nothing more for man; and knew that it could do nothing; and lay down in the hermit's cell to die.

Treves was then "the second metropolis of the empire," boasting, perhaps, even then, as it boasts still, that it was standing thirteen hundred years before Rome was built. Amid the low hills, pierced by rocky dells, and on a strath of richest soil, it had grown, from the mud-hut town of the Treviri, into a noble city of palaces, theatres, baths, triumphal-arches, on either side the broad and clear Moselle. The bridge which Augustus had thrown across the river, four hundred years before the times of hermits and of saints, stood like a cliff through all barbarian invasions, through all the battles and sieges of the Middle Age, till it was blown up by the French in the wars of Louis XIV., and nought remains save the huge piers of black lava stemming the blue stream; while up and down the dwindled city, the colossal fragments of Roman work—the Black Gate, the Heidenthurm, the baths, the Basilica or Hall of Justice, now a Lutheran church—stand out half ruined, like the fossil bones of giants amid the works of weaker, though of happier times; while the amphitheatre was till late years planted thick with vines, fattening in soil drenched with the blood of thousands. Treves had been the haunt of emperor after emperor, men wise and strong, cruel and terrible;—of Constantius, Constantine the Great, Julian, Valentinian, Valens; and lastly, when Potitianus's friends found those poor monks in the garden {27} of Gratian, the gentle hunter who thought day and night on sport, till his arrows were said to be instinct with life, was holding his military court within the walls of Treves, or at that hunting palace on the northern downs, where still on the bath-floors lie the mosaics of hare and deer, and boar and hound, on which the feet of Emperors trod full fifteen hundred years ago.

Still glorious outwardly, like the Roman empire itself, was that great city of Treves; but inwardly it was full of rottenness and weakness. The Roman empire had been, in spite of all its crimes, for four hundred years the salt of the earth: but now the salt had lost its savour; and in one generation more it would be trodden under foot and cast upon the dunghill, and another empire would take its place,—the empire, not of brute strength and self-indulgence, but of sympathy and self-denial,—an empire, not of Caesars, but of hermits. Already was Gratian the friend and pupil of St. Ambrose of Milan; already, too, was he persecuting, though not to the death, heretics and heathens. Nay, some fifty years before (if the legend can be in the least trusted) had St. Helena, the mother of Constantine the Great, returned from Palestine, bearing with her—so men believed—not only the miraculously discovered cross of Christ, but the seamless coat which he had worn; and, turning her palace into a church, deposited the holy coat therein: where—so some believe—it remains until this day. Men felt that a change was coming, but whence it would come, or how terrible it would be, they could not tell. It was to be, as the prophet says, "like the bulging out of a great wall, which bursteth suddenly in an instant." In the very amphitheatre where Gratian sat that afternoon, with all the folk of Treves about him, watching, it may be, lions and antelopes from Africa slaughtered—it may be criminals tortured to death—another and an uglier sight had been twice seen some seventy years before. Constantine, so-called the Great, had there exhibited his "Frankish sports," the "magnificent spectacle," the "famous punishments," as his flattering court-historians called them: thousands of Frank prisoners, many of them of noble, and even of royal blood, torn to pieces by wild beasts, while they stood fearless, smiling with folded arms; and when the wild beasts were gorged, and slew no more, weapons were put into the hands of the survivors, and they were bidden to fight to the death for the amusement of their Roman lords. But fight they would not against their own flesh and blood: and as for life, all chance of that was long gone by. So every man fell joyfully upon his brother's sword, and, dying like a German man, spoilt the sport of the good folk of Treves. And it seemed for a while as if there were no God in heaven who cared to avenge such deeds of blood. For the kinsmen, it may be the very sons, of those Franks were now in Gratian's pay; and the Frank Merobaudes was his "Count of the Domestics," and one of his most successful and trusted generals; and all seemed to go well, and brute force and craft to triumph on the earth.

And yet those two young staff officers, when they left the imperial court for the hermit's cell, judged, on the whole, prudently and well, and chose the better part when they fled from the world to escape the "dangers" of ambition, and the "greater danger still" of success. For they escaped, not merely from vice and worldliness, but, as the event proved, from imminent danger of death if they kept the loyalty which they had sworn to their emperor; or the worse evil of baseness if they turned traitors to him to save their lives.

For little thought Gratian, as he sat in that amphitheatre, that the day was coming when he, the hunter of game—and of heretics—would be hunted in his turn; when, deserted by his army, betrayed by Merobaudes—whose elder kinsfolk were not likely to have kept him ignorant of "the Frankish sports "—he should flee pitiably towards Italy, and die by a German hand; some say near Lyons, some say near Belgrade, calling on Ambrose with his latest breath. {29} Little thought, too, the good folk of Treves, as they sat beneath the vast awning that afternoon, that within the next half century a day of vengeance was coming for them, which should teach them that there was a God who "maketh inquisition for blood;" a day when Treves should be sacked in blood and flame by those very "barbarian" Germans whom they fancied their allies—or their slaves. And least of all did they fancy that, when that great destruction fell upon their city, the only element in it which would pass safely through the fire and rise again, and raise their city to new glory and power, was that which was represented by those poor hermits in the garden-hut outside. Little thought they that above the awful arches of the Black Gate—as if in mockery of the Roman Power—a lean anchorite would take his stand, Simeon of Syracuse by name, a monk of Mount Sinai, and there imitate, in the far West, the austerities of St. Simeon Stylites in the East, and be enrolled in the new Pantheon, not of Caesars, but of Saints.

Under the supposed patronage of those Saints, Treves rose again out of its ruins. It gained its four great abbeys of St. Maximus (on the site of Constantine's palace); St. Matthias, in the crypt whereof the bodies of the monks never decay; {30} St. Martin; and St. Mary of the Four Martyrs, where four soldiers of the famous Theban legion are said to have suffered martyrdom by the house of the Roman prefect. It had its cathedral of St. Peter and St. Helena, supposed to be built out of St. Helena's palace; its exquisite Liebfrauenkirche; its palace of the old Archbishops, mighty potentates of this world, as well as of the kingdom of heaven. For they were princes, arch-chancellors, electors of the empire, owning many a league of fertile land, governing, and that kindly and justly, towns and villages of Christian men, and now and then going out to war, at the head of their own knights and yeomen, in defence of their lands, and of the saints whose servants and trustees they were; and so became, according to their light and their means, the salt of that land for many generations.

And after a while that salt, too, lost its savour, and was, in its turn, trodden under foot. The French republican wars swept away the ecclesiastical constitution and the wealth of the ancient city. The cathedral and churches were stripped of relics, of jewels, of treasures of early art. The Prince-bishop's palace is a barrack; so was lately St. Maximus's shrine; St. Martin's a china manufactory, and St. Matthias's a school. Treves belongs to Prussia, and not to "Holy Church;" and all the old splendours of the "empire of the saints" are almost as much ruinate as those of the "empire of the Romans." So goes the world, because there is a living God.

"The old order changeth, giving place to the new; And God fulfils himself in many ways, Lest one good custom should corrupt the world."

But though palaces and amphitheatres be gone, the gardens outside still bloom on as when Potitianus his friends wandered through them, perpetual as Nature's self; and perpetual as Nature, too, endures whatever is good and true of that afternoon's work, and of that finding of the legend of St. Antony in the monk's cabin, which fixed the destiny of the great genius of the Latin Church.

The story of St. Antony, as it has been handed down to us, {32} runs thus: —

The life and conversation of our holy Father Antony, written and sent to the monks in foreign parts by our Father among the saints, Athanasius, Archbishop of Alexandria.

You have begun a noble rivalry with the monks of Egypt, having determined either to equal or even to surpass them in your training towards virtue; for there are monasteries already among you, and the monastic life is practised. This purpose of yours one may justly praise; and if you pray, God will bring it to perfection. But since you have also asked me about the conversation of the holy Antony, wishing to learn how he began his training, and who he was before it, and what sort of an end he made to his life, and whether what is said of him is true, in order that you may bring yourselves to emulate him, with great readiness I received your command. For to me, too, it is a great gain and benefit only to remember Antony; and I know that you, when you hear of him, after you have wondered at the man, will wish also to emulate his purpose. For the life of Antony is for monks a perfect pattern of ascetic training. What, then, you have heard about him from other informants do not disbelieve, but rather think that you have heard from them a small part of the facts. For in any case, they could hardly relate fully such great matters, when even I, at your request, howsoever much I may tell you in my letter, can only send you a little which I remember about him. But do not cease to inquire of those who sail from hence; for perhaps, if each tells what he knows, at last his history may be worthily compiled. I had wished, indeed, when I received your letter, to send for some of the monks who were wont to be most frequently in his company, that I might learn something more, and send you a fuller account. But since both the season of navigation limited me, and the letter-carrier was in haste, I hastened to write to your piety what I myself know (for I have often seen him), and what I was able to learn from one who followed him for no short time, and poured water upon his hands; always taking care of the truth, in order that no one when he hears too much may disbelieve, nor again, if he learns less than is needful, despise the man.

Antony was an Egyptian by race, born of noble parents, {33} who had a sufficient property of their own: and as they were Christians, he too was Christianly brought up, and when a boy was nourished in the house of his parents, besides whom and his home he knew nought. But when he grew older, he would not be taught letters, {34} not wishing to mix with other boys; but all his longing was (according to what is written of Jacob) to dwell simply in his own house. But when his parents took him into the Lord's house, he was not saucy, like a boy, nor inattentive as he grew older; but was subject to his parents, and attentive to what was read, turning it to his own account. Nor again (as a boy who was moderately well off) did he trouble his parents for various and expensive dainties, nor did he run after the pleasures of this life; but was content with what he found, and asked for nothing more. When his parents died, he was left alone with a little sister, when he was about eighteen or twenty years of age, and took care both of his house and of her. But not six months after their death, as he was going as usual to the Lord's house, and collecting his thoughts, he meditated as he walked how the Apostles had left all and followed the Saviour; and how those in the Acts brought the price of what they had sold, and laid it at the Apostles' feet, to be given away to the poor; and what and how great a hope was laid up for them in heaven. With this in his mind, he entered the church. And it befell then that the Gospel was being read; and he heard how the Lord had said to the rich man, "If thou wilt be perfect, go, sell all thou hast, and give to the poor; and come, follow me, and thou shalt have treasure in heaven." Antony, therefore, as if the remembrance of the saints had come to him from God, and as if the lesson had been read on his account, went forth at once from the Lord's house, and gave away to those of his own village the possessions he had inherited from his ancestors (three hundred plough-lands, fertile and very fair), that they might give no trouble either to him or his sister. All his moveables he sold, and a considerable sum which he received for them he gave to the poor. But having kept back a little for his sister, when he went again into the Lord's house he heard the Lord saying in the Gospel, "Take no thought for the morrow," and, unable to endure any more delay, he went out and distributed that too to the needy. And having committed his sister to known and faithful virgins, and given to her wherewith to be educated in a nunnery, he himself thenceforth devoted himself, outside his house, to training; {35} taking heed to himself, and using himself severely. For monasteries were not then common in Egypt, nor did any monks at all know the wide desert; but each who wished to take heed to himself exercised himself alone, not far from his own village. There was then in the next village an old man, who had trained himself in a solitary life from his youth. When Antony saw him, he emulated him in that which is noble. And first he began to stay outside the village; and then, if he heard of any earnest man, he went to seek him, like a wise bee; and did not return till he had seen him, and having got from him (as it were) provision for his journey toward virtue, went his way. So dwelling there at first, he settled his mind neither to look back towards his parents' wealth nor to recollect his relations; but he put all his longing and all his earnestness on training himself more intensely. For the rest he worked with his hands, because he had heard, "If any man will not work, neither let him eat;" and of his earnings he spent some on himself and some on the needy. He prayed continually, because he knew that one ought to pray secretly, without ceasing. He attended, also, so much to what was read, that, with him, none of the Scriptures fell to the ground, but he retained them all, and for the future his memory served him instead of books. Behaving thus, Antony was beloved by all; and submitted truly to the earnest men to whom he used to go. And from each of them he learnt some improvement in his earnestness and his training: he contemplated the courtesy of one, and another's assiduity in prayer; another's freedom from anger; another's love of mankind: he took heed to one as he watched; to another as he studied: one he admired for his endurance, another for his fasting and sleeping on the ground; he laid to heart the meekness of one, and the long-suffering of another; and stamped upon his memory the devotion to Christ and the mutual love which all in common possessed. And thus filled full, he returned to his own place of training, gathering to himself what he had got from each, and striving to show all their qualities in himself. He never emulated those of his own age, save in what is best; and did that so as to pain no one, but make all rejoice over him. And all in the village who loved good, seeing him thus, called him the friend of God; and some embraced him as a son, some as a brother.

But the devil, who hates and envies what is noble, would not endure such a purpose in a youth: but attempted against him all that he is wont to do; suggesting to him the remembrance of his wealth, care for his sister, relation to his kindred, love of money, love of glory, the various pleasures of luxury, and the other solaces of life; and then the harshness of virtue, and its great toil; and the weakness of his body, and the length of time; and altogether raised a great dust-cloud of arguments in his mind, trying to turn him back from his righteous choice. But when the enemy saw himself to be too weak for Antony's determination, but rather baffled by his stoutness, and overthrown by his great faith, and falling before his continual prayers, then he attacked him with the temptations which he is wont to use against young men; . . . . but he protected his body with faith, prayers, and fastings, . . . setting his thoughts on Christ, and on his own nobility through Christ, and on the rational faculties of his soul, . . . and again on the terrors of the fire, and the torment of the worm, . . . and thus escaped unhurt. And thus was the enemy brought to shame. For he who thought himself to be equal with God was now mocked by a youth; and he who boasted against flesh and blood was defeated by a man clothed in flesh. For the Lord worked with him, who bore flesh on our account, and gave to the body victory over the devil, that each man in his battle may say, "Not I, but the grace of God which is with me." At last, when the dragon could not overthrow Antony even thus, but saw himself thrust out of his heart, then gnashing his teeth (as is written), and as if beside himself, he appeared to the sight, as he is to the reason, as a black child, and as it were falling down before him, no longer attempted to argue (for the deceiver was cast out), but using a human voice, said, "I have deceived many; I have cast down many. But now, as in the case of many, so in thine, I have been worsted in the battle." Then when Antony asked him, "Who art thou who speakest thus to me?" he forthwith replied in a pitiable voice, "I am the spirit of impurity.". . .

Then Antony gave thanks to God, and gaining courage, said, "Thou art utterly despicable; for thou art black of soul, and weak as a child; nor shall I henceforth cast one thought on thee. For the Lord is my helper, and I shall despise my enemies." That black being, hearing this, fled forthwith, cowering at his words, and afraid thenceforth of coming near the man.

This was Antony's first struggle against the devil: or rather this mighty deed in him was the Saviour's, who condemned sin in the flesh that the righteousness of the Lord should be fulfilled in us, who walk not after the flesh, but after the Spirit. But neither did Antony, because the daemon had fallen, grow careless and despise him; neither did the enemy, when worsted by him, cease from lying in ambush against him. For he came round again as a lion, seeking a pretence against him. But Antony had learnt from Scripture that many are the devices of the enemy; and continually kept up his training, considering that, though he had not deceived his heart by pleasure, he would try some other snares. For the daemon delights in sin. Therefore he chastised his body more and more, and brought it into slavery, lest, having conquered in one case, he should be tripped up in others. He determined, therefore, to accustom himself to a still more severe life; and many wondered at him: but the labour was to him easy to bear. For the readiness of the spirit, through long usage, had created a good habit in him, so that, taking a very slight hint from others, he showed great earnestness in it. For he watched so much, that he often passed the whole night without sleep; and that not once, but often, to the astonishment of men. He ate once a day, after the setting of the sun, and sometimes only once in two days, often even in four; his food was bread with salt, his drink nothing but water. To speak of flesh and wine there is no need, for such a thing is not found among other earnest men. When he slept he was content with a rush-mat: but mostly he lay on the bare ground. He would not anoint himself with oil, saying that it was more fit for young men to be earnest in training, than to seek things which softened the body; and that they must accustom themselves to labour, according to the Apostle's saying, "When I am weak, then I am strong;" for that the mind was strengthened as bodily pleasure was weakened. And this argument of his was truly wonderful. For he did not measure the path of virtue, nor his going away into retirement on account of it, by time; but by his own desire and will. So forgetting the past, he daily, as if beginning afresh, took more pains to improve, saying over to himself continually the Apostle's words, "Forgetting what is behind, stretching forward to what is before;" and mindful, too, of Elias' speech, "The Lord liveth, before whom I stand this day." For he held, that by mentioning to-day, he took no account of past time: but, as if he were laying down a beginning, he tried earnestly to make himself day by day fit to appear before God, pure in heart, and ready to obey his will, and no other. And he said in himself that the ascetic ought for ever to be learning his own life from the manners of the great Elias, as from a mirror. Antony, having thus, as it were, bound himself, went to the tombs, which happened to be some way from the village; and having bidden one of his acquaintances to bring him bread at intervals of many days, he entered one of the tombs, and, shutting the door upon himself, remained there alone. But the enemy, not enduring that, but rather terrified lest in a little while he should fill the desert with his training, coming one night with a multitude of daemons, beat him so much with stripes, that he lay speechless from the torture. For he asserted that the pain was so great that no blows given by men could cause such agony. But by the providence of God (for the Lord does not overlook those who hope in him), the next day his acquaintance came, bringing him the loaves. And having opened the door, and seeing him lying on the ground for dead, he carried him to the Lord's house in the village, and laid him on the ground; and many of his kinsfolk and the villagers sat round him, as round a corpse. But about midnight, Antony coming to himself, and waking up, saw them all sleeping, and only his acquaintance awake, and, nodding to him to approach, begged him to carry him back to the tombs, without waking any one. When that was done, the doors were shut, and he remained as before, alone inside. And, because he could not stand on account of the daemons' blows, he prayed prostrate. And after his prayer, he said with a shout, "Here am I, Antony: I do not fly from your stripes; yea, if you do yet more, nothing shall separate me from the love of Christ." And then he sang, "If an host be laid against me, yet shall not my heart be afraid." Thus thought and spoke the man who was training himself. But the enemy, hater of what is noble, and envious, wondering that he dared to return after the stripes, called together his dogs, and bursting with rage,—"Ye see," he said, "that we have not stopped this man by the spirit of impurity; nor by blows: but he is even growing bolder against us. Let us attack him some other way." {41} For it is easy for the devil to invent schemes of mischief. So then in the night they made such a crash, that the whole place seemed shaken, and the daemons, as if breaking in the four walls of the room, seemed to enter through them, changing themselves into the shapes of beasts and creeping things; {42} and the place was forthwith filled with shapes of lions, bears, leopards, bulls, and snakes, asps, scorpions, and wolves, and each of them moved according to his own fashion. The lion roared, longing to attack; the bull seemed to toss; the serpent did not cease creeping, and the wolf rushed upon him; and altogether the noises of all the apparitions were dreadful, and their tempers cruel. But Antony, scourged and pierced by them, felt a more dreadful bodily pain than before: but he lay unshaken and awake in spirit. He groaned at the pain of his body: but clear in intellect, and as it were mocking, he said, "If there were any power in you, it were enough that one of you should come on; but since the Lord has made you weak, therefore you try to frighten me by mere numbers. And a proof of your weakness is, that you imitate the shapes of brute animals." And taking courage, he said again, "If ye can, and have received power against me, delay not, but attack; but if ye cannot, why do ye disturb me in vain? For a seal to us and a wall of safety is our faith in the Lord." The daemons, having made many efforts, gnashed their teeth at him, because he rather mocked at them, than they at him. But neither then did the Lord forget Antony's wrestling, but appeared to help him. For, looking up, he saw the roof as it were opened and a ray of light coming down towards him. The daemons suddenly became invisible, and the pain of his body forthwith ceased, and the building became quite whole. But Antony, feeling the succour, and getting his breath again, and freed from pain, questioned the vision which appeared, saying, "Where wert thou? Why didst thou not appear to me from the first, to stop my pangs?" And a voice came to him, "Antony, I was here, but I waited to see thy fight. Therefore, since thou hast withstood, and not been worsted, I will be to thee always a succour, and will make thee become famous everywhere." Hearing this, he rose and prayed, and was so strong, that he felt that he had more power in his body than he had before. He was then about thirty-and-five years old. And on the morrow he went out, and was yet more eager for devotion to God; and, going to that old man aforesaid, he asked him to dwell with him in the desert. But when he declined, because of his age, and because no such custom had yet arisen, he himself straightway set off to the mountain. But the enemy again, seeing his earnestness, and wishing to hinder it, cast in his way the phantom of a great silver plate. But Antony, perceiving the trick of him who hates what is noble, stopped. And he judged the plate worthless, seeing the devil in it; and said, "Whence comes a plate in the desert? This is no beaten way, nor is there here the footstep of any traveller. Had it fallen, it could not have been unperceived, from its great size; and besides, he who lost it would have turned back and found it, because the place is desert. This is a trick of the devil. Thou shalt not hinder, devil, my determination by this: let it go with thee into perdition." And as Antony said that, it vanished, as smoke from before the face of the fire. Then again he saw, not this time a phantom, but real gold lying in the way as he came up. But whether the enemy showed it him, or whether some better power, which was trying the athlete, and showing the devil that he did not care for real wealth; neither did he tell, nor do we know, save that it was real gold. Antony, wondering at the abundance of it, so stepped over it as over fire, and so passed it by, that he never turned, but ran on in haste, until he had lost sight of the place. And growing even more and more intense in his determination, he rushed up the mountain, and finding an empty inclosure full of creeping things on account of its age, he betook himself across the river, and dwelt in it. The creeping things, as if pursued by some one, straightway left the place: but he blocked up the entry, having taken with him loaves for six months (for the

Thebans do this, and they often remain a whole year fresh), and having water with him, entering, as into a sanctuary, into that monastery, {44} he remained alone, never going forth, and never looking at any one who came. Thus he passed a long time there training himself, and only twice a year received loaves, let down from above through the roof. But those of his acquaintance who came to him, as they often remained days and nights outside (for he did not allow any one to enter), used to hear as it were crowds inside clamouring, thundering, lamenting, crying—"Depart from our ground. What dost thou even in the desert? Thou canst not abide our onset." At first those without thought that there were some men fighting with him, and that they had got in by ladders: but when, peeping in through a crack, they saw no one, then they took for granted that they were daemons, and being terrified, called themselves on Antony. But he rather listened to them than cared for the others. For his acquaintances came up continually, expecting to find him dead, and heard him singing, "Let the Lord arise, and his enemies shall be scattered; and let them who hate him flee before him. As wax melts from before the face of the fire, so shall sinners perish from before the face of God." And again, "All nations compassed me round about, and in the name of the Lord I repelled them." He endured then for twenty years, thus training himself alone; neither going forth, nor seen by any one for long periods of time. But after this, when many longed for him, and wished to imitate his training, and others who knew him came, and were bursting in the door by force, Antony came forth as from some inner shrine, initiated into the mysteries, and bearing the God. {45} And then first he appeared out of the inclosure to those who were coming to him. And when they saw him they wondered; for his body had kept the same habit, and had neither grown fat, nor lean from fasting, nor worn by fighting with the daemons. For he was just such as they had known him before his retirement. They wondered again at the purity of his soul, because it was neither contracted as if by grief, nor relaxed by pleasure, nor possessed by laughter or by depression; for he was neither troubled at beholding the crowd, nor over-joyful at being saluted by too many; but was altogether equal, as being governed by reason, and standing on that which is according to nature. Many sufferers in body who were present did the Lord heal by him; and others he purged from daemons. And he gave to Antony grace in speaking, so that he comforted many who grieved, and reconciled others who were at variance, exhorting all to prefer nothing in the world to the love of Christ, and persuading and exhorting them to be mindful of the good things to come, and of the love of God towards us, who spared not his own son, but delivered him up for us all. He persuaded many to choose the solitary life; and so thenceforth cells sprang up in the mountains, and the desert was colonized by monks, who went forth from their own, and registered themselves in the city which is in heaven.

And when he had need to cross the Arsenoite Canal (and the need was the superintendence of the brethren), the canal was full of crocodiles. And having only prayed, he entered it; and both he and all who were with him went through it unharmed. But when he returned to the cell, he persisted in the noble labours of his youth; and by continued exhortations he increased the willingness of those who were already monks, and stirred to love of training the greater number of the rest; and quickly, as his speech drew men on, the cells became more numerous; and he governed them all as a father. And when he had gone forth one day, and all the monks had come to him desiring to hear some word from him, he spake to them in the Egyptian tongue, thus—"That the Scriptures were sufficient for instruction, but that it was good for us to exhort each other in the faith." . . .

[Here follows a long sermon, historically important, as being the earliest Christian attempt to reduce to a science daemonology and the temptation of daemons: but its involved and rhetorical form proves sufficiently that it could not have been delivered by an unlettered man like Antony. Neither is it, probably, even composed by St. Athanasius; it seems rather, like several other passages in this biography, the interpolation of some later scribe. It has been, therefore, omitted.]

And when Antony had spoken thus, all rejoiced; and in one the love of virtue was increased, in another negligence stirred up, and in others conceit stopped, while all were persuaded to despise the plots of the devil, wondering at the grace which had been given to Antony by the Lord for the discernment of spirits. So the cells in the mountains were like tents filled with divine choirs, singing, discoursing, fasting, praying, rejoicing over the hope of the future, working that they might give alms thereof, and having love and concord with each other. And there was really to be seen, as it were, a land by itself, of piety and justice; for there was none there who did wrong, or suffered wrong: no blame from any talebearer: but a multitude of men training themselves, and in all of them a mind set on virtue. So that any one seeing the cells, and such an array of monks, would have cried out, and said, "How fair are thy dwellings, O Jacob, and thy tents, O Israel; like shady groves and like parks beside a river, and like tents which the Lord hath pitched, and like cedars by the waters." He himself, meanwhile, withdrawing, according to his custom, alone to his own cell, increased the severity of his training. And he groaned daily, considering the mansions in heaven, and setting his longing on them, and looking at the ephemeral life of man. For even when he was going to eat or sleep, he was ashamed, when he considered the rational element of his soul; so that often, when he was about to eat with many other monks, he remembered the spiritual food, and declined, and went far away from them; thinking that he should blush if he was seen by others eating. He ate, nevertheless, by himself, on account of the necessities of the body; and often, too, with the brethren, being bashful with regard to them, but plucking up heart for the sake of saying something that might be useful; and used to tell them that they ought to give all their leisure rather to the soul than to the body; and that they should grant a very little time to the body, for mere necessity's sake: but that their whole leisure should be rather given to the soul, and should seek her profit, that she may not be drawn down by the pleasures of the body, but rather the body be led captive by her. For this (he said) was what was spoken by the Saviour, "Be not anxious for your soul, what ye shall eat; nor for your body, what ye shall put on. And seek not what ye shall eat, nor what ye shall drink, neither let your minds be in suspense: for after all these things the nations of the world seek: but your Father knoweth that ye need all these things. Rather seek first his kingdom; and all these things shall be added unto you."

After these things, the persecution which happened under the Maximinus of that time, {49} laid hold of the Church; and when the holy martyrs were brought to Alexandria, Antony too followed, leaving his cell, and saying, "Let us depart too, that we may wrestle if we be called, or see them wrestling." And he longed to be a martyr himself, but, not choosing to give himself up, he ministered to the confessors in the mines, and in the prisons. And he was very earnest in the judgment-hall to excite the readiness of those who were called upon to wrestle; and to receive and bring on their way, till they were perfected, those of them who went to martyrdom. At last the judge, seeing the fearlessness and earnestness of him and those who were with him, commanded that none of the monks should appear in the judgment-hall, or haunt at all in the city. So all the rest thought good to hide themselves that day; but Antony cared so much for the order, that he all the rather washed his cloak, and stood next day upon a high place, and appeared to the General in shining white. Therefore, when all the rest wondered, and the General saw him, and passed by with his array, he stood fearless, showing forth the readiness of us Christians. For he himself prayed to be a martyr, as I have said, and was like one grieved, because he had not borne his witness. But the Lord was preserving him for our benefit, and that of the rest, that he might become a teacher to many in the training which he had learnt from Scripture. For many, when they only saw his manner of life, were eager to emulate it. So he again ministered continually to the confessors; and, as if bound with them, wearied himself in his services. And when at last the persecution ceased, and the blessed Bishop Peter had been martyred, he left the city, and went back to his cell. And he was there, day by day, a martyr in his conscience, and wrestling in the conflict of faith; for he imposed on himself a much more severe training than before; and his garment was within of hair, without of skin, which he kept till his end. He neither washed his body with water, nor ever cleansed his feet, nor actually endured putting them into water unless it were necessary. And no one ever saw him unclothed till he was dead and about to be buried.

When, then, he retired, and had resolved neither to go forth himself, nor to receive any one, one Martinianus, a captain of soldiers, came and gave trouble to Antony. For he had with him his daughter, who was tormented by a daemon. And while he remained a long time knocking at the door, and expecting him to come to pray to God for the child, Antony could not bear to open, but leaning from above, said, "Man, why criest thou to me? I, too, am a man, as thou art. But if thou believest, pray to God, and it comes to pass." Forthwith, therefore, he believed, and called on Christ; and went away, with his daughter cleansed from the daemon. And many other things the Lord did by him, saying, "Ask, and it shall be given you." For most of the sufferers, when he did not open the door, only sat down outside the cell, and believing, and praying honestly, were cleansed. But when he saw himself troubled by many, and not being permitted to retire, as he wished, being afraid lest he himself should be puffed up by what the Lord was doing by him, or lest others should count of him above what he was, he resolved to go to the Upper Thebaid, to those who knew him not. And, in fact, having taken loaves from the brethren, he sat down on the bank of the river, watching for a boat to pass, that he might embark and go up in it. And as he watched, a voice came to him: "Antony, whither art thou going, and why?" And he, not terrified, but as one accustomed to be often called thus, answered when he heard it, "Because the crowds will not let me be at rest; therefore am I minded to go up to the Upper Thebaid, on account of the many annoyances which befall me; and, above all, because they ask of me things beyond my strength." And the voice said to him, "Even if thou goest up to the Thebaid, even if, as thou art minded to do, thou goest down the cattle pastures, {52a} thou wilt have to endure more, and double trouble; but if thou wilt really be at rest, go now into the inner desert." And when Antony said, "Who will show me the way, for I have not tried it?" forthwith it showed him Saracens who were going to journey that road. So, going to them, and drawing near them, Antony asked leave to depart with them into the desert. But they, as if by an ordinance of Providence, willingly received him; and, journeying three days and three nights with them, he came to a very high mountain; {52b} and there was water under the mountain, clear, sweet, and very cold; and a plain outside; and a few neglected date-palms. Then Antony, as if stirred by God, loved the spot; for this it was what he had pointed out who spoke to him beside the river bank. At first, then, having received bread from those who journeyed with him, he remained alone in the mount, no one else being with him. For he recognised that place as his own home, and kept it thenceforth. And the Saracens themselves, seeing Antony's readiness, came that way on purpose, and joyfully brought him loaves; and he had, too, the solace of the dates, which was then little and paltry. But after this, the brethren, having found out the spot, like children remembering their father, were anxious to send things to him; but Antony saw that, in bringing him bread, some there were put to trouble and fatigue; and, sparing the monks even in that, took counsel with himself, and asked some who came to him to bring him a hoe and a hatchet, and a little corn; and when these were brought, having gone over the land round the mountain, he found a very narrow place which was suitable, and tilled it; and, having plenty of water to irrigate it, he sowed; and, doing this year by year, he got his bread from thence, rejoicing that he should be troublesome to no one on that account, and that he was keeping himself free from obligation in all things. But after this, seeing again some people coming, he planted also a very few pot-herbs, that he who came might have some small solace after the labour of that hard journey. At first, however, the wild beasts in the desert, coming on account of the water, often hurt his crops and his tillage; but he, gently laying hold of one of them, said to them all, "Why do you hurt me, who have not hurt you? Depart, and, in the name of the Lord, never come near this place." And from that time forward, as if they were afraid of his command, they never came near the place. So he was there alone in the inner mountain, having leisure for prayer and for training. But the brethren who ministered to him asked him that, coming every month, they might bring him olives, and pulse, and oil; for, after all, he was old. And while he had his conversation there, what great wrestlings he endured, according to that which is written, "Not against flesh and blood, but against the daemons who are our adversaries," we have known from those who went in to him. For there also they heard tumults, and many voices, and clashing as of arms; and they beheld the mount by night full of wild beasts, and they looked on him, too, fighting, as it were, with beings whom he saw, and praying against them. And those who came to him he bade be of good courage, but he himself wrestled, bending his knees, and praying to the Lord. And it was truly worthy of wonder that, alone in such a desert, he was neither cowed by the daemons who beset him, nor, while there were there so many four-footed and creeping beasts, was at all afraid of their fierceness: but, as is written, trusted in the Lord like the Mount Zion, having his reason unshaken and untost; so that the daemons rather fled, and the wild beasts, as is written, were at peace with him.

Nevertheless, the devil (as David sings) watched Antony, and gnashed upon him with his teeth. But Antony was comforted by the Saviour, remaining unhurt by his craft and manifold artifices. For on him, when he was awake at night, he let loose wild beasts; and almost all the hyaenas in that desert, coming out of their burrows, beset him round, and he was in the midst. And when each gaped on him and threatened to bite him, perceiving the art of the enemy, he said to them all, "If ye have received power against me, I am ready to be devoured by you: but if ye have been set on by daemons, delay not, but withdraw, for I am a servant of Christ." When Antony said this, they fled, pursued by his words as by a whip. Next after a few days, as he was working—for he took care, too, to labour—some one standing at the door pulled the plait that he was working. For he was weaving baskets, which he used to give to those who came, in return for what they brought him. And rising up, he saw a beast, like a man down to his thighs, but having legs and feet like an ass; and Antony only crossed himself and said, "I am a servant of Christ. If thou hast been sent against me, behold, here I am." And the beast with its daemons fled away, so that in its haste it fell and died. Now the death of the beast was the fall of the daemons. For they were eager to do everything to bring him back out of the desert, but could not prevail.

And being once asked by the monks to come down to them, and to visit awhile them and their places, he journeyed with the monks who came to meet him. And a camel carried their loaves and their water; for that desert is all dry, and there is no drinkable water unless in that mountain alone whence they drew their water, and where his cell is. But when the water failed on the journey, and the heat was most intense, they all began to be in danger; for going round to various places, and finding no water, they could walk no more, but lay down on the ground, and they let the camel go, and gave themselves up. But the old man, seeing them all in danger, was utterly grieved, and groaned; and departing a little way from them, and bending his knees and stretching out his hands, he prayed, and forthwith the Lord caused water to come out where he had stopped and prayed. And thus all of them drinking took breath again; and having filled their skins, they sought the camel, and found her; for it befell that the halter had been twisted round a stone, and thus she had been stopped. So, having brought her back, and given her to drink, they put the skins on her, and went through their journey unharmed. And when they came to the outer cells all embraced him, looking on him as a father. And he, as if he brought them guest-gifts from the mountain, gave them away to them in his words, and shared his benefits among them. And there was joy again in the mountains, and zeal for improvement, and comfort through their faith in each other. And he too rejoiced, seeing the willingness of the monks, and his sister grown old in maidenhood, and herself the leader of other virgins. And so after certain days he went back again to the mountain.

And after that many came to him; and others who suffered dared also to come. Now to all the monks who came to him he gave continually this command: To trust in the Lord and love him, and to keep themselves from foul thoughts and fleshly pleasures; and, as is written in the Parables, not to be deceived by fulness of bread; and to avoid vainglory; and to pray continually; and to sing before sleep and after sleep; and to lay by in their hearts the commandment of Scripture; and to remember the works of the saints, in order to have their souls attuned to emulate them. But especially he counselled them to meditate continually on the Apostle's saying, "Let not the sun go down upon your wrath;" and this he said was spoken of all commandments in common, in order that not on wrath alone, but on every other sin, the sun should never go down; for it was noble and necessary that the sun should never condemn us for a baseness by day, nor the moon for a sin or even a thought by night; therefore, in order that that which is noble may be preserved in us, it was good to hear and to keep what the Apostle commanded: for he said: "Judge yourselves, and prove yourselves." Let each then take account with himself, day by day, of his daily and nightly deeds; and if he has not sinned, let him not boast, but let him endure in what is good and not be negligent, neither condemn his neighbour, neither justify himself, as said the blessed Apostle Paul, until the Lord comes who searches secret things. For we often deceive ourselves in what we do, and we indeed know not: but the Lord comprehends all. Giving therefore the judgment to Him, let us sympathise with each other; and let us bear each other's burdens, and examine ourselves; and what we are behind in, let us be eager to fill up. And let this, too, be my counsel for safety against sinning. Let us each note and write down the deeds and motions of the soul as if he were about to relate them to each other; and be confident that, as we shall be utterly ashamed that they should be known, we shall cease from sinning, and even from desiring anything mean. For who when he sins wishes to be harmed thereby? Or who, having sinned, does not rather lie, wishing to hide it? As therefore when in each other's sight we dare not commit a crime, so if we write down our thoughts, and tell them to each other, we shall keep ourselves the more from foul thoughts, for shame lest they should be known. . . . And thus forming ourselves we shall be able to bring the body into slavery, and please the Lord on the one hand, and on the other trample on the snares of the enemy." This was his exhortation to those who met him: but with those who suffered he suffered, and prayed with them. And often and in many things the Lord heard him; and neither when he was heard did he boast; nor when he was not heard did he murmur: but, remaining always the same, gave thanks to the Lord. And those who suffered he exhorted to keep up heart, and to know that the power of cure was none of his, nor of any man's; but only belonged to God, who works when and whatsoever he chooses. So the sufferers received this as a remedy, learning not to despise the old man's words, but rather to keep up heart; and those who were cured learned not to bless Antony, but God alone.

For instance, one called Fronto, who belonged to the palace, and had a grievous disease (for he gnawed his own tongue, and tried to injure his eyes), came to the mountain and asked Antony to pray for him. And when he had prayed he said to Fronto, "Depart, and be healed." And when he resisted, and remained within some days, Antony continued saying, "Thou canst not be healed if thou remainest here; go forth, and as soon as thou enterest Egypt, thou shalt see the sign which shall befall thee." He, believing, went forth; and as soon as he only saw Egypt he was freed from his disease, and became sound according to the word of Antony, which he had learnt by prayer from the Saviour . . .

[Here follows a story of a girl cured of a painful complaint: which need not be translated.]

But when two brethren were coming to him, and water failed them on the journey, one of them died, and the other was about to die. In fact, being no longer able to walk, he too lay upon the ground expecting death. But Antony, as he sat on the mountain, called two monks who happened to be there, and hastened them, saying, "Take a pitcher of water, and run on the road towards Egypt; for of two who are coming hither one has just expired, and the other will do so if you do not hasten. For this has been showed to me as I prayed." So the monks going found the one lying dead, and buried him; and the other they recovered with the water, and brought him to the old man. Now the distance was a day's journey. But if any one should ask why he did not speak before one of them expired, he does not question rightly; for the judgment of that death did not belong to Antony, but to God, who both judged concerning the one; and revealed concerning the other. But this alone in Antony was wonderful, that sitting on the mountain he kept his heart watchful, and the Lord showed him things afar off.

For once again, as he sat on the mountain and looked up, he saw some one carried aloft, and a great rejoicing among some who met him. Then wondering, and blessing such a choir, he prayed to be taught what that might be; and straightway a voice came to him that this was the soul of Ammon, the monk in Nitria, {60} who had persevered as an ascetic to his old age; and the distance from Nitria to the mountain where Antony was, is thirteen days' journey. Those then who were with Antony, seeing the old man wondering, asked the reason, and heard that Ammon had just expired, for he was known to them on account of his having frequently come thither, and many signs having been worked by him, of which this is one. . . .

[Here follows the story (probably an interpolation) of Ammon's being miraculously carried across the river Lycus, because he was ashamed to undress himself.]

But the monks to whom Antony spoke about Ammon's death noted down the day; and when brethren came from Nitria after thirty days, they inquired and learnt that Ammon had fallen asleep at the day and hour in which the old man saw his soul carried aloft. And all on both sides wondered at the purity of Antony's soul; how he had learnt and seen instantly what had happened thirteen days' journey off.

Moreover, Archeleas the Count, finding him once in the outer mountain praying alone, asked him concerning Polycratia, that wonderful and Christ-bearing maiden in Laodicea; for she suffered dreadful internal pain from her extreme training, and was altogether weak in body. Antony, therefore, prayed; and the Count noted down the day on which the prayer was offered. And going back to Laodicea, he found the maiden cured; and asking when and on what day her malady had ceased, he brought out the paper on which he had written down the date of the prayer. And when she told him, he showed at once the writing on the paper. And all found that the Lord had stopped her sufferings while Antony was still praying and calling for her on the goodness of the Saviour.

And concerning those who came to him, he often predicted some days, or even a month, beforehand, and the cause why they were coming. For some came only to see him, and others on account of sickness, and others because they suffered from daemons, and all thought the labour of the journey no trouble nor harm, for each went back aware that he had been benefited. And when he spoke and looked thus, he asked no one to marvel at him on that account, but to marvel rather at the Lord, because he had given us, who are but men, grace to know him according to our powers. And as he was going down again to the outer cells, and was minded to enter a boat and pray with the monks, he alone perceived a dreadfully evil odour, and when those in the boat told him that they had fish and brine on board, and that it was they which smelt, he said that it was a different smell; and while he was yet speaking, a youth, who had an evil spirit, had gone before them and hidden in the boat, suddenly cried out. But the daemon, being rebuked in the name of our Lord Jesus Christ, went out of him, and the man became whole, and all knew that the smell had come from the evil spirit. And there was another man of high rank who came to him, having a daemon, and one so terrible, that the possessed man did not know that he was going to Antony, but [showed the common symptoms of mania]. Those who brought him entreated Antony to pray over him, which he did, feeling for the young man, and he watched beside him all night. But about dawn, the young man, suddenly rushing on Antony, assaulted him. When those who came with him were indignant, Antony said, "Be not hard upon the youth, for it is not he, but the daemon in him; and because he has been rebuked, and commanded to go forth into dry places, he has become furious, and done this. Glorify, therefore, the Lord for his having thus rushed upon me, as a sign to you that the daemon is going out." And as Antony said this, the youth suddenly became sound, and, recovering his reason, knew where he was, and embraced the old man, giving thanks to God. And most of the monks agree unanimously that many like things were done by him: yet are they not so wonderful as what follows. For once, when he was going to eat, and rose up to pray about the ninth hour, he felt himself rapt in spirit; and (wonderful to relate) as he stood he saw himself as it were taken out of himself, and led into the air by some persons; and then others, bitter and terrible, standing in the air, and trying to prevent his passing upwards. And when those who led him fought against them, they demanded whether he was not accountable to them. And when they began to take account of his deeds from his birth, his guides stopped them, saying, "What happened from his birth upwards, the Lord hath wiped out: but of what has happened since he became a monk, and made a promise to God, of that you may demand an account." Then, when they brought accusations against him, and could not prove them, the road was opened freely to him. And straightway he saw himself as if coming back and standing before himself, and was Antony once more. Then, forgetting that he had not eaten, he remained the rest of the day and all night groaning and praying, for he wondered when he saw against how many enemies we must wrestle, and through how many labours a man must traverse the air; and he remembered that it is this which the Apostle means with regard to the Prince of the power of the air; for it is in the air that the enemy has his power, fighting against those who pass through it, and trying to hinder them. Wherefore, also he especially exhorts us: "Take the whole armour of God, that the enemy, having no evil to say about us, may be ashamed." But when we heard this, we remembered the Apostle's saying, "Whether in the body I cannot tell, or out of the body I cannot tell: God knoweth." But Paul was caught up into the third heaven, and, having heard unspeakable words, descended again; but Antony saw himself rapt in the air, and wrestling till he seemed to be free.

Again, he had this grace, that as he was sitting alone in the mountain, if at any time he was puzzled in himself, the thing was revealed to him by Providence as he prayed; and the blessed man was, as Scripture says, taught of God. After this, at all events, when he had been talking with some who came to him concerning the departure of the soul, and what would be its place after this life, the next night some one called him from without, and said, "Rise up, Antony; come out and see." So coming out (for he knew whom he ought to obey), he beheld a tall being, shapeless and terrible, standing and reaching to the clouds, and as it were winged beings ascending; and him stretching out his hands; and some of them hindered by him, and others flying above him, and when they had once passed him, borne upwards without trouble. But against them that tall being gnashed his teeth, while over those who fell, he rejoiced. And there came a voice to Antony, "Consider what thou seest." And when his understanding was opened, he perceived that it was the enemy who envies the faithful, and that those who were in his power he mastered and hindered from passing; but that those who had not obeyed him, over them, as over conquerors, he had no power. Having seen this, and as it were made mindful by it, he struggled more and more daily to improve. Now these things he did not tell of his own accord; but when he was long in prayer, and astonished in himself, those who were with him questioned him and urged him; and he was forced to tell; unable, as a father, to hide anything from his children; and considering, too, that his own conscience was clear, and the story would be profitable for them, when they learned that the life of training bore good fruit, and that visions often came as a solace of their toils.

But how tolerant was his temper, and how humble his spirit; for though he was so great, he both honoured exceedingly the canon of the Church, and wished to put every ecclesiastic before himself in honour. For to the bishops and presbyters he was not ashamed to bow his head; and if a deacon ever came to him for the sake of profit, he discoursed with him on what was profitable, but in prayer he gave place to him, not being ashamed even himself to learn from him. {65} For he often asked questions, and deigned to listen to all present, confessing that he was profited if any one said aught that was useful. Moreover, his countenance had great and wonderful grace; and this gift too he had from the Saviour. For if he was present among the multitude of monks, and any one who did not previously know him wished to see him, as soon as he came he passed by all the rest, and ran to Antony himself, as if attracted by his eyes. He did not differ from the rest in stature or in stoutness, but in the steadiness of his temper, and purity of his soul; for as his soul was undisturbed, his outward senses were undisturbed likewise, so that the cheerfulness of his soul made his face cheerful, and from the movements of his body the stedfastness of his soul could be perceived, according to the Scripture, "When the heart is cheerful the countenance is glad; but when sorrow comes it scowleth." . . . And he was altogether wonderful in faith, and pious, for he never communicated with the Meletian {66a} schismatics, knowing their malice and apostasy from the beginning; nor did he converse amicably with Manichaeans or any other heretics, save only to exhort them to be converted to piety. For he held that their friendship and converse was injury and ruin to the soul. So also he detested the heresy of the Arians, and exhorted all not to approach them, nor hold their misbelief. {66b} In fact, when certain of the Ariomanites came to him, having discerned them and found them impious, he chased them out of the mountain, saying that their words were worse than serpent's poison; and when the Arians once pretended that he was of the same opinion as they, he was indignant and fierce against them. Then being sent for by the bishops and all the brethren, he went down from the mountain, and entering Alexandria he denounced the Arians, saying, that that was the last heresy, and the forerunner of Antichrist; and he taught the people that the Son of God was not a created thing, neither made from nought, but that he is the Eternal Word and Wisdom of the Essence of the Father; wherefore also it is impious to say there was a time when he was not, for he was always the Word co-existent with the Father. Wherefore he said, "Do not have any communication with these most impious Arians; for there is no communion between light and darkness. For you are pious Christians: but they, when they say that the Son of God and the Word, who is from the Father, is a created being, differ nought from the heathen, because they worship the creature instead of God the Creator. {67} Believe rather that the whole creation itself is indignant against them, because they number the Creator and Lord of all, in whom all things are made, among created things." All the people therefore rejoiced at hearing that Christ-opposing heresy anathematized by such a man; and all those in the city ran together to see Antony and the Greeks, {68a} and those who are called their priests {68b} came into the church, wishing to see the man of God; for all called him by that name, because there the Lord cleansed many by him from daemons, and healed those who were out of their mind. And many heathens wished only to touch the old man, believing that it would be of use to them; and in fact as many became

Christians in those few days, as would have been usually converted in a year. And when some thought that the crowd troubled him, and therefore turned all away from him, he quietly said that they were not more numerous than the fiends with whom he wrestled on the mountain. But when he left the city, and we were setting him on his journey, when we came to the gate a certain woman called to him: "Wait, man of God, my daughter is grievously vexed with a devil; wait, I beseech thee, lest I too harm myself with running after thee." The old man hearing it, and being asked by us, waited willingly. But when the woman drew near, the child dashed itself on the ground; and when Antony prayed and called on the name of Christ, it rose up sound, the unclean spirit having gone out; and the mother blessed God, and we all gave thanks: and he himself rejoiced at leaving the city for the mountain, as for his own home.

Now he was very prudent; and what was wonderful, though he had never learnt letters, he was a shrewd and understanding man. Once, for example, two Greek philosophers came to him, thinking that they could tempt Antony. And he was in the outer mountain; and when he went out to them, understanding the men from their countenances, he said through an interpreter, "Why have you troubled yourselves so much, philosophers, to come to a foolish man?" And when they answered that he was not foolish, but rather very wise, he said, "If you have come to a fool, your labour is superfluous, but if ye think me to be wise, become as I am; for we ought to copy what is good, and if I had come to you, I should have copied you; but if you come to me, copy me, for I am a Christian." And they wondering went their way, for they saw that even daemons were afraid of Antony.

And again when others of the same class met him in the outer mountain, and thought to mock him, because he had not learnt letters, Antony answered, "But what do you say? which is first, the sense or the letters? And which is the cause of the other, the sense of the letters, or the letters of the sense?" And when they said that the sense came first, and invented the letters, Antony replied, "If then the sense be sound, the letters are not needed." Which struck them, and those present, with astonishment. So they went away wondering, when they saw so much understanding in an unlearned man. For though he had lived and grown old in the mountain, his manners were not rustic, but graceful and urbane; and his speech was seasoned with the divine salt, so that no man grudged at him, but rather rejoiced over him, as many as came. . . .

[Here follows a long sermon against the heathen worship, attributed to St. Antony, but of very questionable authenticity: the only point about it which is worthy of note is that Antony confutes the philosophers by challenging them to cure some possessed persons, and, when they are unable to do so, casts out the daemons himself by the sign of the cross.]

The fame of Antony reached even the kings, for Constantinus the Augustus, and his sons, Constantius and Constans, the Augusti, hearing of these things, wrote to him as to a father, and begged to receive an answer from him. But he did not make much of the letters, nor was puffed up by their messages; and he was just the same as he was before the kings wrote to him. And he called his monks and said, "Wonder not if a king writes to us, for he is but a man: but wonder rather that God has written his law to man, and spoken to us by his own Son." So he declined to receive their letters, saying he did not know how to write an answer to such things; but being admonished by the monks that the kings were Christians, and that they must not be scandalized by being despised, he permitted the letters to be read, and wrote an answer; accepting them because they worshipped Christ, and counselling them, for their salvation, not to think the present life great, but rather to remember judgment to come; and to know that Christ was the only true and eternal king; and he begged them to be merciful to men, and to think of justice and the poor. And they, when they received the answer, rejoiced. Thus was he kindly towards all, and all looked on him as their father. He then betook himself again into the inner mountain, and continued his accustomed training. But often, when he was sitting and walking with those who came unto him, he was astounded, as is written in Daniel. And after the space of an hour, he told what had befallen to the brethren who were with him, and they perceived that he had seen some vision. Often he saw in the mountain what was happening in Egypt, and told it to Serapion the bishop, who saw him occupied with a vision. Once, for instance, as he sat, he fell as it were into an ecstasy, and groaned much at what he saw. Then, after an hour, turning to those who were with him, he groaned and fell into a trembling, and rose up and prayed, and bending his knees, remained so a long while; and then the old man rose up and wept. The bystanders, therefore, trembling and altogether terrified, asked him to tell them what had happened, and tormented him much, that he was forced to speak. And he groaning greatly—"Ah! my children," he said, "it were better to be dead before what I have seen shall come to pass." And when they asked him again, he said with tears, that "Wrath will seize on the Church, and she will be given over to men like unto brutes, which have no understanding; for I saw the table of the Lord's house, and mules standing all around it in a ring and kicking inwards, as a herd does when it leaps in confusion; and ye all perceived how I groaned, for I heard a voice saying, 'My sanctuary shall be defiled.'"

This the old man saw, and after two years there befell the present inroad of the Arians, {72a} and the plunder of the churches, when they carried off the holy vessels by violence, and made the heathen carry them: and when too they forced the heathens from the prisons to join them, and in their presence did on the holy table what they would. {72b} Then we all perceived that the kicks of those mules presignified to Antony what the Arians are now doing without understanding, like the brutes. But when Antony saw this sight, he exhorted those about him, saying, "Lose not heart, children; for as the Lord has been angry, so will he again be appeased, and the Church shall soon receive again her own order and shine forth as she is wont; and ye shall see the persecuted restored to their place, and impiety retreating again into its own dens, and the pious faith speaking boldly everywhere with all freedom. Only defile not yourselves with the Arians, for this teaching is not of the Apostle but of the daemons, and of their father the devil: barren and irrational and of an unsound mind, like the irrational deeds of those mules." Thus spoke Antony.

But we must not doubt whether so great wonders have been done by a man; for the Saviour's promise is, "If ye have faith as a grain of mustard-seed, ye shall say to this mountain, Pass over from hence, it shall pass over, and nothing shall be impossible to you;" and again, "Verily, verily, I say unto you, if ye shall ask my Father in my name, he shall give it you. Ask, and ye shall receive." And he himself it is who said to his disciples and to all who believe in him, "Heal the sick, cast out devils; freely ye have received, freely give." And certainly Antony did not heal by his own authority, but by praying and calling on Christ; so that it was plain to all that it was not he who did it, but the Lord, who through Antony showed love to men, and healed the sufferers. But Antony's part was only the prayer and the training, for the sake whereof, sitting in the mountain, he rejoiced in the sight of divine things, and grieved when he was tormented by many, and dragged to the outer mountain.

For all the magistrates asked him to come down from the mountain, because it was impossible for them to go in thither to him on account of the litigants who followed him; so they begged him to come, that they might only behold him. And when he declined they insisted, and even sent in to him prisoners under the charge of soldiers, that at least on their account he might come down. So being forced by necessity, and seeing them lamenting, he came to the outer mountain. And his labour this time too was profitable to many, and his coming for their good. To the magistrates, too, he was of use, counselling them to prefer justice to all things, and to fear God, and to know that with what judgment they judged they should be judged in turn. But he loved best of all his life in the mountain. Once again, when he was compelled in the same way to leave it, by those who were in want, and by the general of the soldiers, who entreated him earnestly, he came down, and having spoken to them somewhat of the things which conduced to salvation, he was pressed also by those who were in need. But being asked by the general to lengthen his stay, he refused, and persuaded him by a graceful parable, saying, "Fishes, if they lie long on the dry land, die; so monks who stay with you lose their strength. As the fishes then hasten to the sea, so must we to the mountain, lest if we delay we should forget what is within." The general, hearing this and much more from him, said with surprise that he was truly a servant of God, for whence could an unlearned man have so great sense if he were not loved by God?

Another general, named Balacius, bitterly persecuted us Christians on account of his affection for those abominable Arians. His cruelty was so great that he even beat nuns, and stripped and scourged monks. Antony sent him a letter to this effect:—"I see wrath coming upon thee. Cease, therefore, to persecute the Christians, lest the wrath lay hold upon thee, for it is near at hand." But Balacius, laughing, threw the letter on the ground and spat on it; and insulted those who brought it, bidding them tell Antony, "Since thou carest for monks, I will soon come after thee likewise." And not five days had passed, when the wrath laid hold on him. For Balacius himself, and Nestorius, the Eparch of Egypt, went out to the first station from Alexandria, which is called Chaereas's. Both of them were riding on horses belonging to Balacius, and the most gentle in all his stud: but before they had got to the place, the horses began playing with each other, as is their wont, and suddenly the more gentle of the two, on which Nestorius was riding, attacked Balacius and pulled him off with his teeth, and so tore his thigh that he was carried back to the city, and died in three days. And all wondered that what Antony had so wonderfully foretold was so quickly fulfilled. These were his warnings to the more cruel. But the rest who came to him he so instructed that they gave up at once their lawsuits, and blessed those who had retired from this life. And those who had been unjustly used he so protected that you would think he and not they was the sufferer. And he was so able to be of use to all; so that many who were serving in the army, and many wealthy men, laid aside the burdens of life and became thenceforth monks; and altogether he was like a physician given by God to Egypt. For who met him grieving, and did not go away rejoicing? Who came mourning over his dead, and did not forthwith lay aside his grief? Who came wrathful, and was not converted to friendship? What poor man came wearied out, and when he saw and heard him did not despise wealth and comfort himself in his poverty? What monk who had grown remiss, was not strengthened by coming to him? What young man coming to the mountain and looking upon Antony, did not forthwith renounce pleasure and love temperance? Who came to him tempted by devils, and did not get rest? Who came troubled by doubts, and did not get peace of mind? For this was the great thing in Antony's asceticism, that (as I have said before), having the gift of discerning spirits, he understood their movements, and knew in what direction each of them turned his endeavours and his attacks. And not only he was not deceived by them himself, but he taught those who were troubled in mind how they might turn aside the plots of daemons, teaching them the weakness and the craft of their enemies. How many maidens, too, who had been already betrothed, and only saw Antony from afar, remained unmarried for Christ's sake! Some, too, came from foreign parts to him, and all, having gained some benefit, went back from him as from a father. And now he has fallen asleep, all are as orphans who have lost a parent, consoling themselves with his memory alone, keeping his instructions and exhortations. But what the end of his life was like, it is fit that I should relate, and you hear eagerly. For it too is worthy of emulation. He was visiting, according to his wont, the monks in the outer mountain, and having learned from Providence concerning his own end, he said to the brethren, "This visit to you is my last, and I wonder if we shall see each other again in this life. It is time for me to set sail, for I am near a hundred and five years old." And when they heard that they wept, and embraced and kissed the old man. And he, as if he was setting out from a foreign city to his own, spoke joyfully, and exhorted them not to grow idle in their labours or cowardly in their training, but to live as those who died daily, and (as I said before) to be earnest in keeping their souls from foul thoughts, and to emulate the saints, and not to draw near the Meletian schismatics, for "ye know their evil and profane determinations, nor to have any communion with the Arians, for their impiety also is manifest to all. Neither if ye shall see the magistrates patronising them, be troubled, for their phantasy shall have an end, and is mortal and only for a little while. Keep yourselves therefore rather clean from them, and hold that which has been handed down to you by the fathers, and especially the faith in our Lord Jesus Christ which ye have learned from Scripture, and of which ye have often been reminded by me." And when the brethren tried to force him to stay with them and make his end there, he would not endure it, on many accounts, as he showed by his silence; and especially on this:—The Egyptians are wont to wrap in linen the corpses of good persons, and especially of the holy martyrs, but not to bury them underground, but to lay them upon benches and keep them in their houses; {77} thinking that by this they honour the departed. Now Antony had often asked the bishops to exhort the people about this, and in like manner he himself rebuked the laity and terrified the women; saying that it was a thing neither lawful nor in any way holy; for that the bodies of the patriarchs and prophets are to this day preserved in sepulchres, and that the very body of our Lord was laid in a sepulchre, and a stone placed over it to hide it, till he rose the third day. And thus saying he showed that those broke the law who did not bury the corpses of the dead, even if they were holy; for what is greater or more holy than the Lord's body? Many, then, when they heard him, buried thenceforth underground; and blessed the Lord that they had been taught rightly. Being then aware of this, and afraid lest they should do the same by his body, he hurried himself, and bade farewell to the monks in the outer mountain; and coming to the inner mountain, where he was wont to abide, after a few months he grew sick, and calling those who were by—and there were two of them who had remained there within fifteen years, exercising themselves and ministering to him on account of his old age—he said to them, "I indeed go the way of the fathers, as it is written, for I perceive that I am called by the Lord." . . .

[Then follows a general exhortation to the monk, almost identical with much that has gone before, and ending by a command that his body should be buried in the ground.]

"And let this word of mine be kept by you, so that no one shall know the place, save you alone, for I shall receive it (my body) incorruptible from my Saviour in the resurrection of the dead. And distribute my garments thus. To Athanasius the bishop give one of my sheepskins, and the cloak under me, which was new when he gave it me, and has grown old by me; and to Serapion the bishop give the other sheepskin; and do you have the hair-cloth garment. And for the rest, children, farewell, for Antony is going, and is with you no more."

Saying thus, when they had embraced him, he stretched out his feet, and, as if he saw friends coming to him, and grew joyful on their account (for, as he lay, his countenance was bright), he departed and was gathered to his fathers. And they forthwith, as he had commanded them, preparing the body and wrapping it up, hid it under ground: and no one knows to this day where it is hidden, save those two servants only. And each (i.e. Athanasius and Serapion) having received the sheepskin of the blessed Antony, and the cloak which he had worn out, keeps them as a great possession. For he who looks on them, as it were, sees Antony; and he who puts them on, wears them with joy, as he does Antony's counsels.

Such was the end of Antony in the body, and such the beginning of his training. And if these things are small in comparison with his virtue, yet reckon up from these things how great was Antony, the man of God, who kept unchanged, from his youth up to so great an age, the earnestness of his training; and was neither worsted in his old age by the desire of more delicate food, nor on account of the weakness of his body altered the quality of his garment, nor even washed his feet with water; and yet remained uninjured in all his limbs: for his eyes were undimmed and whole, so that he saw well; and not one of his teeth had fallen out, but they were only worn down to his gums on account of his great age; and he remained sound in hand and foot; and, in a word, appeared ruddier and more ready for exertion than all who use various meats and baths, and different dresses. But that this man should be celebrated everywhere and wondered at by all, and regretted even by those who never saw him, is a proof of his virtue, and that his soul was dear to God. For Antony became known not by writings, not from the wisdom that is from without, not by any art, but by piety alone; and that this was the gift of God, none can deny. For how as far as Spain, as Gaul, as Rome, as Africa, could he have been heard, hidden as he was in a mountain, if it had not been for God, who makes known his own men everywhere, and who had promised Antony this from the beginning? For even if they do their deeds in secret, and wish to be concealed, yet the Lord shows them as lights to all, that so those who hear of them may know that the commandments suffice to put men in the right way, and may grow zealous of the path of virtue.

Read then these things to the other brethren, that they may learn what the life of monks should be, and may believe that the Lord Jesus Christ our Saviour will glorify those who glorify him, and that those who serve him to the end he will not only bring to the kingdom of heaven, but that even if on earth they hide themselves and strive to get out of the way, he will make them manifest and celebrated everywhere, for the sake of their own virtue, and for the benefit of others. But if need be, read this also to the heathens, that even thus they may learn that our Lord Jesus Christ is not only Lord and the Son of God, but that those who truly serve him, and believe piously on him, not only prove that those daemons whom the Greeks think are gods to be no gods, but even tread them under foot, and chase them out as deceivers and corrupters of men, through Jesus Christ our Lord, to whom be glory and honour for ever and ever. Amen.

Thus ends this strange story. What we are to think of the miracles and wonders contained in it, will be discussed at a later point in this book. Meanwhile there is a stranger story still connected with the life of St. Antony. It professes to have been told by him himself to his monks; and whatever groundwork of fact there may be in it is doubtless his. The form in which we have it was given it by the famous St. Jerome, who sends the tale as a letter to Asella, one of the many noble Roman ladies whom he persuaded to embrace the monastic life. The style is as well worth preserving as the matter. Its ruggedness and awkwardness, its ambition and affectation, contrasted with the graceful simplicity of Athanasius's "Life of Antony," mark well the difference between the cultivated Greek and the ungraceful and half-barbarous Roman of the later Empire. I have, therefore, given it as literally as possible, that readers may judge for themselves how some of the Great Fathers of the fifth century wrote, and what they believed.

THE LIFE OF SAINT PAUL, THE FIRST HERMIT

BY THE DIVINE HIERONYMUS THE PRIEST. (ST. JEROME.)

PROLOGUE

Many have often doubted by which of the monks the desert was first inhabited. For some, looking for the beginnings of Monachism in earlier ages, have deduced it from the blessed Elias and John; of whom Elias seems to us to have been rather a prophet than a monk; and John to have begun to prophesy before he was born. But others (an opinion in which all the common people are agreed) assert that Antony was the head of this rule of life, which is partly true. For he was not so much himself the first of all, as the man who excited the earnestness of all. But Amathas and Macarius, Antony's disciples (the former of whom buried his master's body), even now affirm that a certain Paul, a Theban, was the beginner of the matter; which (not so much in name as in opinion) we also hold to be true. Some scatter about, as the fancy takes them, both this and other stories; inventing incredible tales of a man in a subterranean cave, hairy down to his heels, and many other things, which it is tedious to follow out. For, as their lie is shameless, their opinion does not seem worth refuting.

Therefore, because careful accounts of Antony, both in Greek and Roman style, have been handed down, I have determined to write a little about the beginning and end of Paul's life; more because the matter has been omitted, than trusting to my own wit. But how he lived during middle life, or what stratagems of Satan he endured, is known to none.

THE LIFE OF PAUL

Under Decius and Valerius, the persecutors, at the time when Cornelius at Rome, and Cyprian at Carthage, were condemned in blessed blood, a cruel tempest swept over many Churches in Egypt and the Thebaid.

Christian subjects in those days longed to be smitten with the sword for the name of Christ. But the crafty enemy, seeking out punishments which delayed death, longed to slay souls, not bodies. And as Cyprian himself (who suffered by him) says: "When they longed to die, they were not allowed to be slain." In order to make his cruelty better known, we have set down two examples for remembrance.

A martyr, persevering in the faith, and conqueror amid racks and red-hot irons, he commanded to be anointed with honey and laid on his back under a burning sun, with his hands tied behind him; in order, forsooth, that he who had already conquered the fiery gridiron, might yield to the stings of flies.

* * *

In those days, in the Lower Thebaid, was Paul left at the death of both his parents, in a rich inheritance, with a sister already married; being about fifteen years old, well taught in Greek and Egyptian letters, gentle tempered, loving God much; and, when the storm of persecution burst, he withdrew into a distant city. But

"To what dost thou not urge the human breast Curst hunger after gold?"

His sister's husband was ready to betray him whom he should have concealed. Neither the tears of his wife, the tie of blood, or God who looks on all things from on high, could call him back from his crime. He was at hand, ready to seize him, making piety a pretext for cruelty. The boy discovered it, and fled into the desert hills. Once there he changed need into pleasure, and going on, and then stopping awhile, again and again, reached at last a stony cliff, at the foot whereof was, nigh at hand, a great cave, its mouth closed with a stone. Having moved which away (as man's longing is to know the hidden), exploring more greedily, he sees within a great hall, open to the sky above, but shaded by the spreading boughs of an ancient palm; and in it a clear spring, the rill from which, flowing a short space forth, was sucked up again by the same soil which had given it birth. There were besides in that cavernous mountain not a few dwellings, in which he saw rusty anvils and hammers, with which coin had been stamped of old. For this place (so books say) was the workshop for base coin in the days when Antony lived with Cleopatra.

Therefore, in this beloved dwelling, offered him as it were by God, he spent all his life in prayer and solitude, while the palm-tree gave him food and clothes; which lest it should seem impossible to some, I call Jesus and his holy angels to witness that I have seen monks one of whom, shut up for thirty years, lived on barley bread and muddy water; another in an old cistern, which in the country speech they call the Syrian's bed, was kept alive on five figs each day. These things, therefore, will seem incredible to those who do not believe; for to those who do believe all things are possible.

But to return thither whence I digressed. When the blessed Paul had been leading the heavenly life on earth for 113 years, and Antony, ninety years old, was dwelling in another solitude, this thought (so Antony was wont to assert) entered his mind—that no monk more perfect than he had settled in the desert. But as he lay still by night, it was revealed to him that there was another monk beyond him far better than he, to visit whom he must set out. So when the light broke, the venerable old man, supporting his weak limbs on a staff, began to will to go, he knew not whither. And now the mid day, with the sun roasting above, grew fierce; and yet he was not turned from the journey he had begun, saying, "I trust in my God, that he will show his servant that which he has promised." And as he spake, he sees a man half horse, to whom the poets have given the name of Hippocentaur. Seeing whom, he crosses his forehead with the salutary impression of the Cross, and, "Here!" he says, "in what part here does a servant of God dwell?" But he, growling I know not what barbarous sound, and grinding rather than uttering, the words, attempted a courteous speech from lips rough with bristles, and, stretching out his right hand, pointed to the way; then, fleeing swiftly across the open plains, vanished from the eyes of the wondering Antony. But whether the devil took this form to terrify him; or whether the desert, fertile (as is its wont) in monstrous animals, begets that beast likewise, we hold as uncertain.

So Antony, astonished, and thinking over what he had seen, goes forward. Soon afterwards, he sees in a stony valley a short manikin, with crooked nose and brow rough with horns, whose lower parts ended in goat's feet. Undismayed by this spectacle likewise, Antony seized, like a good warrior, the shield of faith and habergeon of hope; the animal, however, was bringing him dates, as food for his journey, and a pledge of peace. When he saw that, Antony pushed on, and, asking him who he was, was answered, "I am a mortal, and one of the inhabitants of the desert, whom the Gentiles, deluded by various errors, worship by the name of Fauns, Satyrs, and Incubi. I come as ambassador from our herd, that thou mayest pray for us to the common God, who, we know, has come for the salvation of the world, and his sound is gone out into all lands." As he spoke thus, the aged wayfarer bedewed his face plenteously with tears, which the greatness of his joy had poured forth as signs of his heart. For he rejoiced at the glory of Christ, and the destruction of Satan; and, wondering at the same time that he could understand the creature's speech, he smote on the ground with his staff, and said, "Woe to thee, Alexandria, who worshippest portents instead of God! Woe to thee, harlot city, into which all the demons of the world have flowed together! What wilt thou say now? Beasts talk of Christ, and thou worshippest portents instead of God." He had hardly finished his words, when the swift beast fled away as upon wings. Lest this should move a scruple in any one on account of its incredibility, it was corroborated, in the reign of Constantine, by the testimony of the whole world. For a man of that kind, being led alive to Alexandria, afforded a great spectacle to the people; and afterwards the lifeless carcase, being salted lest it should decay in the summer heat, was brought to Antioch, to be seen by the Emperor.

But—to go on with my tale—Antony went on through that region, seeing only the tracks of wild beasts, and the wide waste of the desert. What he should do, or whither turn, he knew not. A second day had now run by. One thing remained, to be confident that he could not be deserted by Christ. All night through he spent a second darkness in prayer, and while the light was still dim, he sees afar a she-wolf, panting with heat and thirst, creeping in at the foot of the mountain. Following her with his eyes, and drawing nigh to the cave when the beast was gone, he began to look in: but in vain; for the darkness stopped his view. However, as the Scripture saith, perfect love casteth out fear; with gentle step and bated breath the cunning explorer entered, and going forward slowly, and stopping often, watched for a sound. At length he saw afar off a light through the horror of the darkness; hastened on more greedily; struck his foot against a stone; and made a noise, at which the blessed Paul shut and barred his door, which had stood open.

Then Antony, casting himself down before the entrance, prayed there till the sixth hour, and more, to be let in, saying, "Who I am, and whence, and why I am come, thou knowest. I know that I deserve not to see thy face; yet, unless I see thee, I will not return. Thou who receivest beasts, why repellest thou a man? I have sought, and I have found. I knock, that it may be opened to me: which if I win not, here will I die before thy gate. Surely thou shalt at least bury my corpse."

"Persisting thus he spoke, and stood there fixed: To whom the hero shortly thus replied."

"No one begs thus to threaten. No one does injury with tears. And dost thou wonder why I do not let thee in, seeing thou art a mortal guest?"

Then Paul, smiling, opened the door. They mingled mutual embraces, and saluted each other by their names, and committed themselves in common to the grace of God. And after the holy kiss, Paul sitting down with Antony thus began—

"Behold him, whom thou hast sought with such labour; with limbs decayed by age, and covered with unkempt white hair. Behold, thou seest but a mortal, soon to become dust. But, because charity bears all things, tell me, I pray thee, how fares the human race? whether new houses are rising in the ancient cities? by what emperor is the world governed? whether there are any left who are led captive by the deceits of the devil?" As they spoke thus, they saw a raven settle on a bough; who, flying gently down, laid, to their wonder, a whole loaf before them. When he was gone, "Ah," said Paul, "the Lord, truly loving, truly merciful, hath sent us a meal. For sixty years past I have received daily half a loaf, but at thy coming Christ hath doubled his soldiers' allowance." Then, having thanked God, they sat down on the brink of the glassy spring.

But here a contention arising as to which of them should break the loaf, occupied the day till well-nigh evening. Paul insisted, as the host; Antony declined, as the younger man. At last it was agreed that they should take hold of the loaf at opposite ends, and each pull towards himself, and keep what was left in his hand. Next they stooped down, and drank a little water from the spring; then, immolating to God the sacrifice of praise, passed the night watching.

And when day dawned again, the blessed Paul said to Antony, "I knew long since, brother, that thou wert dwelling in these lands; long since God had promised thee to me as a fellow servant: but because the time of my falling asleep is now come, and (because I always longed to depart, and to be with Christ) there is laid up for me when I have finished my course a crown of righteousness; therefore thou art sent from the Lord to cover my corpse with mould, and give back dust to dust."

Antony, hearing this, prayed him with tears and groans not to desert him, but take him as his companion on such a journey. But he said, "Thou must not seek the things which are thine own, but the things of others. It is expedient for thee, indeed, to cast off the burden of the flesh, and to follow the Lamb: but it is expedient for the rest of the brethren that they should be still trained by thine example. Wherefore go, unless it displease thee, and bring the cloak which Athanasius the bishop gave thee, to wrap up my corpse." But this the blessed Paul asked, not because he cared greatly whether his body decayed covered or bare (as one who for so long a time was used to clothe himself with woven palm leaves), but that Antony's grief at his death might be lightened when he left him. Antony astounded that he had heard of Athanasius and his own cloak, seeing as it were Christ in Paul, and venerating the God within his breast, dared answer nothing: but keeping in silence, and kissing his eyes and hands, returned to the monastery, which afterwards was occupied by the Saracens. His steps could not follow his spirit; but, although his body was empty with fastings, and broken with old age, yet his courage conquered his years. At last, tired and breathless, he arrived at home. There two disciples met him, who had been long sent to minister to him, and asked him, "Where hast thou tarried so long, father?" He answered, "Woe to me a sinner, who falsely bear the name of a monk. I have seen Elias; I have seen John in the desert; I have truly seen Paul in Paradise;" and so, closing his lips, and beating his breast, he took the cloak from his cell, and when his disciples asked him to explain more fully what had befallen, he said, "There is a time to be silent, and a time to speak." Then going out, and not taking even a morsel of food, he returned by the way he had come. For he feared—what actually happened—lest Paul in his absence should render up the soul he owed to Christ.

And when the second day had shone, and he had retraced his steps for three hours, he saw amid hosts of angels, amid the choirs of prophets and apostles, Paul shining white as snow, ascending up on high; and forthwith falling on his face, he cast sand on his head, and weeping and wailing, said, "Why dost thou dismiss me, Paul? Why dost thou depart without a farewell? So late known, dost thou vanish so soon?" The blessed Antony used to tell afterwards, how he ran the rest of the way so swiftly that he flew like a bird. Nor without cause. For entering the cave he saw, with bended knees, erect neck, and hands spread out on high, a lifeless corpse. And at first, thinking that it still lived, he prayed in like wise. But when he heard no sighs (as usual) come from the worshipper's breast, he fell to a tearful kiss, understanding how the very corpse of the saint was praying, in seemly attitude, to that God to whom all live.

So, having wrapped up and carried forth the corpse, and chanting hymns of the Christian tradition, Antony grew sad, because he had no spade, wherewith to dig the ground; and thinking over many plans in his mind, said, "If I go back to the monastery, it is a three days' journey. If I stay here, I shall be of no more use. I will die, then, as it is fit; and, falling beside thy warrior, Christ, breathe my last breath."

As he was thinking thus to himself, lo! two lions came running from the inner part of the desert, their manes tossing on their necks; seeing whom he shuddered at first; and then, turning his mind to God, remained fearless, as though he were looking upon doves. They came straight to the corpse of the blessed old man, and crouched at his feet, wagging their tails, and roaring with mighty growls, so that Antony understood them to lament, as best they could. Then not far off they began to claw the ground with their paws, and, carrying out the sand eagerly, dug a place large enough to hold a man: then at once, as if begging a reward for their work, they came to Antony, drooping their necks, and licking his hands and feet. But he perceived that they prayed a blessing from him; and at once, bursting into praise of Christ, because even dumb animals felt that he was God, he saith, "Lord, without whose word not a leaf of the tree drops, nor one sparrow falls to the ground, give to them as thou knowest how to give." And, signing to them with his hand, he bade them go.

And when they had departed, he bent his aged shoulders to the weight of the holy corpse; and laying it in the grave, heaped earth on it, and raised a mound as is the wont. And when another dawn shone, lest the pious heir should not possess aught of the goods of the intestate dead, he kept for himself the tunic which Paul had woven, as baskets are made, out of the leaves of the palm; and returning to the monastery, told his disciples all throughout; and, on the solemn days of Easter and Pentecost, always clothed himself in Paul's tunic.

I am inclined, at the end of my treatise, to ask those who know not the extent of their patrimonies; who cover their houses with marbles; who sew the price of whole farms into their garments with a single thread—What was ever wanting to this naked old man? Ye drink from a gem; he satisfied nature from the hollow of his hands. Ye weave gold into your tunics; he had not even the vilest garment of your bond-slave. But, on the other hand, to that poor man Paradise is open; you, gilded as you are, Gehenna will receive. He, though naked, kept the garment of Christ; you, clothed in silk, have lost Christ's robe. Paul lies covered with the meanest dust, to rise in glory; you are crushed by wrought sepulchres of stone, to burn with all your works. Spare, I beseech you, yourselves; spare, at least, the riches which you love. Why do you wrap even your dead in golden vestments? Why does not ambition stop amid grief and tears? Cannot the corpses of the rich decay, save in silk? I beseech thee, whosoever thou art that readest this, to remember Hieronymus the sinner, who, if the Lord gave him choice, would much sooner choose Paul's tunic with his merits, than the purple of kings with their punishments.

This is the story of Paul and Antony, as told by Jerome. But, in justice to Antony himself, it must be said that the sayings recorded of him seem to show that he was not the mere visionary ascetic which his biographers have made him. Some twenty sermons are attributed to him, seven of which only are considered to be genuine. A rule for monks, too, is called his: but, as it is almost certain that he could neither read nor write, we have no proof that any of these documents convey his actual language. If the seven sermons attributed to him be really his, it must be said for them that they are full of sound doctrine and vital religion, and worthy, as wholes, to be preached in any English church, if we only substitute for the word "monk," the word "man."

But there are records of Antony which represent him as a far more genial and human personage; full of a knowledge of human nature, and of a tenderness and sympathy, which account for his undoubted power over the minds of men; and showing, too, at times, a certain covert and "pawky" humour which puts us in mind, as does the humour of many of the Egyptian hermits, of the old-fashioned Scotch. These reminiscences are contained in the "Words of the Elders," a series of anecdotes of the desert fathers collected by various hands; which are, after all, the most interesting and probably the most trustworthy accounts of them and their ways. I shall have occasion to quote them later. I insert here some among them which relate to Antony.

SAYINGS OF ANTONY, FROM THE "WORDS OF THE ELDERS."

A monk gave away his wealth to the poor, but kept back some for himself. Antony said to him, "Go to the village and buy meat, and bring it to me on thy bare back." He did so: and the dogs and birds attacked him, and tore him as well as the meat. Quoth Antony, "So are those who renounce the world, and yet must needs have money, torn by daemons."

Antony heard high praise of a certain brother; but, when he tested him, he found that he was impatient under injury. Quoth Antony, "Thou art like a house which has a gay porch, but is broken into by thieves through the back door."

Antony, as he sat in the desert, was weary in heart, and said, "Lord, I long to be saved, but my wandering thoughts will not let me. Show me what I shall do." And looking up, he saw one like himself twisting ropes, and rising up to pray. And the angel (for it was one) said to him, "Work like me, Antony, and you shall be saved."

One asked him how he could please God. Quoth Antony, "Have God always before thine eyes; whatever work thou doest, take example for it out of Holy Scripture: wherever thou stoppest, do not move thence in a hurry, but abide there in patience. If thou keepest these three things, thou shalt be saved."

Quoth Antony, "If the baker did not cover the mill-horse's eyes he would eat the corn, and take his own wages. So God covers our eyes, by leaving us to sordid thoughts, lest we should think of our own good works, and be puffed up in spirit."

Quoth Antony, "I saw all the snares of the enemy spread over the whole earth. And I sighed, and said, 'Who can pass through these?' And a voice came to me, saying, 'Humility alone can pass through, Antony, where the proud can in no wise go.'"

Antony was sitting in his cell, and a voice said to him, "Thou hast not yet come to the stature of a currier, who lives in Alexandria." Then he took his staff, and went down to Alexandria; and the currier, when he found him, was astonished at seeing so great a man. Said Antony, "Tell me thy works; for on thy account have I come out of the desert." And he answered, "I know not that I ever did any good; and, therefore, when I rise in the morning, I say that this whole city, from the greatest to the least, will enter into the kingdom of God for their righteousness: while I, for my sins, shall go to eternal pain. And this I say over again, from the bottom of my heart, when I lie down at night." When Antony heard that, he said, "Like a good goldsmith, thou hast gained the kingdom of God sitting still in thy house; while I, as one without discretion, have been haunting the desert all my time, and yet not arrived at the measure of thy saying."

Quoth Antony, "If a monk could tell his elders how many steps he walks, or how many cups of water he drinks, in his cell, he ought to tell them, for fear of going wrong therein."

At Alexandria, Antony met one Didymus, most learned in the Scriptures, witty, and wise: but he was blind. Antony asked him, "Art thou not grieved at thy blindness?" He was silent: but being pressed by Antony, he confessed that he was sad thereat. Quoth Antony, "I wonder that a prudent man grieves over the loss of a thing which ants, and flies, and gnats have, instead of rejoicing in that possession which the holy Apostles earned. For it is better to see with the spirit than with the flesh."

A Father asked Antony, "What shall I do?" Quoth the old man, "Trust not in thine own righteousness; regret not the thing which is past; bridle thy tongue and thy stomach."

Quoth Antony, "He who sits still in the desert is safe from three enemies: from hearing, from speech, from sight: and has to fight against only one, his own heart."

A young monk came and told Antony how he had seen some old men weary on their journey, and had bidden the wild asses to come and carry him, and they came. Quoth Antony, "That monk looks to me like a ship laden with a precious cargo; but whether it will get into port is uncertain." And after some days he began to tear his hair and weep; and when they asked him why, he said, "A great pillar of the Church has just fallen;" and he sent brothers to see the young man, and found him sitting on his mat, weeping over a great sin which he had done; and he said, "Tell Antony to give me ten days' truce, and I hope I shall satisfy him;" and in five days he was dead.

Abbot Elias fell into temptation, and the brethren drove him out. Then he went to the mountain to Antony. After awhile, Antony sent him home to his brethren; but they would not receive him. Then the old man sent to them, and saying, "A ship has been wrecked at sea, and lost all its cargo; and, with much toil, the ship is come empty to land. Will you sink it again in the sea?" So they took Elias back.

Quoth Antony, "There are some who keep their bodies in abstinence: but, because they have no discretion, they are far from God."

A hunter came by, and saw Antony rejoicing with the brethren, and it displeased him. Quoth Antony, "Put an arrow in thy bow, and draw;" and he did. Quoth Antony, "Draw higher;" and again, "Draw higher still." And he said, "If I overdraw, I shall break my bow." Quoth Antony, "So it is in the work of God. If we stretch the brethren beyond measure, they fail."

A brother said to Antony, "Pray for me." Quoth he, "I cannot pity thee, nor God either, unless thou pitiest thyself, and prayest to God."

Quoth Antony, "The Lord does not permit wars to arise in this generation, because he knows that men are weak, and cannot bear them."

Antony, as he considered the depths of the judgments of God, failed; and said, "Lord, why do some die so early, and some live on to a decrepit age? Why are some needy, and others rich? Why are the unjust wealthy, and the just poor?" And a voice came to him, "Antony, look to thyself. These are the judgments of God, which are not fit for thee to know."

Quoth Antony to Abbot Pastor, "This is a man's great business—to lay each man his own fault on himself before the Lord, and to expect temptation to the last day of his life."

Quoth Antony, "If a man works a few days, and then is idle, and works again and is idle again, he does nothing, and will not possess the perseverance of patience."

Quoth Antony to his disciples, "If you try to keep silence, do not think that you are exercising a virtue, but that you are unworthy to speak."

Certain old men came once to Antony; and he wished to prove them, and began to talk of holy Scripture, and to ask them, beginning at the youngest, what this and that text meant. And each answered as best they could. But he kept on saying, "You have not yet found it out."

And at last he asked Abbot Joseph, "And what dost thou think this text means?" Quoth Abbot Joseph, "I do not know." Quoth Antony, "Abbot Joseph alone has found out the way, for he says he does not know it."

Quoth Antony, "I do not now fear God, but love Him, for love drives out fear."

He said again, "Life and death are very near us; for if we gain our brother, we gain God: but if we cause our brother to offend, we sin against Christ."

A philosopher asked Antony, "How art thou content, father, since thou hast not the comfort of books?" Quoth Antony, "My book is the nature of created things. In it, when I choose, I can read the words of God."

Brethren came to Antony, and asked of him a saying by which they might be saved. Quoth he, "Ye have heard the Scriptures, and know what Christ requires of you." But they begged that he would tell them something of his own. Quoth he, "The Gospel says, 'If a man smite you on one cheek, turn to him the other.'" But they said that they could not do that. Quoth he, "You cannot turn the other cheek to him? Then let him smite you again on the same one." But they said they could not do that either. Then said he, "If you cannot, at least do not return evil for evil." And when they said that neither could they do that, quoth Antony to his disciples, "Go, get them something to eat, for they are very weak." And he said to them, "If you cannot do the one, and will not have the other, what do you want? As I see, what you want is prayer. That will heal your weakness."

Quoth Antony, "He who would be free from his sins must be so by weeping and mourning; and he who would be built up in virtue must be built up by tears."

Quoth Antony, "When the stomach is full of meat, forthwith the great vices bubble out, according to that which the Saviour says: 'That which entereth into the mouth defileth not a man; but that which cometh out of the heart sinks a man in destruction.'"

[This may be a somewhat paradoxical application of the text: but the last anecdote of Antony which I shall quote is full of wisdom and humanity.]

A monk came from Alexandria, Eulogius by name, bringing with him a man afflicted with elephantiasis. Now Eulogius had been a scholar, learned, and rich, and had given away all he had save a very little, which he kept because he could not work with his own hands.

And he told Antony how he had found that wretched man lying in the street fifteen years before, having lost then nearly every member save his tongue, and how he had taken him home to his cell, nursed him, bathed him, physicked him, fed him; and how the man had returned him nothing save slanders, curses, and insults; how he had insisted on having meat, and had had it; and on going out in public, and had company brought to him; and how he had at last demanded to be put down again whence he had been taken, always cursing and slandering. And now Eulogius could bear the man no longer, and was minded to take him at his word.

Then said Antony with an angry voice, "Wilt thou cast him out, Eulogius? He who remembers that he made him, will not cast him out. If thou cast him out, he will find a better friend than thee. God will choose some one who will take him up when he is cast away." Eulogius was terrified at these words, and held his peace.

Then went Antony to the sick man, and shouted at him, "Thou elephantiac, foul with mud and dirt, not worthy of the third heaven, wilt thou not stop shouting blasphemies against God? Dost thou not know that he who ministers to thee is Christ? How darest thou say such things against Christ?" And he bade Eulogius and the sick man go back to their cell, and live in peace, and never part more. Both went back, and, after forty days, Eulogius died, and the sick man shortly after, "altogether whole in spirit."

HILARION

I would gladly, did space allow, give more biographies from among those of the Egyptian hermits: but it seems best, having shown the reader Antony as the father of Egyptian monachism, to go on to his great pupil Hilarion, the father of monachism in Palestine. His life stands written at length by St. Jerome, who himself died a monk at Bethlehem; and is composed happily in a less ambitious and less rugged style than that of Paul, not without elements of beauty, even of tragedy.

The Hermits

PROLOGUE

Remember me in thy holy prayers, glory and honour of virgins, nun Asella. Before beginning to write the life of the blessed Hilarion, I invoke the Holy Spirit which dwelt in him, that, as he largely bestowed virtues on Hilarion, he may give to me speech wherewith to relate them; so that his deeds may be equalled by my language. For those who (as Crispus says) "have wrought virtues" are held to have been worthily praised in proportion to the words in which famous intellects have been able to extol them. Alexander the Great, the Macedonian (whom Daniel calls either the brass, or the leopard, or the he-goat), on coming to the tomb of Achilles, "Happy art thou, youth," he said, "who hast been blest with a great herald of thy worth"—meaning Homer. But I have to tell the conversation and life of such and so great a man, that even Homer, were he here, would either envy my matter, or succumb under it.

For although St. Epiphanius, bishop of Salamina in Cyprus, who had much intercourse with Hilarion, has written his praise in a short epistle, which is commonly read, yet it is one thing to praise the dead in general phrases, another to relate his special virtues. We therefore set to work rather to his advantage than to his injury; and despise those evil-speakers who lately carped at Paul, and will perhaps now carp at my Hilarion, unjustly blaming the former for his solitary life, and the latter for his intercourse with men; in order that the one, who was never seen, may be supposed not to have existed; the other, who was seen by many, may be held cheap. This was the way of their ancestors likewise, the Pharisees, who were neither satisfied with John's desert life and fasting, nor with the Lord Saviour's public life, eating and drinking. But I shall lay my hand to the work which I have determined, and pass by, with stopped ears, the hounds of Scylla. I pray that thou mayest persevere in Christ, and be mindful of me in thy prayers, most sacred virgin.

THE LIFE

Hilarion was born in the village of Thabatha, which lies about five miles to the south of Gaza, in Palestine. He had parents given to the worship of idols, and blossomed (as the saying is) a rose among the thorns. Sent by them to Alexandria, he was entrusted to a grammarian, and there, as far as his years allowed, gave proof of great intellect and good morals. He was soon dear to all, and skilled in the art of speaking. And, what is more than all, he believed in the Lord Jesus, and delighted neither in the madness of the circus, in the blood of the arena, or in the luxury of the theatre: but all his heart was in the congregation of the Church.

But hearing the then famous name of Antony, which was carried throughout all Egypt, he was fired with a longing to visit him, and went to the desert. As soon as he saw him he changed his dress, and stayed with him about two months, watching the order of his life, and the purity of his manner; how frequent he was in prayers, how humble in receiving brethren, severe in reproving them, eager in exhorting them; and how no infirmity ever broke through his continence, and the coarseness of his food. But, unable to bear longer the crowd which assembled round Antony, for various diseases and attacks of devils, he said that it was not consistent to endure in the desert the crowds of cities, but that he must rather begin where Antony had begun. Antony, as a valiant man, was receiving the reward of victory: he had not yet begun to serve as a soldier. He returned, therefore, with certain monks to his own country; and, finding his parents dead, gave away part of his substance to the brethren, part to the poor, and kept nothing at all for himself, fearing what is told in the Acts of the Apostles, the example or punishment, of Ananias and Sapphira; and especially mindful of the Lord's saying—"He that leaveth not all that he hath, he cannot be my disciple."

He was then fifteen years old. So, naked, but armed in Christ, he entered the desert, which, seven miles from Maiuma, the port of Gaza, turns away to the left of those who go along the shore towards Egypt. And though the place was blood-stained by robbers, and his relations and friends warned him of the imminent danger, he despised death, in order to escape death. All wondered at his spirit, wondered at his youth. Save that a certain fire of the bosom and spark of faith glittered in his eyes, his cheeks were smooth, his body delicate and thin, unable to bear any injury, and liable to be overcome by even a light chill or heat.

So, covering his limbs only with a sackcloth, and having a cloak of skin, which the blessed Antony had given him at starting, and a rustic cloak, between the sea and the swamp, he enjoyed the vast and terrible solitude, feeding on only fifteen figs after the setting of the sun; and because the region was, as has been said above, of ill-repute from robberies, no man had ever stayed before in that place. The devil, seeing what he was doing and whither he had gone, was tormented. And though he, who of old boasted, saying, "I shall ascend into heaven, I shall sit above the stars of heaven, and shall be like unto the Most High," now saw that he had been conquered by a boy, and trampled under foot by him, ere, on account of his youth, he could commit sin. He therefore began to tempt his senses; but he, enraged with himself, and beating his breast with his fist, as if he could drive out thoughts by blows, "I will force thee, mine ass," said he, "not to kick; and feed thee with straw, not barley. I will wear thee out with hunger and thirst; I will burden thee with heavy loads; I will hunt thee through heat and cold, till thou thinkest more of food than of play." He therefore sustained his fainting spirit with the juice of herbs and a few figs, after each three or four days, praying frequently, and singing psalms, and digging the ground with a mattock, to double the labour of fasting by that of work. At the same time, by weaving baskets of rushes, he imitated the discipline of the Egyptian monks, and the Apostle's saying—"He that will not work, neither let him eat"—till he was so attenuated, and his body so exhausted, that it scarce clung to his bones.

One night he began to hear the crying {108} of infants, the bleating of sheep, the wailing of women, the roaring of lions, the murmur of an army, and utterly portentous and barbarous voices; so that he shrank frightened by the sound ere he saw aught. He understood these to be the insults of devils; and, falling on his knees, he signed the cross of Christ on his forehead, and armed with that helmet, and girt with the breastplate of faith, he fought more valiantly as he lay, longing somehow to see what he shuddered to hear, and looking round him with anxious eyes: when, without warning, by the bright moonshine he saw a chariot with fiery horses rushing upon him. But when he had called on Jesus, the earth opened suddenly, and the whole pomp was swallowed up before his eyes. Then said he, "The horse and his rider he hath drowned in the sea;" and "Some glory themselves in chariots, and some in horses: but we in the name of the Lord our

God." Many were his temptations, and various, by day and night, the snares of the devils. If we were to tell them all, they would make the volume too long. How often did women appear to him; how often plenteous banquets when he was hungry. Sometimes as he prayed, a howling wolf ran past him, or a barking fox; or as he sang, a fight of gladiators made a show for him: and one of them, as if slain, falling at his feet, prayed for sepulture. He prayed once with his head bowed to the ground, and— as is the nature of man—his mind wandered from his prayer, and thought of I know not what, when a mocking rider leaped on his back, and spurring his sides, and whipping his neck, "Come," he cries, "come, run! why do you sleep?" and, laughing loudly over him, asked him if he were tired, or would have a feed of barley.

So from his sixteenth to his twentieth year, he was sheltered from the heat and rain in a tiny cabin, which he had woven of rush and sedge. Afterwards he built a little cell, which remains to this day, four feet wide and five feet high—that is, lower than his own stature—and somewhat longer than his small body needed, so that you would believe it to be a tomb rather than a dwelling. He cut his hair only once a year, on Easter-day, and lay till his death on the bare ground and a layer of rushes, never washing the sack in which he was clothed, and saying that it was superfluous to seek for cleanliness in haircloth. Nor did he change his tunic, till the first was utterly in rags. He knew the Scriptures by heart, and recited them after his prayers and psalms as if God were present. And, because it would take up too much time to tell his great deeds one by one, I will give a short account of them.

[Then follows a series of miracles, similar to those attributed to St. Antony, and, indeed, to all these great Hermit Fathers. But it is unnecessary to relate more wonders which the reader cannot be expected to believe. These miracles, however, according to St. Jerome, were the foundations of Hilarion's fame and public career. For he says, "When they were noised abroad, people flowed to him eagerly from Syria to Egypt, so that many believed in Christ, and professed themselves to be monks—for no one had known of a monk in Syria before the holy Hilarion. He was the first founder and teacher of this conversation and study in the province. The Lord Jesus had in Egypt the old man Antony; he had in Palestine the young Hilarion . . . He was raised, indeed, by the Lord to such a glory, that the blessed Antony, hearing of his conversation, wrote to him, and willingly received his letters; and if rich people came to him from the parts of Syria, he said to them, 'Why have you chosen to trouble yourselves by coming so far, when you have at home my son Hilarion?' So by his example innumerable monasteries arose throughout all Palestine, and all monks came eagerly to him . . . But what a care he had, not to pass by any brother, however humble or however poor, may be shown by this; that once going into the Desert of Kadesh, to visit one of his disciples, he came, with an infinite crowd of monks, to Elusa, on the very day, as it chanced, on which a yearly solemnity had gathered all the people of the town to the Temple of Venus; for they honour her on account of the morning star, to the worship of which the nation of the Saracens is devoted. The town itself too is said to be in great part semi- barbarous, on account of its remote situation. Hearing, then, that the holy Hilarion was passing by—for he had often cured Saracens possessed with daemons—they came out to meet him in crowds, with their wives and children, bowing their necks, and crying in the Syrian tongue, 'Barech!' that is, 'Bless!' He received them courteously and humbly, entreating them to worship God rather than stones, and wept abundantly, looking up to heaven, and promising them that, if they would believe in Christ, he would come oftener to them. Wonderful was the grace of the Lord. They would not let him depart till he had laid the foundations of a future church, and their priest, crowned as he was, had been consecrated with the sign of Christ.

****

He was now sixty-three years old. He saw about him a great monastery, a multitude of brethren, and crowds who came to be healed of diseases and unclean spirits, filling the solitude around; but he wept daily, and remembered with incredible regret his ancient life. "I have returned to the world," he said, "and received my reward in this life. All Palestine and the neighbouring provinces think me to be worth somewhat; while I possess a farm and household goods, under the pretext of the brethren's advantage." On which the brethren, and especially Hesychius, who bore him a wondrous love, watched him narrowly.

When he had lived thus sadly for two years, Aristaeneta, the Prefect's wife, came to him, wishing him to go with her to Antony, "I would go," he said, weeping, "if I were not held in the prison of this monastery, and if it were of any use. For two days since, the whole world was robbed of such a father." She believed him, and stopped. And Antony's death was confirmed a few days after. Others may wonder at the signs and portents which he did, at his incredible abstinence, his silence, his miracles: I am astonished at nothing so much as that he was able to trample under foot that glory and honour.

Bishops and clergy, monks and Christian matrons (a great temptation), people of the common sort, great men, too, and judges crowded to him, to receive from him blessed bread or oil. But he was thinking of nothing but the desert, till one day he determined to set out, and taking an ass (for he was so shrunk with fasting that he could hardly walk), he tried to go his way. The news got wind; the desolation and destruction of Palestine would ensue; ten thousand souls, men and women, tried to stop his way; but he would not hear them. Smiting on the ground with his staff, he said, "I will not make my God a liar. I cannot bear to see churches ruined, the altars of Christ trampled down, the blood of my sons spilt." All who heard thought that some secret revelation had been made to him: but yet they would not let him go. Whereon he would neither eat nor drink, and for seven days he persevered fasting, till he had his wish, and set out for Bethulia, with forty monks, who could march without food till sundown. On the fifth day he came to Pelusium, then to the camp Thebatrum, to see Dracontius; and then to Babylon to see Philo. These two were bishops and confessors exiled by Constantius, who favoured the Arian heresy. Then he came to Aphroditon, where he met Barsanes the deacon, who used to carry water to Antony on dromedaries, and heard from him that the anniversary Antony's death was near, and would be celebrated by a vigil at his tomb. Then through a vast and horrible wilderness, he went for three days to a very high mountain, and found there two monks, Isaac and Pelusianus, of whom Isaac had been Antony's interpreter.

A high and rocky hill it was, with fountains gushing out at its foot. Some of them the sand sucked up; some formed a little rill, with palms without number on its banks. There you might have seen the old man wandering to and fro with Antony's disciples. "Here," they said, "he used to sing, here to pray, here to work, here to sit when tired. These vines, these shrubs, he planted himself; that plot he laid out with his own hands. This pond to water the garden he made with heavy toil; that hoe he kept for many years." Hilarion lay on his bed, and kissed the couch, as if it were still warm. Antony's cell was only large enough to let a man lie down in it; and on the mountain top, reached by a difficult and winding stair, were two other cells of the same size, cut in the stony rock, to which he used to retire from the visitors and disciples, when they came to the garden. "You see," said Isaac, "this orchard, with shrubs and vegetables. Three years since a troop of wild asses laid it waste. He bade one of their leaders stop; and beat it with his staff. 'Why do you eat,' he asked it, 'what you did not sow?' And after that the asses, though they came to drink the waters, never touched his plants."

Then Hilarion asked them to show him Antony's grave. They led him apart; but whether they showed it to him, no man knows. They hid it, they said, by Antony's command, lest one Pergamius, who was the richest man of those parts, should take the corpse to his villa, and build a chapel over it.

Then he went back to Aphroditon, and with only two brothers, dwelt in the desert, in such abstinence and silence that (so he said) he then first began to serve Christ. Now it was then three years since the heaven had been shut, and the earth dried up: so that they said commonly, the very elements mourned the death of Antony. But Hilarion's fame spread to them; and a great multitude, brown and shrunken with famine, cried to him for rain, as to the blessed Antony's successor. He saw them, and grieved over them; and lifting up his hand to heaven, obtained rain at once. But the thirsty and sandy land, as soon as it was watered by showers, sent forth such a crowd of serpents and venomous animals that people without number were stung, and would have died, had they not run together to Hilarion. With oil blessed by him, the husbandmen and shepherds touched their wounds, and all were surely healed.

But when he saw that he was marvellously honoured, he went to Alexandria, meaning to cross the desert to the further oasis. And because since he was a monk he had never stayed in a city, he turned aside to some brethren known to him in the Brucheion {115} not far from Alexandria. They received him with joy: but, when night came on, they suddenly heard him bid his disciples saddle the ass. In vain they entreated, threw themselves across the threshold. His only answer was, that he was hastening away, lest he should bring them into trouble; they would soon know that he had not departed without good reason. The next day, men of Gaza came with the Prefect's lictors, burst into the monastery, and when they found him not—"Is it not true," they said, "what we heard? He is a sorcerer, and knows the future." For the citizens of Gaza, after Hilarion was gone, and Julian had succeeded to the empire, had destroyed his monastery, and begged from the Emperor the death of Hilarion and

Hesychius. So letters had been sent forth, to seek them throughout the world.

So Hilarion went by the pathless wilderness into the Oasis; {116} and after a year, more or less—because his fame had gone before him even there, and he could not lie hid in the East—he was minded to sail away to lonely islands, that the sea at least might hide what the land would not.

But just then Hadrian, his disciple, came from Palestine, telling him that Julian was slain, and that a Christian emperor was reigning; so that he ought to return to the relics of his monastery. But he abhorred the thought; and, hiring a camel, went over the vast desert to Paraetonia, a sea town of Libya. Then the wretched Hadrian, wishing to go back to Palestine and get himself glory under his master's name, packed up all that the brethren had sent by him to his master, and went secretly away. But—as a terror to those who despise their masters—he shortly after died of jaundice.

Then, with Zananas alone, Hilarion went on board ship to sail for Sicily. And when, almost in the middle of Adria, {117a} he was going to sell the Gospels which he had written out with his own hand when young, to pay his fare withal, then the captain's son was possessed with a devil, and cried out, "Hilarion, servant of God, why can we not be safe from thee even at sea? Give me a little respite till I come to the shore, lest, if I be cast out here, I fall headlong into the abyss." Then said he, "If my God lets thee stay, stay. But if he cast thee out, why dost thou lay the blame on me, a sinner and a beggar?" Then he made the captain and the crew promise not to betray him: and the devil was cast out. But the captain would take no fare when he saw that they had nought but those Gospels, and the clothes on their backs. And so Hilarion came to Pachynum, a cape of Sicily, {117b} and fled twenty miles inland into a deserted farm; and there every day gathered a bundle of firewood, and put it on Zananas's back, who took it to the town, and bought a little bread thereby.

But it happened, according to that which is written, "A city set on an hill cannot be hid," one Scutarius was tormented by a devil in the Basilica of St. Peter at Rome; and the unclean spirit cried out in him, "A few days since Hilarion, the servant of Christ, landed in Sicily, and no man knows him, and he thinks himself hid. I will go and betray him." And forthwith he took ship with his slaves, and came to

Pachynum, and, by the leading of the devil, threw himself down before the old man's hut, and was cured.

The frequency of his signs in Sicily drew to him sick people and religious men in multitudes; and one of the chief men was cured of dropsy the same day that he came, and offered Hilarion boundless gifts: but he obeyed the Saviour's saying, "Freely ye have received; freely give."

While this was happening in Sicily, Hesychius, his disciple, was seeking the old man through the world, searching the shores, penetrating the desert, and only certain that, wherever he was, he could not long be hid. So, after three years were past, he heard at Methone {118} from a Jew, who was selling old clothes, that a prophet of the Christians had appeared in Sicily, working such wonders that he was thought to be one of the old saints. But he could give no description of him, having only heard common report. He sailed for Pachynum, and there, in a cottage on the shore, heard of Hilarion's fame—that which most surprised all being that, after so many signs and miracles, he had not accepted even a bit of bread from any man.

So, "not to make the story too long," as says St. Jerome, Hesychius fell at his master's knees, and watered his feet with tears, till at last he raised him up. But two or three days after he heard from Zananas, how the old man could dwell no longer in these regions, but was minded to go to some barbarous nation, where both his name and his speech should be unknown. So he took him to Epidaurus, {119a} a city of Dalmatia, where he lay a few days in a little farm, and yet could not be hid; for a dragon of wondrous size—one of those which, in the country speech, they call boas, because they are so huge that they can swallow an ox—laid waste the province, and devoured not only herds and flocks, but husbandmen and shepherds, which he drew to him by the force of his breath. {119b} Hilarion commanded a pile of wood to be prepared, and having prayed to Christ, and called the beast forth, commanded him to ascend the pile, and having put fire under, burnt him before all the people. Then fretting over what he should do, or whither he should turn, he went alone over the world in imagination, and mourned that, when his tongue was silent, his miracles still spoke.

In those days, at the earthquake over the whole world, which befell after Julian's death, the sea broke its bounds; and, as if God was threatening another flood, or all was returning to the primaeval chaos, ships were carried up steep rocks, and hung there. But when the Epidauritans saw roaring waves and mountains of water borne towards the shore, fearing lest the town should be utterly overthrown, they went out to the old man, and, as if they were leading him out to battle, stationed him on the shore. And when he had marked three signs of the Cross upon the sand, and stretched out his hands against the waves, it is past belief to what a height the sea swelled, and stood up before him, and then, raging long as if indignant at the barrier, fell back little by little into itself.

All Epidaurus, and all that region, talk of this to this day; and mothers teach it their children, that they may hand it down to posterity. Truly, that which was said to the Apostles, "If ye believe, ye shall say to this mountain, Be removed, and cast into the sea; and it shall be done," can be fulfilled even to the letter, if we have the faith of the Apostles, and such as the Lord commanded them to have. For which is more strange, that a mountain should descend into the sea; or that mountains of water should stiffen of a sudden, and, firm as a rock only at an old man's feet, should flow softly everywhere else? All the city wondered; and the greatness of the sign was bruited abroad even at Salo.

When the old man discovered that, he fled secretly by night in a little boat, and finding a merchantman after two days, sailed for Cyprus. Between Maleae and Cythera {121} they were met by pirates, who had left their vessels under the shore, and came up in two large galleys, worked not with sails, but oars. As the rowers swept the billows, all on board began to tremble, weep, run about, get handspikes ready, and, as if one messenger was not enough, vie with each other in telling the old man that pirates were at hand. He looked out at them and smiled. Then turning to his disciples, "O ye of little faith," he said; "wherefore do ye doubt? Are these more in number than Pharaoh's army? Yet they were all drowned when God so willed." While he spoke, the hostile keels, with foaming beaks, were but a short stone's throw off. He then stood on the ship's bow, and stretching out his hand against them, "Let it be enough," he said, "to have come thus far."

O wondrous faith! The boats instantly sprang back, and made stern-way, although the oars impelled them in the opposite direction. The pirates were astonished, having no wish to return back-foremost, and struggled with all their might to reach the ship; but were carried to the shore again, much faster than they had come.

I pass over the rest, lest by telling every story I make the volume too long. This only I will say, that, while he sailed prosperously through the Cyclades, he heard the voices of foul spirits, calling here and there out of the towns and villages, and running together on the beaches. So he came to Paphos, the city of Cyprus, famous once in poets' songs, which now, shaken down by frequent earthquakes, only shows what it has been of yore by the foundations of its ruins. There he dwelt meanly near the second milestone out of the city, rejoicing much that he was living quietly for a few days. But not three weeks were past, ere throughout the whole island whosoever had unclean spirits began to cry that Hilarion the servant of Christ was come, and that they must hasten to him. Salonica, Curium, Lapetha, and the other towns, all cried this together, most saying that they knew Hilarion, and that he was truly a servant of God; but where he was they knew not. Within a month, nearly 200 men and women were gathered together to him. Whom when he saw, grieving that they would not suffer him to rest, raging, as it were to revenge himself, he scourged them with such an instancy of prayer, that some were cured at once, some after two or three days, and all within a week.

So staying there two years, and always meditating flight, he sent Hesychius to Palestine, to salute the brethren, visit the ashes of the monastery, and return in the spring. When he returned, and Hilarion was longing to sail again to Egypt,—that is, to the cattle pastures, {123a} because there is no Christian there, but only a fierce and barbarous folk,—he persuaded the old man rather to withdraw into some more secret spot in the island itself. And looking round it long till he had examined it all over, he led him away twelve miles from the sea, among lonely and rough mountains, where they could hardly climb up, creeping on hands and knees. When they were within, they beheld a spot terrible and very lonely, surrounded with trees, which had, too, waters falling from the brow of a cliff, and a most pleasant little garden, and many fruit-trees- -the fruit of which, however, Hilarion never ate—and near it the ruin of a very ancient temple, {123b} out of which (so he and his disciples averred) the voices of so many daemons resounded day and night, that you would have fancied an army there. With which he was exceedingly delighted, because he had his foes close to him; and dwelt therein five years; and (while Hesychius often visited him) he was much cheered up in this last period of his life, because owing to the roughness and difficulty of the ground, and the multitude of ghosts (as was commonly reported), few, or none, ever dare climb up to him.

But one day, going out of the little garden, he saw a man paralytic in all his limbs, lying before the gate; and having asked Hesychius who he was, and how he had come, he was told that the man was the steward of a small estate, and that to him the garden, in which they were, belonged. Hilarion, weeping over him, and stretching a hand to him as he lay, said, "I say to thee, in the name of Jesus Christ our Lord, arise and walk." Wonderful was the rapidity of the effect. The words were yet in his mouth, when the limbs, strengthened, raised the man upon his feet. As soon as it was known, the needs of many conquered the difficulty of the ground, and the want of a path, while all in the neighbourhood watched nothing so carefully, as that he should not by some plan slip away from them. For the report had been spread about him, that he could not remain long in the same place; which nevertheless he did not do from any caprice, or childishness, but to escape honour and importunity; for he always longed after silence, and an ignoble life.

So, in the eightieth year of his age, while Hesychius was absent, he wrote a short letter, by way of testament, with his own hand, leaving to Hesychius all his riches; namely, his Gospel-book, and a sackcloth-shirt, hood, and mantle. For his servant had died a few days before. Many religious men came to him from Paphos while he was sick, especially because they had heard that he had said that now he was going to migrate to the Lord, and be freed from the chains of the body. There came also Constantia, a high-born lady, whose son-in-law and daughter he had delivered from death by anointing them with oil. And he made them all swear, that he should not be kept an hour after his death, but covered up with earth in that same garden, clothed, as he was, in his haircloth shirt, hood, and rustic cloak. And now little heat was left in his body, and nothing of a living man was left, except his reason: and yet, with open eyes, he went on saying, "Go forth, what fearest thou? Go forth, my soul, what doubtest thou? Nigh seventy years hast thou served Christ, and dost thou fear death?" With these words, he breathed out his soul. They covered him forthwith in earth, and told them in the city that he was buried, before it was known that he was dead.

The holy man Hesychius heard this in Palestine; reached Cyprus; and pretending, in order to prevent suspicion on the part of the neighbours, who guarded the spot diligently, that he wished to dwell in that same garden, he, after some ten months, with extreme peril of his life, stole the corpse. He carried it to Maiuma, followed by whole crowds of monks and townsfolk, and placed it in the old monastery, with the shirt, hood, and cloak unhurt; the whole body perfect, as if alive, and fragrant with such strong odour, that it seemed to have had unguents poured over it.

I think that I ought not, in the end of my book, to be silent about the devotion of that most holy woman Constantia, who, hearing that the body of Hilarion, the servant of God, was gone to Palestine, straightway gave up the ghost, proving by her very death her true love for the servant of God. For she was wont to pass nights in watching his sepulchre, and to converse with him as if he were present, in order to assist her prayers. You may see, even to this day, a wonderful contention between the folk of Palestine and the Cypriots, the former saying that they have the body, the latter that they have the soul, of Hilarion. And yet, in both places, great signs are worked daily; but most in the little garden in Cyprus; perhaps because he loved that place the best.

Such is the story of Hilarion. His name still lingers in "the place he loved the best." "To this day," I quote this fact from M. de Montalembert's work, "the Cypriots, confounding in their memories legends of good and of evil, the victories of the soul and the triumph of the senses, give to the ruins of one of those strong castles built by the Lusignans, which command their isle, the double name of the Castle of St. Hilarion, and the Castle of the God of Love." But how intense must have been the longing for solitude which drove the old man to travel on foot from Syria to the Egyptian desert, across the pathless westward waste, even to the Oasis and the utmost limits of the Egyptian province; and then to Sicily, to the Adriatic, and at last to a distant isle of Greece. And shall we blame him for that longing? He seems to have done his duty earnestly, according to his own light, towards his fellow-creatures whenever he met them. But he seems to have found that noise and crowd, display and honour, were not altogether wholesome for his own soul; and in order that he might be a better man he desired again and again to flee, that he might collect himself, and be alone with Nature and with God. We, here in England, like the old Greeks and Romans, dwellers in the busy mart of civilized life, have got to regard mere bustle as so integral an element of human life, that we consider a love of solitude a mark of eccentricity, and, if we meet any one who loves to be alone, are afraid that he must needs be going mad: and that with too great solitude comes the danger of too great self-consciousness, and even at last of insanity, none can doubt. But still we must remember, on the other hand, that without solitude, without contemplation, without habitual collection and re- collection of our own selves from time to time, no great purpose is carried out, and no great work can be done; and that it is the bustle and hurry of our modern life which causes shallow thought, unstable purpose, and wasted energy, in too many who would be better and wiser, stronger and happier, if they would devote more time to silence and meditation; if they would commune with their own heart in their chamber, and be still. Even in art and in mechanical science, those who have done great work upon the earth have been men given to solitary meditation. When Brindley, the engineer, it is said, had a difficult problem to solve, he used to go to bed, and stay there till he had worked it out. Turner, the greatest nature- painter of this or any other age, spent hours upon hours in mere contemplation of nature, without using his pencil at all. It is said of him that he was seen to spend a whole day, sitting upon a rock, and throwing pebbles into a lake; and when at evening his fellow painters showed their day's sketches, and rallied him upon having done nothing, he answered them, "I have done this at least: I have learnt how a lake looks when pebbles are thrown into it." And if this silent labour, this steadfast thought are required even for outward arts and sciences, how much more for the highest of all arts, the deepest of all sciences, that which involves the questions— who are we? and where are we? who is God? and what are we to God, and He to us?—namely, the science of being good, which deals not with time merely, but with eternity. No retirement, no loneliness, no period of earnest and solemn meditation, can be misspent which helps us towards that goal.

And therefore it was that Hilarion longed to be alone; alone with God; and with Nature, which spoke to him of God. For these old hermits, though they neither talked nor wrote concerning scenery, nor painted pictures of it as we do now, had many of them a clear and intense instinct of the beauty and the meaning of outward Nature; as Antony surely had when he said that the world around was his book, wherein he read the mysteries of God. Hilarion seems, from his story, to have had a special craving for the sea. Perhaps his early sojourn on the low sandhills of the Philistine shore, as he watched the tideless Mediterranean, rolling and breaking for ever upon the same beach, had taught him to say with the old prophet as he thought of the wicked and still half idolatrous cities of the Philistine shore, "Fear ye not? saith the Lord; Will ye not tremble at my presence who have placed the sand for the bound of the sea, for a perpetual decree, that it cannot pass it? And though the waves thereof toss themselves, yet can they not prevail; though they roar, yet can they not pass over. But this people has a revolted and rebellious heart, they are revolted and gone." Perhaps again, looking down from the sunny Sicilian cliffs of Taormino, or through the pine-clad gulfs and gullies of the Cypriote hills upon the blue Mediterranean below,

"And watching from his mountain wall The wrinkled sea beneath him crawl,"

he had enjoyed and profited by all those images which that sight has called up in so many minds before and since. To him it may be, as to the Psalmist, the storm-swept sea pictured the instability of mortal things, while secure upon his cliff he said with the Psalmist, "The Lord hath set my feet upon a rock, and ordered my goings;" and again, "The wicked are like a troubled sea, casting up mire and dirt." Often, again, looking upon that far horizon, must his soul have been drawn, as many a soul has been drawn since, to it, and beyond it, as it were into a region of boundless freedom and perfect peace, while he said again with David, "Oh that I had wings like a dove; then would I flee away and be at rest!" and so have found, in the contemplation of the wide ocean, a substitute at least for the contemplation of those Eastern deserts which seemed the proper home for the solitary and meditative philosopher.

For indeed in no northern country can such situations be found for the monastic cell as can be found in those great deserts which stretch from Syria to Arabia, from Arabia to Egypt, from Egypt to Africa properly so called. Here and there a northern hermit found, as Hilarion found, a fitting home by the seaside, on some lonely island or storm-beat rock, like St. Cuthbert, off the coast of Northumberland; like St. Rule, on his rock at St. Andrew's; and St. Columba, with his ever-venerable company of missionaries, on Iona. But inland, the fens and the forests were foul, unwholesome, depressing, the haunts of fever, ague, delirium, as St. Guthlac found at Crowland, and St. Godric at Finkhale. {130} The vast pine-woods which clothe the Alpine slopes, the vast forests of beech and oak which then spread over France and Germany, gave in time shelter to many a holy hermit. But their gloom, their unwholesomeness, and the severity of the climate, produced in them, as in most northern ascetics, a temper of mind more melancholy, and often more fierce; more given to passionate devotion, but more given also to dark superstition and cruel self-torture, than the genial climate of the desert produced in old monks of the East. When we think of St. Antony upon his mountain, we must not picture to ourselves, unless we, too, have been in the East, such a mountain as we have ever seen. We must not think of a brown northern moorland, sad, savage, storm-swept, snow-buried, save in the brief and uncertain summer months. We must not picture to ourselves an Alp, with thundering avalanches, roaring torrents, fierce alternations of heat and cold, uninhabitable by mortal man, save during that short period of the year when the maidens in the sennhutt watch the cattle upon the upland pastures. We must picture to ourselves mountains blazing day after day, month after month, beneath the glorious sun and cloudless sky, in an air so invigorating that the Arabs can still support life there upon a few dates each day; and where, as has been said,—"Man needs there hardly to eat, drink, or sleep, for the act of breathing will give life enough;" an atmosphere of such telescopic clearness as to explain many of the strange stories which have been lately told of Antony's seemingly preternatural powers of vision; a colouring, which, when painters dare to put it on canvas, seems to our eyes, accustomed to the quiet greys and greens of England, exaggerated and impossible—distant mountains, pink and lilac, quivering in pale blue haze—vast sheets of yellow sand, across which the lonely rock or a troop of wild asses or gazelles throw intense blue-black shadows—rocks and cliffs not shrouded, as here, in soil, much less in grass and trees, or spotted with lichens and stained with veins; but keeping each stone its natural colour, as it wastes—if, indeed, it wastes at all—under the action of the all but rainless air, which has left the paintings on the old Egyptian temples fresh and clear for thousands of years; rocks, orange and purple, black, white, and yellow; and again and again beyond them {131} glimpses, it may be, of the black Nile, and of the long green garden of Egypt, and of the dark blue sea. The eastward view from Antony's old home must be one of the most glorious in the world, save for its want of verdure and of life. For Antony, as he looked across the blue waters of the Gulf of Akaba, across which, far above, the Israelites had passed in old times, could see the sacred goal of their pilgrimage, the red granite peaks of Sinai, flaming against the blue sky with that intensity of hue which is scarcely exaggerated, it is said, by the bright scarlet colour in which Sinai is always painted in mediaeval illuminations.

But the gorgeousness of colouring, though it may interest us, was not, of course, what produced the deepest effect upon the minds of those old hermits. They enjoyed Nature, not so much for her beauty, as for her perfect peace. Day by day the rocks remained the same. Silently out of the Eastern desert, day by day, the rising sun threw aloft those arrows of light, which the old Greeks had named "the rosy fingers of the dawn." Silently he passed in full blaze almost above their heads throughout the day; and silently he dipped behind the western desert in a glory of crimson and orange, green and purple; and without an interval of twilight, in a moment, all the land was dark, and the stars leapt out, not twinkling as in our damper climate here, but hanging like balls of white fire in that purple southern night, through which one seems to look beyond the stars into the infinite abyss, and towards the throne of God himself. Day after day, night after night, that gorgeous pageant passed over the poor hermit's head without a sound; and though sun and moon and planet might change their places as the year rolled round, the earth beneath his feet seemed not to change. Every morning he saw the same peaks in the distance, the same rocks, the same sand-heaps around his feet. He never heard the tinkle of a running stream. For weeks together he did not even hear the rushing of the wind. Now and then a storm might sweep up the pass, whirling the sand in eddies, and making the desert for a while literally a "howling wilderness;" and when that was passed all was as it had been before. The very change of seasons must have been little marked to him, save by the motions, if he cared to watch them, of the stars above; for vegetation there was none to mark the difference between summer and winter. In spring of course the solitary date-palm here and there threw out its spathe of young green leaves, to add to the number of those which, grey or brown, hung drooping down the stem, withering but not decaying for many a year in that dry atmosphere; or perhaps the accacia bushes looked somewhat gayer for a few weeks, and the Retama broom, from which as well as from the palm leaves he plaited his baskets, threw out its yearly crop of twigs; but any greenness there might be in the vegetation of spring, turned grey in a few weeks beneath that burning sun; and be rest of the year was one perpetual summer of dust and glare and rest. Amid such scenes they had full time for thought. Nature and man alike left it in peace; while the labour required for sustaining life (and the monk wished for nothing more than to sustain mere life) was very light. Wherever water could be found, the hot sun and the fertile soil would repay by abundant crops, perhaps twice in the year, the toil of scratching the ground and putting in the seed. Moreover, the labour of the husbandman, so far from being adverse to the contemplative life, is of all occupations, it may be, that which promotes most quiet and wholesome meditation in the mind which cares to meditate. The life of the desert, when once the passions of youth were conquered, seems to have been not only a happy, but a healthy one. And when we remember that the monk, clothed from head to foot in woollen, and sheltered, too, by his sheepskin cape, escaped those violent changes of temperature which produce in the East so many fatal diseases, and which were so deadly to the linen-clothed inhabitants of the green lowlands of the Nile, we need not be surprised when we read of the vast longevity of many of the old abbots; and of their death, not by disease, but by gentle, and as it were wholesome natural decay.

But if their life was easy, it was surely not ill-spent. If having few wants, and those soon supplied, they found too much time for the luxury of quiet thought, those need not blame them, who having many wants, and those also easily supplied, are wont to spend their superfluous leisure in any luxury save that of thought, above all save that of thought concerning God. For it was upon God that these men, whatever their defects or ignorances may have been, had set their minds. That man was sent into the world to know and to love, to obey and thereby to glorify, the Maker of his being, was the cardinal point of their creed, as it has been of every creed which ever exercised any beneficial influence on the minds of men. Dean Milman in his "History of Christianity," vol. iii. page 294, has, while justly severe upon the failings and mistakes of the Eastern monks, pointed out with equal justice that the great desire of knowing God was the prime motive in the mind of all their best men:- -

"In some regions of the East, the sultry and oppressive heat, the general relaxation of the physical system, dispose constitutions of a certain temperament to a dreamy inertness. The indolence and prostration of the body produce a kind of activity in the mind, if that may properly be called activity which is merely giving loose to the imagination and the emotions as they follow out the wild train of incoherent thought, or are agitated by impulses of spontaneous and ungoverned feeling. Ascetic Christianity ministered new aliment to this common propensity. It gave an object, both vague and determinate enough to stimulate, yet never to satisfy or exhaust. The regularity of stated hours of prayer, and of a kind of idle industry, weaving mats or plaiting baskets, alternated with periods of morbid reflection on the moral state of the soul, and of mystic communion with the Deity. It cannot indeed be wondered that this new revelation, as it were, of the Deity, this profound and rational certainty of his existence, this infelt consciousness of his perpetual presence, these as yet unknown impressions of his infinity, his power, and his love, should give a higher character to this eremitical enthusiasm, and attract men of loftier and more vigorous minds within its sphere. It was not merely the pusillanimous dread of encountering the trials of life which urged the humbler spirits to seek a safe retirement; or the natural love of peace, and the weariness and satiety of life, which commended this seclusion to those who were too gentle to mingle in, or who were exhausted with, the unprofitable turmoil of the world; nor was it always the anxiety to mortify the rebellious and refractory body with more advantage. The one absorbing idea of the Majesty of the Godhead almost seemed to swallow up all other considerations. The transcendent nature of the Triune Deity, the relation of the different persons of the Godhead to each other, seemed the only worthy object of men's contemplative faculties."

And surely the contemplation of the Godhead is no unworthy occupation for the immortal soul of any human being. But it would be unjust to these hermits did we fancy that their religion consisted merely even in this; much less that it consisted merely in dreams and visions, or in mere stated hours of prayer. That all did not fulfil the ideal of their profession is to be expected, and is frankly confessed by the writers of the Lives of the Fathers; that there were serious faults, even great crimes, among them is not denied. Those who wrote concerning them were so sure that they were on the whole good men, that they were not at all afraid of saying that some of them were bad,—not afraid, even, of recording, though only in dark hints, the reason why the Arab tribes around once rose and laid waste six churches with their monasteries in the neighbourhood of Scetis. St. Jerome in like manner does not hesitate to pour out bitter complaints against many of the monks in the neighbourhood of Bethlehem. It is notorious, too, that many became monks merely to escape slavery, hunger, or conscription into the army: Unruly and fanatical spirits, too, grew fond of wandering. Bands of monks on the great roads and public places of the empire, Massalians or Gyrovagi, as they were called, wandered from province to province, and cell to cell, living on the alms which they extorted from the pious, and making up too often for protracted fasts by outbursts of gluttony and drunkenness. And doubtless the average monk, even when well-conducted himself and in a well-conducted monastery, was, like average men of every creed, rank, or occupation, a very common-place person, acting from very mixed and often very questionable motives; and valuing his shaven crown and his sheepskin cloak, his regular hours of prayer and his implicit obedience to his abbot, more highly than he valued the fear and the love of God.

It is so in every creed. With some, even now, the strict observance of the Sabbath; with others, outward reverence at the Holy Communion; with others, the frequent hearing of sermons which suit heir own views; with others, continual reading of pious books (on the lessons of which they do not act), covers, instead of charity, a multitude of sins. But the saint, abbot, or father among these hermits was essentially the man who was not a common-place person; who was more than an ascetic, and more than a formalist; who could pierce beyond the letter to the spirit, and see, beyond all forms of doctrine or modes of life, that virtue was the one thing needful.

The Historia Lausiaca and the Pratum Spirituale have many a story and many a saying as weighty, beautiful, and instructive now as they were fifteen hundred years ago; stories which show that graces and virtues such as the world had never seen before, save in the persecuted and half-unknown Christians of the first three centuries, were cultivated to noble fruitfulness by the monks of the East. For their humility, obedience, and reverence for their superiors it is not wise to praise them just now; for those are qualities which are not at present considered virtues, but rather (save by the soldier) somewhat abject vices; and indeed they often carried them, as they did their abstinence, to an extravagant pitch. But it must be remembered, in fairness, that if they obeyed their supposed superiors, they had first chosen their superiors themselves; that as the becoming a monk at all was an assertion of self-will and independence, whether for good or evil, so their reverence for their abbots was a voluntary loyalty to one who they fancied had a right to rule them, because he was wiser and better than they; a feeling which some have found not degrading, but ennobling; and the parent, not of servility, but of true freedom. And as for the obsolete virtue of humility, that still remains true which a voice said to Antony, when he saw the snares which were spread over the whole earth, and asked, sighing, "Who can pass safely over these?" and the voice answered, "Humility alone."

For the rest, if the Sermon on the Mount mean anything, as a practical rule of life for Christian men, then these monks were surely justified in trying to obey it, for to obey it they surely tried.

The Words of the Elders, to which I have already alluded, and the Lausiaca of Palladius likewise, are full of precious scraps of moral wisdom, sayings, and anecdotes, full of nobleness, purity, pathos, insight into character, and often instinct with a quiet humour, which seems to have been, in the Old world, peculiar to the Egyptians, as it is, in the New, almost peculiar to the old- fashioned God-fearing Scotsman.

Take these examples, chosen almost at random.

Serapion the Sindonite was so called because he wore nothing but a sindon, or linen shirt. Though he could not read, he could say all the Scriptures by heart. He could not (says Palladius) sit quiet in his cell, but wandered over the world in utter poverty, so that he "attained to perfect impassibility, for with that nature he was born; for there are differences of natures, not of substances."

So says Palladius, and goes on to tell how Serapion sold himself to certain play-actors for twenty gold pieces, and laboured for them as a slave till he had won them to Christ, and made them renounce the theatre; after which he made his converts give the money to the poor, and went his way.

On one of his journeys he came to Athens, and, having neither money nor goods, starved there for three days. But on the fourth he went up, seemingly to the Areopagus, and cried, "Men of Athens, help!" And when the crowd questioned him, he told them that he had, since he left Egypt, fallen into the hands of three usurers, two of whom he had satisfied, but the third would not leave him.

On being promised assistance, he told them that his three usurers were avarice, sensuality, and hunger. Of the two first he was rid, having neither money nor passions: but, as he had eaten nothing for three days, the third was beginning to be troublesome, and demanded its usual debt, without paying which he could not well live; whereon certain philosophers, seemly amused by his apologue, gave him a gold coin. He went to a baker's shop, laid down the coin, took up a loaf, and went out of Athens for ever. Then the philosophers knew that he was endowed with true virtue; and when they had paid the baker the price of the loaf, got back their gold.

When he went into Lacedaemon, he heard that a great man there was a Manichaean, with all his family, though otherwise a good man. To him Serapion sold himself as a slave, and within two years converted him and his wife, who thenceforth treated him not as a slave, but as their own brother.

After awhile, this "Spiritual adamant," as Palladius calls him, bought his freedom of them, and sailed for Rome. At sundown first the sailors, and then the passengers, brought out each man his provisions, and ate. Serapion sat still. The crew fancied that he was sea-sick; but when he had passed a second, third, and fourth day fasting, they asked, "Man, why do you not eat?" "Because I have nothing to eat." They thought that some one had stolen his baggage: but when they found that the man had absolutely nothing, they began to ask him not only how he would keep alive, but how he would pay his fare. He only answered, "That he had nothing; that they might cast him out of the ship where they had found him."

But they answered, "Not for a hundred gold pieces, so favourable was the wind," and fed him all the way to Rome, where we lose sight of him and his humour.

To go on with almost chance quotations:—

Some monks were eating at a festival, and one said to the serving man, "I eat nothing cooked; tell them to bring me salt." The serving man began to talk loudly: "That brother eats no cooked meat; bring him a little salt." Quoth Abbot Theodore: "It were more better for thee, brother, to eat meat in thy cell than to hear thyself talked about in the presence of thy brethren."

Again: a brother came to Abbot Silvanus, in Mount Sinai, and found the brethren working, and said, "Why labour you for the meat which perisheth? Mary chose the good part." The abbot said, "Give him a book to read, and put him in an empty cell." About the ninth hour the brother looked out, to see if he would be called to eat, and at last came to the abbot, and asked, "Do not the brethren eat to-day, abbot?" "Yes." "Then why was not I called?" Then quoth Abbot Silvanus: "Thou art a spiritual man: and needest not their food. We are carnal, and must eat, because we work: but thou hast chosen the better part." Whereat the monk was ashamed.

As was also John the dwarf, who wanted to be "without care like the angels, doing nothing but praise God." So he threw away his cloak, left his brother the abbot, and went into the desert. But after seven days he came back, and knocked at the door. "Who is there?" asked his brother. "John." "Nay, John is turned into an angel, and is no more among men." So he left him outside all night; and in the morning gave him to understand that if he was a man he must work, but that if he was an angel, he had no need to live in a cell.

Consider again the saying of the great Antony, when some brethren were praising another in his presence. But Antony tried him, and found that he could not bear an injury. Then said the old man, "Brother, thou art like a house with an ornamented porch, while the thieves break into it by the back door."

Or this, of Abbot Isidore, when the devil tempted him to despair, and told him that he would be lost after all: "If I do go into torment, I shall still find you below me there."

Or this, of Zeno the Syrian, when some Egyptian monks came to him and began accusing themselves: "The Egyptians hide the virtues which they have, and confess vices which they have not. The Syrians and Greeks boast of virtues which they have not, and hide vices which they have."

Or this: One old man said to another, "I am dead to this world." "Do not trust yourself," quoth the other, "till you are out of this world. If you are dead, the devil is not."

Two old men lived in the same cell, and had never disagreed. Said one to the other, "Let us have just one quarrel, like other men." Quoth the other: "I do not know what a quarrel is like." Quoth the first: "Here—I will put a brick between us, and say that it is mine: and you shall say it is not mine; and over that let us have a contention and a squabble." But when they put the brick between them, and one said, "It is mine," the other said, "I hope it is mine." And when the first said, "It is mine, it is not yours," he answered, "If it is yours, take it." So they could not find out how to have a quarrel.

Anger, malice, revenge, were accursed things in the eyes of these men. There was enough of them, and too much, among their monks; but far less, doubt not, than in the world outside. For within the monastery it was preached against, repressed, punished; and when repented of, forgiven, with loving warnings and wise rules against future transgression.

Abbot Agathon used to say, "I never went to sleep with a quarrel against any man; nor did I, as far as lay in me, let one who had a quarrel against me sleep till he had made peace."

Abbot Isaac was asked why the devils feared him so much. "Since I was made a monk," he said, "I settled with myself that no angry word should come out of my mouth."

An old man said, "Anger arises from these four things: from the lust of avarice, in giving and receiving; from loving one's own opinion; from wishing to be honoured; and from fancying oneself a teacher and hoping to be wiser than everybody. And anger obscures human reason by these four ways: if a man hate his neighbour; or if he envy him; or if he look on him as nought; or if he speak evil of him."

A brother being injured by another, came to Abbot Sidonius, told his story, and said, "I wish to avenge myself, father." The abbot begged him to leave vengeance to God: but when he refused, said, "Then let us pray." Whereon the old man rose, and said, "God, thou art not necessary to us any longer, that thou shouldest be careful of us: for we, as this brother says, both will and can avenge ourselves." At which that brother fell at his feet, and begged pardon, promising never to strive with his enemy.

Abbot Poemen said often, "Let malice never overcome thee. If any man do thee harm, repay him with good, that thou mayest conquer evil with good."

In a congregation at Scetis, when many men's lives and conversation had been talked over, Abbot Pior held his tongue. After it was over, he went out, and filled a sack with sand, and put it on his back. Then he took a little bag, filled it likewise with sand, and carried it before him. And when the brethren asked him what he meant, he said, "The sack behind is my own sins, which are very many: yet I have cast them behind my back, and will not see them, nor weep over them.

But I have put these few sins of my brother's before my eyes, and am tormenting myself over them, and condemning my brother."

A brother having committed a fault, went to Antony, and his brethren followed, upbraiding him, and wanting to bring him back; while he denied having done the wrong. Abbot Paphnutius was there, and spoke a parable to them:—

"I saw on the river bank a man sunk in the mud up to his knees. And men came to pull him out, and thrust him in up to the neck."

Then said Antony of Paphnutius, "Behold a man who can indeed save souls."

Abbot Macarius was going up to the mountain of Nitria, and sent his disciple on before. The disciple met an idol-priest hurrying on, and carrying a great beam: to whom he cried, "Where art thou running, devil?" At which he was wroth, and beat him so that he left him half dead, and then ran on, and met Macarius, who said, "Salvation to thee, labourer, salvation!" He answered, wondering, "What good hast thou seen in me that thou salutest me?" "Because I saw thee working and running, though ignorantly." To whom the priest said, "Touched by thy salutation, I knew thee to be a great servant of God; for another—I know not who—miserable monk met me and insulted me, and I gave him blows for his words." Then laying hold of Macarius's feet he said, "Unless thou make me a monk I will not leave hold of thee."

After all, of the best of these men are told (with much honesty) many sayings which show that they felt in their minds and hearts that the spirit was above the letter: sayings which show that they had at least at times glimpses of a simpler and more possible virtue; foretastes of a perfection more human, and it may be more divine.

"Better," said Abbot Hyperichius, "to eat flesh and drink wine, than to eat our brethren's flesh with bitter words."

A brother asked an elder, "Give me, father one thing which I may keep, and be saved thereby." The elder answered, "If thou canst be injured and insulted, and hear and be silent, that is a great thing, and above all the other commandments."

One of the elders used to say, "Whatever a man shrinks from let him not do to another. Dost thou shrink if any man detracts from thee? Speak not ill of another. Dost thou shrink if any man slanders thee, or if any man takes aught from thee? Do not that or the like to another man. For he that shall have kept this saying, will find it suffice for his salvation."

"The nearer," said Abbot Muthues, "a man approaches God, the more he will see himself to be a sinner."

Abbot Sisois, when he lay dying, begged to live a little longer, that he might repent; and when they wondered, he told them that he had not yet even begun repentance. Whereby they saw that he was perfect in the fear of the Lord.

But the most startling confession of all must have been that wrung from the famous Macarius the elder. He had been asked once by a brother, to tell him a rule by which he might be saved; and his answer had been this:—to fly from men, to sit in his cell, and to lament for his sins continually; and, what was above all virtues, to keep his tongue in order as well as his appetite.

But (whether before or after that answer is not said) he gained a deeper insight into true virtue, on the day when (like Antony when he was reproved by the example of the tanner in Alexandria) he heard a voice telling him that he was inferior to two women who dwelt in the nearest town. Catching up his staff, like Antony, he went off to see the wonder. The women, when questioned by him as to their works, were astonished. They had been simply good wives for years past, married to two brothers, and living in the same house. But when pressed by him, they confessed that they had never said a foul word to each other, and never quarrelled. At one time they had agreed together to retire into a nunnery, but could not, for all their prayers, obtain the consent of their husbands. On which they had both made an oath, that they would never, to their deaths, speak one worldly word.

Which when the blessed Macarius had heard, he said, "In truth there is neither virgin, nor married woman, nor monk, nor secular; but God only requires the intention, and ministers the spirit of life to all."

ARSENIUS

I shall give one more figure, and that a truly tragical one, from these "Lives of the Egyptian Fathers," namely, that of the once great and famous Arsenius, the Father (as he was at one time called) of the Emperors. Theodosius, the great statesman and warrior, who for some twenty years kept up by his single hand the falling empire of Rome, heard how Arsenius was at once the most pious and the most learned of his subjects; and wishing—half barbarian as he was himself—that his sons should be brought up, not only as scholars, but as Christians, he sent for Arsenius to his court, and made him tutor to his two young sons Honorius and Arcadius. But the two lads had neither their father's strength nor their father's nobleness. Weak and profligate, they fretted Arsenius's soul day by day; and, at last, so goes the story, provoked him so far that, according to the fashion of a Roman pedagogue, he took the ferula and administered to one of the princes a caning, which he no doubt deserved. The young prince, in revenge, plotted against his life. Among the parasites of the Palace it was not difficult to find those who would use steel and poison readily enough in the service of an heir-apparent, and Arsenius fled for his life: and fled, as men were wont in those days, to Egypt and the Thebaid. Forty years old he was when he left the court, and forty years more he spent among the cells at Scetis, weeping day and night. He migrated afterwards to a place called Troe, and there died at the age of ninety-five, having wept himself, say his admirers, almost blind. He avoided, as far as possible, beholding the face of man; upon the face of woman he would never look. A noble lady, whom he had known probably in the world, came all the way from Rome to see him; but he refused himself to her sternly, almost roughly. He had known too much of the fine ladies of the Roman court; all he cared for was peace. There is a story of him that, changing once his dwelling-place, probably from Scetis to Troe, he asked, somewhat peevishly, of the monks around him, "What that noise was?" They told him it was only the wind among the reeds. "Alas!" he said, "I have fled everywhere in search of silence, and yet here the very reeds speak." The simple and comparatively unlearned monks around him looked with a profound respect on the philosopher, courtier, scholar, who had cast away the real pomps and vanities of this life, such as they had never known. There is a story told, plainly concerning Arsenius, though his name is not actually mentioned in it, how a certain old monk saw him lying upon a softer mat than his fellows, and indulged with a few more comforts; and complained indignantly of his luxury, and the abbot's favouritism. Then asked the abbot, "What didst thou eat before thou becamest a monk?" He confessed he had been glad enough to fill his stomach with a few beans. "How wert thou dressed?" He was glad enough, again he confessed, to have any clothes at all on his back. "Where didst thou sleep?" "Often enough on the bare ground in the open air," was the answer. "Then," said the abbot, "thou art, by thy own confession, better off as a monk than thou wast as a poor labouring man: and yet thou grudgest a little comfort to one who has given up more luxury than thou hast ever beheld. This man slept beneath silken canopies; he was carried in gilded litters, by trains of slaves; he was clothed in purple and fine linen; he fed upon all the delicacies of the great city: and he has given up all for Christ. And what hast thou given up, that thou shouldst grudge him a softer mat, or a little more food each day?" And so the monk was abashed, and held his peace.

As for Arsenius's tears, it is easy to call his grief exaggerated or superstitious: but those who look on them with human eyes will pardon them, and watch with sacred pity the grief of a good man, who felt that his life had been an utter failure. He saw his two pupils, between whom, at their father's death, the Roman Empire was divided into Eastern and Western, grow more and more incapable of governing. He saw a young barbarian, whom he must have often met at the court in Byzantium, as Master of the Horse, come down from his native forests, and sack the Eternal City of Rome. He saw evil and woe unspeakable fall on that world which he had left behind him, till the earth was filled with blood, and Antichrist seemed ready to appear, and the day of judgment to be at hand. And he had been called to do what he could to stave off this ruin, to make those young princes decree justice and rule in judgment by the fear of God. But he had failed; and there was nothing left to him save self-accusation and regret, and dread lest some, at least, of the blood which had been shed might be required at his hands. Therefore, sitting upon his palm-mat there in Troe, he wept his life away; happier, nevertheless, and more honourable in the sight of God and man than if, like a Mazarin or a Talleyrand, and many another crafty politician, both in Church and State, he had hardened his heart against his own mistakes, and, by crafty intrigue and adroit changing of sides at the right moment, had contrived to secure for himself, out of the general ruin, honour and power and wealth, and delicate food, and a luxurious home, and so been one of those of whom the Psalmist says, with awful irony, "So long as thou doest well unto thyself, men will speak good of thee."

One good deed at least Arsenius had seen done—a deed which has lasted to all time, and done, too, to the eternal honour of his order, by a monk—namely, the abolition of gladiator shows. For centuries these wholesale murders had lasted through the Roman Republic and through the Roman Empire. Human beings in the prime of youth and health, captives or slaves, condemned malefactors, and even free-born men, who hired themselves out to death, had been trained to destroy each other in the amphitheatre for the amusement, not merely of the Roman mob, but of the Roman ladies. Thousands sometimes, in a single day, had been

"Butchered to make a Roman holiday."

The training of gladiators had become a science. By their weapons and their armour, and their modes of fighting, they had been distinguished into regular classes, of which the antiquaries count up full eighteen: Andabatae, who wore helmets without any opening for the eyes, so that they were obliged to fight blindfold, and thus excited the mirth of the spectators; Hoplomachi, who fought in a complete suit of armour; Mirmillones, who had the image of a fish upon their helmets, and fought in armour with a short sword, matched usually against the Retiarii, who fought without armour, and whose weapons were a casting-net and a trident. These, and other species of fighters, were drilled and fed in "families" by Lanistae; or regular trainers, who let them out to persons wishing to exhibit a show. Women, even high-born ladies, had been seized in former times with the madness of fighting, and, as shameless as cruel, had gone down into the arena to delight with their own wounds and their own gore the eyes of the Roman people.

And these things were done, and done too often, under the auspices of the gods, and at their most sacred festivals. So deliberate and organized a system of wholesale butchery has never perhaps existed on this earth before or since, not even in the worship of those Mexican gods whose idols Cortez and his soldiers found fed with human hearts, and the walls of their temples crusted with human gore. Gradually the spirit of the Gospel had been triumphing over this abomination. Ever since the time of Tertullian, in the second century, Christian preachers and writers had lifted up their voice in the name of humanity. Towards the end of the third century, the Emperors themselves had so far yielded to the voice of reason, as to forbid by edicts the gladiatorial fights. But the public opinion of the mob in most of the great cities had been too strong both for saints and for emperors. St. Augustine himself tells us of the horrible joy which he, in his youth, had seen come over the vast ring of flushed faces at these horrid sights; and in Arsenius's own time, his miserable pupil, the weak Honorius, bethought himself of celebrating once more the heathen festival of the Secular Games, and formally to allow therein an exhibition of gladiators. But in the midst of that show sprang down into the arena of the Colosseum of Rome an unknown monk, some said from Nitria, some from Phrygia, and with his own hands parted the combatants in the name of Christ and God. The mob, baulked for a moment of their pleasure, sprang on him, and stoned him to death. But the crime was followed by a sudden revulsion of feeling. By an edict of the Emperor the gladiatorial sports were forbidden for ever; and the Colosseum, thenceforth useless, crumbled slowly away into that vast ruin which remains unto this day, purified, as men well said, from the blood of tens of thousands, by the blood of one true and noble martyr.

THE HERMITS OF ASIA

The impulse which, given by Antony, had been propagated in Asia by his great pupil, Hilarion, spread rapidly far and wide. Hermits took possession of the highest peaks of Sinai; and driven from thence, so tradition tells, by fear of those mysterious noises which still haunt its cliffs, settled at that sheltered spot where now stands the convent of St. Catharine. Massacred again and again by the wild Arab tribes, their places were filled up by fresh hermits, and their spiritual descendants hold the convent to this day.

Through the rich and luxuriant region of Syria, and especially round the richest and most luxurious of its cities, Antioch, hermits settled, and bore, by the severity of their lives, a noble witness against the profligacy of its inhabitants, who had half renounced the paganism of their forefathers without renouncing in the least, it seems, those sins which drew down of old the vengeance of a righteous God upon their forefathers, whether in Canaan or in Syria itself.

At Antioch, about the year 347, was born the famous Chrysostom, John of the Golden Mouth; and near Antioch he became a hermit, and dwelt, so legends say, several years alone in the wilderness: till, nerved by that hard training, he went forth again into the world to become, whether at Antioch or at Constantinople, the bravest as well as the most eloquent preacher of righteousness and rebuker of sin which the world had seen since the times of St. Paul. The labours of Chrysostom belong not so much to this book as to a general ecclesiastical history: but it must not be forgotten that he, like all the great men of that age, had been a monk, and kept up his monastic severity, even in the midst of the world, until his dying day.

At Nisibis, again, upon the very frontier of Persia, appeared another very remarkable personage, known as the Great Jacob or Great St. James. Taking (says his admiring biographer, Theodoret of Cyra) to the peaks of the loftiest mountains., he passed his life on them, in spring and summer haunting the woods, with the sky for a roof, but sheltering himself in winter in a cave. His food was wild fruits and mountain herbs. He never used a fire, and, clothed in a goats' hair garment, was perhaps the first of those Boscoi, or "browsing hermits," who lived literally like the wild animals in the flesh, while they tried to live like angels in the spirit.

Some of the stories told of Jacob savour of that vindictiveness which Giraldus Cambrensis, in after years, attributed to the saints in Ireland. He was walking one day over the Persian frontier, "to visit the plants of true religion" and "bestow on them due care," when he passed at a fountain a troop of damsels washing clothes and treading them with their feet. They seem, according to the story, to have stared at the wild man, instead of veiling their faces or letting down their garments. No act or word of rudeness is reported of them: but Jacob's modesty or pride was so much scandalized that he cursed both the fountain and the girls. The fountain of course dried up forthwith, and the damsels' hair turned grey. They ran weeping into the town. The townsfolk came out, and compelled Jacob, by their prayers, to restore the water to their fountain; but the grey hair he refused to restore to its original hue unless the damsels would come and beg pardon publicly themselves. The poor girls were ashamed to come, and their hair remained grey ever after.

A story like this may raise a smile in some of my readers, in others something like indignation or contempt. But as long as such legends remain in these hermit lives, told with as much gravity as any other portion of the biography, and eloquently lauded, as this deed is, by Bishop Theodoret, as proofs of the holiness and humanity of the saint, an honest author is bound to notice some of them at least, and not to give an alluring and really dishonest account of these men and their times, by detailing every anecdote which can elevate them in the mind of the reader, while he carefully omits all that may justly disgust him.

Yet, after all, we are not bound to believe this legend, any more than we are bound to believe that when Jacob saw a Persian judge give an unjust sentence, he forthwith cursed, not him, but a rock close by, which instantly crumbled into innumerable fragments, so terrifying that judge that he at once revoked his sentence, and gave a just decision.

Neither, again, need we believe that it was by sending, as men said in his own days, swarms of mosquitos against the Persian invaders, that he put to flight their elephants and horses: and yet it may be true that, in the famous siege of Nisibis, Jacob played the patriot and the valiant man. For when Sapor, the Persian king, came against Nisibis with all his forces, with troops of elephants, and huge machines of war, and towers full of archers wheeled up to the walls, and at last, damming the river itself, turned its current against the fortifications of unburnt brick, until a vast breach was opened in the walls, then Jacob, standing in the breach, encouraged by his prayers his fellow-townsmen to stop it with stone, brick, timber, and whatsoever came to hand; and Sapor, the Persian Sultan, saw "that divine man," and his goats'-hair tunic and cloak seemed transformed into a purple robe and royal diadem. And, whether he was seized with superstitious fear, or whether the hot sun or the marshy ground had infected his troops with disease, or whether the mosquito swarms actually became intolerable, the great King of Persia turned and went away.

So Nisibis was saved for a while; to be shamefully surrendered to the Persians a few years afterwards by the weak young Emperor Jovian. Old Ammianus Marcellinus, brave soldier as he was, saw with disgust the whole body of citizens ordered to quit the city within three days, and "men appointed to compel obedience to the order, with threats of death to every one who delayed his departure; and the whole city was a scene of mourning and lamentation, and in every quarter nothing was heard but one universal wail, matrons tearing their hair, and about to be driven from the homes in which they had been born and brought up; the mother who had lost her children, or the wife who had lost her husband, about to be torn from the place rendered sacred by their shades, clinging to their doorposts, embracing their thresholds, and pouring forth floods of tears. Every road was crowded, each person struggling away as he could. Many, too, loaded themselves with as much of their property as they thought they could carry, while leaving behind them abundant and costly furniture, which they could not remove for want of beasts of burden." {159}

One treasure, however, they did remove, of which the old soldier Ammianus says nothing, and which, had he seen it pass him on the road, he would have treated with supreme contempt. And that, says Theodoret, was the holy body of "their prince and defender," St. James the mountain hermit, round which the emigrants chanted, says Theodoret, hymns of regret and praise, "for, had he been alive, that city would have never passed into barbarian hands."

There stood with Jacob in the breach, during that siege of Nisibis, a man of gentler temperament, a disciple of his, who had received baptism at his hands, and who was, like himself, a hermit—Ephraim, or Ephrem, of Edessa, as he is commonly called, for, though born at Nisibis, his usual home was at Edessa, the metropolis of a Syrian-speaking race. Into the Syrian tongue Ephrem translated the doctrines of the Christian faith and the Gospel history, and spread abroad, among the heathen round, a number of delicate and graceful hymns, which remain to this day, and of which some have lately been translated into English. {160} Soft, sad, and dreamy as they were, they had strength and beauty enough in them to supersede the Gnostic hymns of Bardesanes and his son Harmonius, which had been long popular among the Syrians; and for centuries afterwards, till Christianity was swept away by the followers of Mahomet, the Syrian husbandman beguiled his toil with the pious and plaintive melodies of St. Ephrem.

But Ephrem was not only a hermit and a poet: he was a preacher and a missionary. If he wept, as it was said, day and night for his own sins and the sins of mankind, he did his best at least to cure those sins. He was a demagogue, or leader of the people, for good and not for evil, to whom the simple Syrians looked up for many a year as their spiritual father. He died in peace, as he said himself, like the labourer who has finished his day's work, like the wandering merchant who returns to his fatherland, leaving nothing behind him save prayers and counsels, for "Ephrem," he added, "had neither wallet nor pilgrim's staff."

"His last utterance" (I owe this fact to M. de Montalembert's book, "Moines d'Occident") "was a protest on behalf of the dignity of man redeemed by the Son of God."

"The young and pious daughter of the Governor of Edessa came weeping to receive his latest breath. He made her swear never again to be carried in a litter by slaves, 'The neck of man,' he said, 'should bear no yoke save that of Christ.'" This anecdote is one among many which go to prove that from the time that St. Paul had declared the great truth that in Christ Jesus was neither bond nor free, and had proclaimed the spiritual brotherhood of all men in Christ, slavery, as an institution, was doomed to slow but certain death. But that death was accelerated by the monastic movement, wherever it took root. A class of men who came not to be ministered unto, but to minister to others; who prided themselves upon needing fewer luxuries than the meanest slaves; who took rank among each other and among men not on the ground of race, nor of official position, nor of wealth, nor even of intellect, but simply on the ground of virtue, was a perpetual protest against slavery and tyranny of every kind; a perpetual witness to the world that, whether all men were equal or not in the sight of God, the only rank among them of which God would take note, would be their rank in goodness.

The Hermits

BASIL

On the south shore of the Black Sea, eastward of Sinope, there dwelt in those days, at the mouth of the River Iris, a hermit as gentle and as pure as Ephrem of Edessa. Beside a roaring waterfall, amid deep glens and dark forests, with distant glimpses of the stormy sea beyond, there lived on bread and water a graceful gentleman, young and handsome; a scholar too, who had drunk deeply at the fountains of Pagan philosophy and poetry, and had been educated with care at Constantinople and at Athens, as well as at his native city of Caesaraea, in the heart of Asia Minor, now dwindled under Turkish misrule into a wretched village. He was heir to great estates; the glens and forests round him were his own: and that was the use which he made of them. On the other side of the torrent, his mother and his sister, a maiden of wonderful beauty, lived the hermit life, on a footing of perfect equality with their female slaves, and the pious women who had joined them.

Basil's austerities—or rather the severe climate of the Black Sea forests—brought him to an early grave. But his short life was spent well enough. He was a poet, with an eye for the beauty of Nature— especially for the beauty of the sea—most rare in those times; and his works are full of descriptions of scenery as healthy- minded as they are vivid and graceful.

In his travels through Egypt, Palestine, and Syria, he had seen the hermits, and longed to emulate them; but (to do him justice) his ideal of the so-called "religious life" was more practical than those of the solitaries of Egypt, who had been his teachers. "It was the life" (says Dean Milman {163}) "of the industrious religious community, not of the indolent and solitary anchorite, which to Basil was the perfection of Christianity. . . . The indiscriminate charity of these institutions was to receive orphans" (of which there were but too many in those evil days) "of all classes, for education and maintenance: but other children only with the consent or at the request of parents, certified before witnesses; and vows were by no means to be enforced upon these youthful pupils. Slaves who fled to the monasteries were to be admonished and sent back to their owners. There is one reservation" (and that one only too necessary then), "that slaves were not bound to obey their master, if he should order what is contrary to the law of God. Industry was to be the animating principle of these settlements. Prayer and psalmody were to have their stated hours, but by no means to intrude on those devoted to useful labour. These labours were strictly defined; such as were of real use to the community, not those which might contribute to vice or luxury. Agriculture was especially recommended. The life was in no respect to be absorbed in a perpetual mystic communion with the Deity."

The ideal which Basil set before him was never fulfilled in the East. Transported to the West by St. Benedict, "the father of all monks," it became that conventual system which did so much during the early middle age, not only for the conversion and civilization, but for the arts and the agriculture of Europe.

Basil, like his bosom friend, Gregory of Nazianzen, had to go forth from his hermitage into the world, and be a bishop, and fight the battles of the true faith. But, as with Gregory, his hermit- training had strengthened his soul, while it weakened his body. The Emperor Valens, supporting the Arians against the orthodox, sent to Basil his Prefect of the Praetorium, an officer of the highest rank. The prefect argued, threatened; Basil was firm. "I never met," said he at last, "such boldness." "Because," said Basil, "you never met a bishop." The prefect returned to his Emperor. "My lord, we are conquered; this bishop is above threats. We can do nothing but by force." The Emperor shrank from that crime, and Basil and the orthodoxy of his diocese were saved. The rest of his life and of Gregory's belongs, like that of Chrysostom, to general history, and we need pursue it no further here.

I said that Basil's idea of what monks should be was never carried out in the East, and it cannot be denied that, as the years went on, the hermit life took a form less and less practical, and more and more repulsive also. Such men as Antony, Hilarion, Basil, had valued the ascetic training, not so much because it had, as they thought, a merit in itself, but because it enabled the spirit to rise above the flesh; because it gave them strength to conquer their passions and appetites, and leave their soul free to think and act.

But their disciples, especially in Syria, seem to have attributed more and more merit to the mere act of inflicting want and suffering on themselves. Their souls were darkened, besides, more and more, by a doctrine unknown to the Bible, unknown to the early Christians, and one which does not seem to have had any strong hold of the mind of Antony himself—namely, that sins committed after baptism could only be washed away by tears, and expiated by penance; that for them the merits of him who died for the sins of the whole world were of little or of no avail.

Therefore, in perpetual fear of punishment hereafter, they set their whole minds to punish themselves on earth, always tortured by the dread that they were not punishing themselves enough, till they crushed down alike body, mind, and soul into an abject superstition, the details of which are too repulsive to be written here. Some of the instances of this self-invented misery which are recorded, even as early as the time of Theodoret, bishop of Cyra, in the middle of the fifth century, make us wonder at the puzzling inconsistencies of the human mind. Did these poor creatures really believe that God could be propitiated by the torture of his own creatures? What sense could Theodoret (who was a good man himself) have put upon the words, "God is good," or "God is love," while he was looking with satisfaction, even with admiration and awe, on practices which were more fit for worshippers of Moloch?

Those who think these words too strong, may judge for themselves how far they apply to his story of Marana and Cyra.

Marana, then, and Cyra were two young ladies of Berhoea, who had given up all the pleasures of life to settle themselves in a roofless cottage outside the town. They had stopped up the door with stones and clay, and allowed it only to be opened at the feast of Pentecost. Around them lived certain female slaves who had voluntarily chosen the same life, and who were taught and exhorted through a little window by their mistresses; or rather, it would seem, by Marana alone: for Cyra (who was bent double by her "training") was never to speak. Theodoret, as a priest, was allowed to enter the sacred enclosure, and found them shrouded from head to foot in long veils, so that neither their faces or hands could be seen; and underneath their veils, burdened on every limb, poor wretches, with such a load of iron chains and rings that a strong man, he says, could not have stood under the weight. Thus had they endured for two-and-forty years, exposed to sun and wind, to frost and rain, taking no food at times for many days together. I have no mind to finish the picture, and still less to record any of the phrases of rapturous admiration with which Bishop Theodoret comments upon their pitiable superstition.

The Hermits

SIMEON STYLITES

Of all such anchorites of the far East, the most remarkable, perhaps, was the once famous Simeon Stylites—a name almost forgotten, save by antiquaries and ecclesiastics, till Mr. Tennyson made it once more notorious in a poem as admirable for its savage grandness, as for its deep knowledge of human nature. He has comprehended thoroughly, as it seems to me, that struggle between self-abasement and self-conceit, between the exaggerated sense of sinfulness and the exaggerated ambition of saintly honour, which must have gone on in the minds of these ascetics—the temper which could cry out one moment with perfect honesty—

"Although I be the basest of mankind, From scalp to sole one slough and crust of sin;"

at the next—

"I will not cease to grasp the hope I hold Of saintdom; and to clamour, mourn, and sob, Battering the gates of heaven with storms of prayer. Have mercy, Lord, and take away my sin. Let this avail, just, dreadful, mighty God, This not be all in vain, that thrice ten years Thrice multiplied by superhuman pangs, * * * * * * A sign between the meadow and the cloud, Patient on this tall pillar I have borne Rain, wind, frost, heat, hail, damp, and sleet, and snow; And I had hoped that ere this period closed Thou wouldst have caught me up into thy rest, Denying not these weather-beaten limbs The meed of saints, the white robe and the palm. O take the meaning, Lord: I do not breathe, Not whisper any murmur of complaint. Pain heaped ten hundred-fold to this, were still Less burthen, by ten-hundred-fold, to bear Than were those lead-like tons of sin, that crush'd My spirit flat before thee."

Admirably also has Mr. Tennyson conceived the hermit's secret doubt of the truth of those miracles, which he is so often told that he has worked, that he at last begins to believe that he must have worked them; and the longing, at the same time, to justify himself to himself, by persuading himself that he has earned miraculous powers. On this whole question of hermit miracles I shall speak at length hereafter. I have given specimens enough of them already, and shall give as few as possible henceforth. There is a sameness about them which may become wearisome to those who cannot be expected to believe them. But what the hermits themselves thought of them, is told (at least, so I suspect) only too truly by Mr. Tennyson—

"O Lord, thou knowest what a man I am; A sinful man, conceived and born in sin: 'Tis their own doing; this is none of mine; Lay it not to me. Am I to blame for this, That here come those who worship me? Ha! ha! The silly people take me for a saint, And bring me offerings of fruit and flowers: And I, in truth (thou wilt bear witness here), Have all in all endured as much, and more Than many just and holy men, whose names Are register'd and calendar'd for saints. Good people, you do ill to kneel to me. What is it I can have done to merit this? It may be I have wrought some miracles, And cured some halt and maimed: but what of that? It may be, no one, even among the saints, Can match his pains with mine: but what of that? Yet do not rise; for you may look on me, And in your looking you may kneel to God. Speak, is there any of you halt and maimed? I think you know I have some power with heaven From my long penance; let him speak his wish. Yes, I can heal him. Power goes forth from me. They say that they are heal'd. Ah, hark! they shout, 'St. Simeon Stylites!' Why, if so, God reaps a harvest in me. O my soul, God reaps a harvest in thee. If this be, Can I work miracles, and not be saved? This is not told of any. They were saints. It cannot be but that I shall be saved; Yea, crowned a saint." . . .

I shall not take the liberty of quoting more: but shall advise all who read these pages to study seriously Mr. Tennyson's poem if they wish to understand that darker side of the hermit life which became at last, in the East, the only side of it. For in the East the hermits seem to have degenerated, by the time of the Mahomedan conquest, into mere self-torturing fakeers, like those who may be seen to this day in Hindostan. The salt lost its savour, and in due tune it was trampled under foot; and the armies of the Moslem swept out of the East a superstition which had ended by enervating instead of ennobling humanity.

But in justice, not only to myself, but to Mr. Tennyson (whose details of Simeon's asceticism may seem to some exaggerated and impossible), I have thought fit to give his life at length, omitting only many of his miracles, and certain stories of his penances, which can only excite horror and disgust, without edifying the reader.

There were, then, three hermits of this name, often confounded; and all alike famous (as were Julian, Daniel, and other Stylites) for standing for many years on pillars. One of the Simeons is said by Moschus to have been struck by lightning, and his death to have been miraculously revealed to Julian the Stylite, who lived twenty-four miles off. More than one Stylite, belonging to the Monophysite heresy of Severus Acephalus, was to be found, according to Moschus, in the East at the beginning of the seventh century. This biography is that of the elder Simeon, who died (according to Cedrenus) about 460, after passing some forty or fifty years upon pillars of different heights. There is much discrepancy in the accounts, both of his date and of his age; but that such a person really existed, and had his imitators, there can be no doubt. He is honoured as a saint alike by the Latin and by the Greek Churches.

His life has been written by a disciple of his named Antony, who professes to have been with him when he died; and also by Theodoret, who knew him well in life. Both are to be found in Rosweyde, and there seems no reason to doubt their authenticity. I have therefore interwoven them both, marking the paragraphs taken from each.

Theodoret, who says that he was born in the village of Gesa, between Antioch and Cilicia, calls him that "famous Simeon—that great miracle of the whole world, whom all who obey the Roman rule know; whom the Persians also know, and the Indians, and AEthiopians; nay, his fame has even spread to the wandering Scythians, and taught them his love of toil and love of wisdom;" and says that he might be compared with Jacob the patriarch, Joseph the temperate, Moses the legislator, David the king and prophet, Micaiah the prophet, and the divine men who were like them. He tells how Simeon, as a boy, kept his father's sheep, and, being forced by heavy snow to leave them in the fold, went with his parents to the church, and there heard the Gospel which blesses those who mourn and weep, and calls those miserable who laugh, and those enviable who have a pure heart. And when he asked a bystander what he would gain who did each of these things, the man propounded to him the solitary life, and pointed out to him the highest philosophy.

This, Theodoret says, he heard from the saint's own tongue. His disciple Antony gives the story of his conversion somewhat differently.

St. Simeon (says Antony) was chosen by God from his birth, and used to study how to obey and please him. Now his father's name was Susocion, and he was brought up by his parents.

When he was thirteen years old, he was feeding his father's sheep; and seeing a church he left the sheep and went in, and heard an epistle being read. And when he asked an elder, "Master, what is that which is read?" the old man replied, "For the substance (or very being) of the soul, that a man may learn to fear God with his whole heart, and his whole mind." Quoth the blessed Simeon, "What is to fear God?" Quoth the elder, "Wherefore troublest thou me, my son?" Quoth he, "I inquire of thee, as of God. For I wish to learn what I hear from thee, because I am ignorant and a fool." The elder answered, "If any man shall have fasted continually, and offered prayers every moment, and shall have humbled himself to every man, and shall not have loved gold, nor parents, nor garments, nor possessions, and if he honours his father and mother, and follows the priests of God, he shall inherit the eternal kingdom: but he who, on the contrary, does not keep those things, he shall inherit the outer darkness which God hath prepared for the devil and his angels. All these things, my son, are heaped together in a monastery."

Hearing this, the blessed Simeon fell at his feet, saying, "Thou art my father and my mother, and my teacher of good works, and guide to the kingdom of heaven. For thou hast gained my soul, which was already being sunk in perdition. May the Lord repay thee again for it. For these are the things which edify. I will now go into a monastery, where God shall choose; and let his will be done on me." The elder said, "My son, before thou enterest, hear me. Thou shalt have tribulation; for thou must watch and serve in nakedness, and sustain ills without ceasing; and again thou shalt be comforted, thou vessel precious to God."

And forthwith the blessed Simeon, going out of the church, went to the monastery of the holy Timotheus, a wonder-working man; and falling down before the gate of the monastery, he lay five days, neither eating nor drinking. And on the fifth day, the abbot, coming out, asked him, "Whence art thou, my son? And what parents hast thou, that thou art so afflicted? Or what is thy name, lest perchance thou hast done some wrong? Or perchance thou art a slave, and fleest from thy master?" Then the blessed Simeon said with tears, "By no means, master; but I long to be a servant of God, if he so will, because I wish to save my lost soul. Bid me, therefore, enter the monastery, and leave all; and send me away no more." Then the Abbot, taking his hand, introduced him into the monastery, saying to the brethren, "My sons, behold I deliver you this brother; teach him the canons of the monastery." Now he was in the monastery about four months, serving all without complaint, in which he learnt the whole Psalter by heart, receiving every day divine food. But the food which he took with his brethren he gave away secretly to the poor, not caring for the morrow. So the brethren ate at even: but he only on the seventh day.

But one day, having gone to the well to draw water, he took the rope from the bucket with which the brethren drew water, and wound it round his body from his loins to his neck: and going in, said to the brethren, "I went out to draw water, and found no rope on the bucket." And they said, "Hold thy peace, brother, lest the abbot know it; till the thing has passed over." But his body was wounded by the tightness and roughness of the rope, because it cut him to the bone, and sank into his flesh till it was hardly seen. But one day, some of the brethren going out, found him giving his food to the poor; and when they returned, said to the abbot, "Whence hast thou brought us that man? We cannot abstain like him, for he fasts from Lord's day to Lord's day, and gives away his food." . . . Then the abbot, going out, found as was told him, and said, "Son, what is it which the brethren tell of thee? Is it not enough for thee to fast as we do? Hast thou not heard the Gospel, saying of teachers, that the disciple is not above his master?" . . . The blessed Simeon stood and answered nought. And the abbot, being angry, bade strip him, and found the rope round him, so that only its outside appeared; and cried with a loud voice, saying, "Whence has this man come to us, wanting to destroy the rule of the monastery? I pray thee depart hence, and go whither thou wiliest." And with great trouble they took off the rope, and his flesh with it, and taking care of him, healed him.

But after he was healed he went out of the monastery, no man knowing of it, and entered a deserted tank, in which was no water, where unclean spirits dwelt. And that very night it was revealed to the abbot, that a multitude of people surrounded the monastery with clubs and swords, saying, "Give us Simeon the servant of God, Timotheus; else we will burn thee with thy monastery, because thou hast angered a just man." And when he woke, he told the brethren the vision, and how he was much disturbed thereby. And another night he saw a multitude of strong men standing and saying, "Give us Simeon the servant of God; for he is beloved by God and the angels: why hast thou vexed him? He is greater than thou before God; for all the angels are sorry on his behalf. And God is minded to set him on high in the world, that by him many signs may be done, such as no man has done." Then the abbot, rising, said with great fear to the brethren, "Seek me that man, and bring him hither, lest perchance we all die on his account. He is truly a saint of God, for I have heard and seen great wonders of him." Then all the monks went out and searched, but in vain, and told the abbot how they had sought him everywhere, save in the deserted tank. . . . Then the abbot went, with five brethren, to the tank. And making a prayer, he went down into it with the brethren. And the blessed Simeon, seeing him, began to entreat, saying, "I beg you, servants of God, let me alone one hour, that I may render up my spirit; for yet a little, and it will fail. But my soul is very weary, because I have angered the Lord." But the abbot said to him, "Come, servant of God, that we may take thee to the monastery; for I know concerning thee that thou art a servant of God." But when he would not, they brought him by force to the monastery. And all fell at his feet, weeping, and saying, "We have sinned against thee, servant of God; forgive us." But the blessed Simeon groaned, saying, "Wherefore do ye burden an unhappy man and a sinner? You are the servants of God, and my fathers." And he stayed there about one year.

After this (says Theodoret) he came to the Telanassus, under the peak of the mountain on which he lived till his death; and having found there a little house, he remained in it shut up for three years. But eager always to increase the riches of virtue, he longed, in imitation of the divine Moses and Elias, to fast forty days; and tried to persuade Bassus, who was then set over the priests in the villages, to leave nothing within by him, but to close up the door with clay. He spoke to him of the difficulty, and warned him not to think that a violent death was a virtue. "Put by me then, father," he said, "ten loaves, and a cruse of water, and if I find my body need sustenance, I will partake of them." At the end of the days, that wonderful man of God, Bassus, removed the clay, and going in, found the food and water untouched, and Simeon lying unable to speak or move. Getting a sponge, he moistened and opened his lips and then gave him the symbols of the divine mysteries; and, strengthened by them, he arose, and took some food, chewing little by little lettuces and succory, and such like.

From that time, for twenty-eight years (says Theodoret), he had remained fasting continually for forty days at a time. But custom had made it more easy to him. For on the first days he used to stand and praise God; after that, when through emptiness he could stand no longer, he used to sit and perform the divine office; and on the last day, even lie down. For when his strength failed slowly, he was forced to lie half dead. But after he stood on the column he could not bear to lie down, but invented another way by which he could stand. He fastened a beam to the column, and tied himself to it by ropes, and so passed the forty days. But afterwards, when he had received greater grace from on high, he did not want even that help: but stood for the forty days, taking no food, but strengthened by alacrity of soul and divine grace.

When he had passed three years in that little house, he took possession of the peak which has since been so famous; and when he had commanded a wall to be made round him, and procured an iron chain, twenty cubits long, he fastened one end of it to a great stone, and the other to his right foot, so that he could not, if he wished, leave those bounds. There he lived, continually picturing heaven to himself, and forcing himself to contemplate things which are above the heavens; for the iron bond did not check the flight of his thoughts. But when the wonderful Meletius, to whom the care of the episcopate of Antioch was then commended (a man of sense and prudence, and adorned with shrewdness of intellect), told him that the iron was superfluous, since the will is able enough to impose on the body the chains of reason, he gave way, and obeyed his persuasion. And having sent for a smith, he bade him strike off the chain.

[Here follow some painful details unnecessary to be translated.]

When, therefore, his fame was flying far and wide everywhere, all ran together, not only the neighbours, but those who were many days' journey off, some bringing the palsied, some begging health for the sick, some that they might become fathers, and all wishing to receive from him what they had not received from nature; and when they had received, and gained their request, they went back joyful, proclaiming the benefits they had obtained, and sending many more to beg the same. So, as all are coming up from every quarter, and the road is like a river, one may see gathered in that place an ocean of men, which receives streams from every side; not only of those who live in our region, but Ishmaelites, and Persians, and the Armenians who are subject to them, and Iberi, and Homerites, and those who dwell beyond them. Many have come also from the extreme west, Spaniards, and Britons, and Gauls who live between the two. Of Italy it is superfluous to speak; for they say that at Rome the man has become so celebrated that they have put little images of him in all the porches of the shops, providing thereby for themselves a sort of safeguard and security.

When, therefore, they came innumerable (for all tried to touch him, and receive some blessing from those skin garments of his), thinking it in the first place absurd and unfit that such exceeding honour should be paid him, and next, disliking the labour of the business, devised that station on the pillar, bidding one be built, first of six cubits, then of twelve, next of twenty-two, and now of thirty- six. For he longs to fly up to heaven, and be freed from this earthly conversation.

But I believe that this station was made not without divine counsel. Wherefore I exhort fault-finders to bridle their tongue, and not let it rashly loose, but rather consider that the Lord has often devised such things, that he might profit those who were too slothful.

In proof of which, Theodoret quotes the examples of Isaiah, Hosea, and Ezekiel; and then goes on to say how God in like manner ordained this new and admirable spectacle, by the novelty of it drawing all to look, and exhibiting to those who came, a lesson which they could trust. For the novelty of the spectacle (he says) is a worthy warrant for the teaching; and he who came to see goes away instructed in divine things. And as those whose lot it is to rule over men, after a certain period of time, change the impressions on their coins, sometimes stamping them with images of lions, sometimes of stars, sometimes of angels, and trying, by a new mark, to make the gold more precious; so the King of all, adding to piety and true religion these new and manifold modes of living, as certain stamps on coin, excites to praise the tongues not only of the children of faith, but of those who are diseased with unbelief. And that so it is, not only words bear witness, but facts proclaim aloud. For many myriads of Ishmaelites, who were enslaved in the darkness of impiety, have been illuminated by that station on the column. For this most shining lamp, set as it were upon a candlestick, sent forth all round its rays, like of the sun: and one may see (as I said) Iberi coming, and Persians, and Armenians, and accepting divine baptism. But the Ishmaelites, coming by tribes, 200 and 300 at a time, and sometimes even 1,000, deny, with shouts, the error of their fathers; and breaking in pieces, before that great illuminator, the images which they had worshipped, and renouncing the orgies of Venus (for they had received from ancient times the worship of that daemon), they receive the divine sacraments, and take laws from that holy tongue, bidding farewell to their ancestral rites, and renouncing the eating of wild asses and camels. And this I have seen with my own eyes, and have heard them renouncing the impiety of their fathers, and assenting to the Evangelic doctrine.

But once I was in the greatest danger: for he himself told them to go to me, and receive priestly benediction, saying that they would thence obtain great advantage. But they, having run together in somewhat too barbarous fashion, some dragged me before, some behind, some sideways; and those who were further off, scrambling over the others, and stretching out their hands, plucked my beard, or seized my clothes; and I should have been stifled by their too warm onset, had not he, shouting out, dispersed them all. Such usefulness has that column, which is mocked at by scornful men, poured forth; and so great a ray of the knowledge of God has it sent forth into the minds of barbarians.

I know also of his having done another thing of this kind:—One tribe was beseeching the divine man, that he would send forth some prayer and blessing for their chief: but another tribe which was present retorted that he ought not to bless that chief, but theirs; for the one was a most unjust man, but the other averse to injustice. And when there had been a great contention and barbaric wrangling between them, they attacked each other. But I, using many words, kept exhorting them to be quiet, seeing that the divine man was able enough to give a blessing to both. But the one tribe kept saying, that the first chief ought not to have it; and the other tribe trying to deprive the second chief of it. Then he, by threatening them from above, and calling them dogs, hardly stilled the quarrel. This I have told, wishing to show their great faith. For they would not have thus gone mad against each other, had they not believed that the divine man's blessing possesses some very great power.

I saw another miracle, which was very celebrated. One coming up (he, too, was a chief of a Saracen tribe) besought the divine personage that he would help a man whose limbs had given way in paralysis on the road; and he said the misfortune had fallen on him in Callinicus, which is a very large camp. When he was brought into the midst, the saint bade him renounce the impiety of his forefathers; and when he willingly obeyed, he asked him if he believed in the Father, the only-begotten Son, and the Holy Spirit. And when he confessed that he believed—"Believing," said he, "in their names, Arise." And when the man had risen, he bade him carry away his chief (who was a very large man) on his shoulders to his tent. He took him up, and went away forthwith; while those who were present raised their voices in praise of God. This he commanded, imitating the Lord, who bade the paralytic carry his bed. Let no man call this imitation tyranny. For his saying is, "He who believeth in me, the works which I do, he shall do also, and more than these shall he do." And, indeed, we have seen the fulfilment of this promise. For though the shadow of the Lord never worked a miracle, the shadow of the great Peter both loosed death, and drove out diseases, and put daemons to flight. But the Lord it was who did also these miracles by his servants; and now likewise, using his name, the divine Simeon works his innumerable wonders.

It befell also that another wonder was worked, by no means inferior to the last. For among those who had believed in the saving name of the Lord Christ, an Ishmaelite, of no humble rank, had made a vow to God, with Simeon as witness. Now his promise was this, that he would henceforth to the end abstain from animal food. Transgressing this promise once, I know not how, he slew a bird, and dared to eat it. But God being minded to bring him by reproof to conversion, and to honour his servant, who was a witness to the broken vow, the flesh of the bird was changed into the nature of a stone, so that, even if he wished, he could not thenceforth eat it. For how could he, when the body meant for food had turned to stone? The barbarian, stupified by this unexpected sight, came with great haste to the holy man, bringing to the light the sin which he had hidden, and proclaimed his transgression to all, begging pardon from God, and invoking the help of the saint, that by his all-powerful prayers he might loose him from the bonds of his sin. Now many saw that miracle, and felt that the part of the bird about the breast consisted of bone and stone.

But I was not only an ear-witness of his wonders, but also an ear-witness of his prophecies concerning futurity. For that drought which came, and the great dearth of that year, and the famine and pestilence which followed together, he foretold two years before, saying that he saw a rod which was laid on man, stripes which would be inflicted by it. Moreover, he at another time foretold an invasion of locusts, and that it would bring no great harm, because the divine clemency soon follows punishment. But when thirty days were past, an innumerable multitude of them hung aloft, so that they even cut off the sun's rays and threw a shadow; and that we all saw plainly: but it only damaged the cattle pastures, and in no wise hurt the food of man. To me, too, who was attacked by a certain person, he signified that the quarrel would end ere a fortnight was past; and I learned the truth of the prediction by experience.

Moreover there were seen by him once two rods, which came down from the skies, and fell on the eastern and western lands. Now the divine man said that they signified the rising of the Persian and Scythian nations against the Romans; and told the vision to those who were by, and with many tears and assiduous prayers, warded that disaster, the threat whereof hung over the earth. Certainly the Persian nation, when already armed and prepared to invade the Romans, was kept back (the divine will being against them) from their attempt, and occupied at home with their own troubles. But while I know many other cases of this kind, I shall pass them over to avoid prolixity. These are surely enough to show the spiritual contemplation of his mind.

His fame was great, also, with the King of the Persians; for as the ambassadors told, who came to him, he diligently inquired what was his life, and what his miracles. But they say that the King's wife also begged oil honoured by his blessing, and accepted it as the greatest of gifts. Moreover, all the King's courtiers, being moved by his fame, and having heard many slanders against him from the Magi, inquired diligently, and having learnt the truth, called him a divine man; while the rest of the crowd, coming to the muleteers and servants and soldiers, both offered money, and begged for a share in the oil of benediction. The Queen, too, of the Ishmaelites, longing to have a child, sent first some of her most noble subjects to the saint, beseeching him that she might become a mother. And when her prayer had been granted, and she had her heart's desire, she took the son who had been born, and went to the divine old man; and (because women were not allowed to approach him) sent the babe, entreating his blessing on it . . . [Here Theodoret puts into the Queen's mouth words which it is unnecessary to quote.]

But how long do I strive to measure the depths of the Atlantic sea? For as they are unfathomable by man, so do the things which he does daily surpass narration. I, however, admire above all these things his endurance; for night and day he stands, so as to be seen by all. For as the doors are taken away, and a large part of the wall around pulled down, he is set forth as a new and wondrous spectacle to all; now standing long, now bowing himself frequently, and offering adoration to God. Many of those who stand by count these adorations; and once a man with me, when he had counted 1,244, and then missed, gave up counting: but always, when he bows himself, he touches his feet with his forehead. For as his stomach takes food only once in the week, and that very little—no more than is received in the divine sacraments,—his back admits of being easily bent. . . . But nothing which happens to him overpowers his philosophy; he bears nobly both voluntary and involuntary pains, and conquers both by readiness of will.

There came once from Arabena a certain good man, and honoured with the ministry of Christ. He, when he had come to that mountain peak,—"Tell me," he cried, "by the very truth which converts the human race to itself—Art thou a man, or an incorporeal nature?" But when all there were displeased with the question, the saint bade them all be silent, and said to him, "Why hast thou asked me this?" He answered, "Because I hear every one saying publicly, that thou neither eatest nor sleepest; but both are properties of man, and no one who has a human nature could have lived without food and sleep." Then the saint bade them set a ladder to the column, and him to come up; and first to look at his hands, and then feel inside his cloak of skins; and to see not only his feet, but a severe wound. But when he saw that he was a man, and the size of that wound, and learnt from him how he took nourishment, he came down and told me all.

At the public festivals he showed an endurance of another kind. For from the setting of the sun till it had come again to the eastern horizon, he stood all night with hands uplift to heaven, neither soothed with sleep nor conquered by fatigue. But in toils so great, and so great a magnitude of deeds, and multitude of miracles, his self-esteem is as moderate as if he were in dignity the least of all men. Beside his modesty, he is easy of access of speech, and gracious, and answers every man who speaks to him, whether he be handicraftsman, beggar, or rustic. And from the bounteous God he has received also the gift of teaching, and making his exhortations twice a day, he delights the ears of those who hear, discoursing much on grace, and setting forth the instructions of the Divine Spirit to look up and fly toward heaven, and depart from the earth, and imagine the kingdom which is expected, and fear the threats of Gehenna, and despise earthly things, and wait for things to come. He may be seen, too, acting as judge, and giving right and just decisions. This, and the like, is done after the ninth hour. For all night, and through the day to the ninth hour, he prays perpetually. After that, he first sets forth the divine teaching to those who are present; then having heard each man's petition, after he has performed some cures, he settles the quarrels of those between whom there is any dispute. About sunset he begins the rest of his converse with God. But though he is employed in this way, and does all this, he does not give up the care of the holy Churches, sometimes fighting with the impiety of the Greeks, sometimes checking the audacity of the Jews, sometimes putting to flight the bands of heretics, and sometimes sending messages concerning these last to the Emperor; sometimes, too, stirring up rulers to zeal for God, and sometimes exhorting the pastors of the Churches to bestow more care upon their flocks.

I have gone through these facts, trying to show the shower by one drop, and to give those who meet with my writing a taste on the finger of the sweetness of the honey. But there remains (as is to be expected) much more; and if he should live longer, he will probably add still greater wonders. . . .

Thus far Theodoret. Antony gives some other details of Simeon's life upon the column.

The devil, he says, in envy transformed himself into the likeness of an angel, shining in splendour, with fiery horses, and a fiery chariot, and appeared close to the column on which the blessed Simeon stood, and shone with glory like an angel. And the devil said with bland speeches, "Simeon, hear my words, which the Lord hath commanded thee. He has sent me, his angel, with a chariot and horses of fire, that I may carry thee away, as I carried Elias. For thy time is come. Do thou, in like wise, ascend now with me into the chariot, because the Lord of heaven and earth has sent it down. Let us ascend together into the heavens, that the angels and archangels may see thee, with Mary the mother of the Lord, with the Apostles and martyrs, the confessors and prophets; because they rejoice to see thee, that thou mayest pray to the Lord, who hast made thee after his own image. Verily I have spoken to thee: delay not to ascend." Simeon, having ended his prayer, said, "Lord, wilt thou carry me, a sinner, into heaven?" And lifting his right foot that he might step into the chariot, he lifted also his right hand, and made the sign of

Christ. When he had made the sign of the cross, forthwith the devil appeared nowhere, but vanished with his device, as dust before the face of the wind. Then understood Simeon that it was an art of the devil.

Having recovered himself, therefore, he said to his foot, "Thou shalt not return back hence, but stand here until my death, when the Lord shall send for me a sinner."

[Here follow more painful stories, which had best be omitted.]

But after much time, his mother, hearing of his fame, came to see him, but was forbidden, because no woman entered that place. But when the blessed Simeon heard the voice of his mother, he said to her, "Bear up, my mother, a little while, and we shall see each other, if God will." But she, hearing this, began to weep, and tearing her hair, rebuked him, saying, "Son, why hast thou done this? In return for the body in which I bore thee, thou hast filled me full of grief. For the milk with which I nourished thee, thou hast given me tears. For the kiss with which I kissed thee, thou hast given me bitter pangs of heart. For the grief and labour which I have suffered, thou hast laid on me cruel stripes." And she spoke so much that she made us all weep. The blessed Simeon, hearing the voice of her who bore him, put his face in his hands and wept bitterly; and commanded her, saying, "Lady mother, be still a little time, and we shall see each other in eternal rest." But she began to say, "By Christ, who formed thee, if there is a probability of seeing thee, who hast been so long a stranger to me, let me see thee; or if not, let me only hear thy voice and die at once; for thy father is dead in sorrow because of thee. And now do not destroy me for very bitterness, my son." Saying this, for sorrow and weeping she fell asleep; for during three days and three nights she had not ceased entreating him. Then the blessed Simeon prayed the Lord for her, and she forthwith gave up the ghost.

But they took up her body, and brought it where he could see it. And he said, weeping, "The Lord receive thee in joy, because thou hast endured tribulation for me, and borne me, and nursed and nourished me with labour." And as he said that, his mother's countenance perspired, and her body was stirred in the sight of us all. But he, lifting up his eyes to heaven, said, "Lord God of virtues, who sittest above the cherubim, and searchest the foundations of the abyss, who knewest Adam before he was; who hast promised the riches of the kingdom of heaven to those who love thee; who didst speak to Moses in the bush of fire; who blessedst Abraham our father; who bringest into Paradise the souls of the just, and sinkest the souls of the impious to perdition; who didst humble the lions, and mitigate for thy servants the strong fires of the Chaldees; who didst nourish Elisha by the ravens which brought him food — receive her soul in peace, and put her in the place of the holy fathers, for thine is the power for ever and ever."

Antony then goes on to relate the later years of the saint's life.

He tells how Simeon, some time after this, ascended the column of forty cubits; how a great dragon (serpent) crawled towards it, and coiled round it, entreating (so it seemed) to be freed from a spike of wood which had entered its eye; and how, St. Simeon took pity on it, he caused the spike (which was a cubit long) to come out.

He tells how a woman, drinking water from a jar at night, swallowed a snake unawares, which grew within her, till she was brought to the blessed Simeon, who commanded some of the water of the monastery to be given her; on which the serpent crawled out of her mouth, three cubits long, and burst immediately; and was hung up there seven days, as a testimony to many.

He tells how, when there was great want of water, St. Simeon prayed till the earth opened on the east of the monastery, and a cave full of water was discovered, which had never failed them to that day.

He tells how men, sitting beneath a tree, on their way to the saint, saw a doe go by, and commanded her to stop, "by the prayers of St. Simeon;" which when she had done, they killed and ate her, and came to St. Simeon with the skin. But they were all struck dumb, and hardly cured after two years. And the skin of the doe they hung up, for a testimony to many.

He tells of a huge leopard, which slew men and cattle all around; and how St. Simeon bade sprinkle in his haunts soil or water from the monastery; and when men went again, they found the leopard dead.

He tells how, when St. Simeon cured any one, he bade him go home, and honour God who had healed him, and not dare to say that Simeon had cured him, lest a worse thing should suddenly come to him; and not to presume to swear by the name of the Lord, for it was a grave sin; but to swear, "whether justly or unjustly, by him, lowly and a sinner. Wherefore all the Easterns, and barbarous tribes in those regions, swear by Simeon."

He tells how a robber from Antioch, Jonathan by name, fled to St. Simeon, and embraced the column, weeping bitterly, and saying how he had committed every crime, and had come thither to repent. And how the saint said, "Of such is the kingdom of heaven: but do not try to tempt me, lest thou be found again in the sins which thou hast cast away." Then came the officials from Antioch, demanding that he should be given up, to be cast to the wild beasts. But Simeon answered, "My sons, I brought him not hither, but One greater than I; for he helps such as this man, and of such is the kingdom of heaven. But if you can enter, carry him hence; I cannot give him up, for I fear him who has sent the man to me." And they, struck with fear, went away. Then Jonathan lay for seven days embracing the column, and then asked the saint leave to go. The saint asked him if he were going back to sin? "No, lord," he said; "but my time is fulfilled," and straightway he gave up the ghost; and when officials came again from Antioch, demanding him, Simeon replied: "He who brought him came with a multitude of the heavenly host, and is able to send into Tartarus your city, and all who dwell in it, who also has reconciled this man to himself; and I was afraid lest he should slay me suddenly. Therefore weary me no more, a humble man and poor."

But after a few years (says Antony) it befell one day that he bowed himself in prayer, and remained so three days—that is, the Friday, the Sabbath, and the Lord's day. Then I was terrified, and went up to him, and stood before his face, and said to him, "Master, arise: bless us; for the people have been waiting three days and three nights for a blessing from thee." And he answered me not; and I said again to him: "Wherefore dost thou grieve me, lord? or in what have I offended? I beseech thee, put out thy hand to me; or, perchance, thou hast already departed from us?"

And seeing that he did not answer, I thought to tell no one; for I feared to touch him: and, standing about half an hour, I bent down, and put my ear to listen; and there was no breathing: but a fragrance as of many scents rose from his body. And so I understood that he rested in the Lord; and, turning faint, I wept most bitterly; and, bending down, I kissed his eyes, and clasped his beard and hair, and reproaching him, I said: "To whom dost thou leave me, lord? or where shall I seek thy angelic doctrine? What answer shall I make for thee? or whose soul will look at this column, without thee, and not grieve? What answer shall I make to the sick, when they come here to seek thee, and find thee not? What shall I say, poor creature that I am? To-day I see thee; to-morrow I shall look right and left, and not find thee. And what covering shall I put upon thy column? Woe to me, when folk shall come from afar, seeking thee, and shall not find thee!" And, for much sorrow, I fell asleep.

And forthwith he appeared to me, and said: "I will not leave this column, nor this place, and this blessed mountain, where I was illuminated. But go down, satisfy the people, and send word secretly to Antioch, lest a tumult arise. For I have gone to rest, as the Lord willed: but do thou not cease to minister in this place, and the Lord shall repay thee thy wages in heaven."

But, rising from sleep, I said, in terror, "Master, remember me in thy holy rest." And, lifting up his garments, I fell at his feet, and kissed them; and, holding his hands, I laid them on my eyes, saying, "Bless me, I beseech thee, my lord!" And again I wept, and said, "What relics shall I carry away from thee as memorials?" And as I said that his body was moved; therefore I was afraid to touch him.

And, that no one might know, I came down quickly, and sent a faithful brother to the Bishop at Antioch. He came at once with three Bishops, and with them Ardaburius, the master of the soldiers, with his people, and stretched curtains round the column, and fastened their clothes around it. For they were cloth of gold.

And when they laid him down by the altar before the column, and gathered themselves together, birds flew round the column, crying, and as it were lamenting, in all men's sight; and the wailing of the people and of the cattle resounded for seven miles away; yea, even the hills, and the fields, and the trees were sad around that place; for everywhere a dark cloud hung about it. And I watched an angel coming to visit him; and, about the seventh hour, seven old men talked with that angel, whose face was like lightning, and his garments as snow. And I watched his voice, in fear and trembling, as long as I could hear it; but what he said I cannot tell.

But when the holy Simeon lay upon the bier, the Pope of Antioch, wishing to take some of his beard for a blessing, stretched out his hand; and forthwith it was dried up; and prayers were made to God for him, and so his hand was restored again.

Then, laying the corpse on the bier, they took it to Antioch, with psalms and hymns. But all the people round that region wept, because the protection of such mighty relics was taken from them, and because the Bishop of Antioch had sworn that no man should touch his body.

But when they came to the fifth milestone from Antioch, to the village which is called Meroe, no one could move him. Then a certain man, deaf and dumb for forty years, who had committed a very great crime, suddenly fell down before the bier, and began to cry, "Thou art well come, servant of God; for thy coming will save me: and if I shall obtain the grace to live, I will serve thee all the days of my life." And, rising, he caught hold of one of the mules which carried the bier, and forthwith moved himself from that place. And so the man was made whole from that hour.

Then all going out of the city of Antioch received the body of the holy Simeon on gold and silver, with psalms and hymns, and with many lamps brought it into the greater church, and thence to another church, which is called Penitence. Moreover, many virtues are wrought at his tomb, more than in his life; and the man who was made whole served there till the day of his death. But many offered treasures to the Bishop of Antioch for the faith, begging relics from the body: but, on account of his oath, he never gave them.

I, Antony, lowly and a sinner, have set forth briefly, as far as I could, this lesson. But blessed is he who has this writing in a book, and reads it in the church and house of God; and when he shall have brought it to his memory, he shall receive a reward from the Most High; to whom is honour, power, and virtue, for ever and ever. Amen.

After such a fantastic story as this of Simeon, it is full time (some readers may have thought that it was full time long since) to give my own opinion of the miracles, visions, daemons, and other portents which occur in the lives of these saints. I have refrained from doing so as yet, because I wished to begin by saying everything on behalf of these old hermits which could honestly be said, and to prejudice my readers' minds in their favour rather than against them; because I am certain that if we look on them merely with scorn and ridicule, —

if we do not acknowledge and honour all in them which was noble, virtuous, and honest,—we shall never be able to combat their errors, either in our own hearts or in those of our children: and that we may have need to do so is but too probable. In this age, as in every other age of materialism and practical atheism, a revulsion in favour of superstition is at hand; I may say is taking place round us now. Doctrines are tolerated as possibly true,— persons are regarded with respect and admiration, who would have been looked on, even fifty years ago, if not with horror, yet with contempt, as beneath the serious notice of educated English people. But it is this very contempt which has brought about the change of opinion concerning them. It has been discovered that they were not altogether so absurd as they seemed; that the public mind, in its ignorance, has been unjust to them; and, in hasty repentance for that injustice, too many are ready to listen to those who will tell them that these things are not absurd at all—that there is no absurdity in believing that the leg-bone of St. Simon Stock may possess miraculous powers, or that the spirits of the departed communicate with their friends by rapping on the table. The ugly after-crop of superstition which is growing up among us now is the just and natural punishment of our materialism—I may say, of our practical atheism. For those who will not believe in the real spiritual world, in which each man's soul stands face to face all day long with Almighty God, the Father, the Son, and the Holy Ghost, are sure at last to crave after some false spiritual world, and seek, like the evil and profligate generation of the Jews, after visible signs and material wonders. And those who will not believe that the one true and living God is above their path and about their bed and spieth out all their ways, and that in him they live and move and have their being, are but too likely at last to people with fancied saints and daemons that void in the imagination and in the heart which their own unbelief has made.

Are we then to suppose that these old hermits had lost faith in God? On the contrary, they were the only men in that day who had faith in God. And, if they had faith in any other things or persons beside God, they merely shared in the general popular ignorance and mistakes of their own age; and we must not judge those who, born in an age of darkness, were struggling earnestly toward the light, as we judge those who, born in an age of scientific light, are retiring of their own will back into the darkness.

Before I enter upon the credibility of these alleged saints' miracles, I must guard my readers carefully from supposing that I think miracles impossible. Heaven forbid. He would be a very rash person who should do that, in a world which swarms with greater wonders than those recorded in the biography of a saint. For, after all, which is more wonderful, that God should be able to restore the dead to life, or that he should be able to give life at all? Again, as for these miracles being contrary to our experience, that is no very valid argument against them; for equally contrary to our experience is every new discovery of science, every strange phenomenon among plants and animals, every new experiment in a chemical lecture.

The more we know of science the more we must confess, that nothing is too strange to be true: and therefore we must not blame or laugh at those who in old times believed in strange things which were not true. They had an honest and rational sense of the infinite and wonderful nature of the universe, and of their own ignorance about it; and they were ready to believe anything, as the truly wise man will be ready also. Only, from ignorance of the laws of the universe, they did not know what was likely to be true and what was not; and therefore they believed many things which experience has proved to be false; just as Seba or any of the early naturalists were ready to believe in six-legged dragons, or in the fatal power of the basilisk's eye; fancies which, if they had been facts, would not have been nearly as wonderful as the transformation of the commonest insect, or the fertilization of the meanest weed: but which are rejected now, not because they are too wonderful, but simply because experience has proved them to be untrue. And experience, it must be remembered, is the only sound test of truth. As long as men will settle beforehand for themselves, without experience, what they ought to see, so long will they be perpetually fancying that they or others have seen it; and their faith, as it is falsely called, will delude not only their reason, but their very hearing, sight, and touch.

In this age we see no supernatural prodigies, because there are none to see; and when we are told that the reason why we see no prodigies is because we have no faith, we answer (if we be sensible), Just so. As long as people had faith, in plain English believed, that they could be magically cured of a disease, they thought that they or others were so cured. As long as they believed that ghosts could be seen, every silly person saw them. As long as they believed that daemons transformed themselves into an animal's shape, they said, "The devil croaked at me this morning in the shape of a raven; and therefore my horse fell with me." As long as they believed that witches could curse them, they believed that an old woman in the next parish had overlooked them, their cattle, and their crops; and that therefore they were poor, diseased, and unfortunate. These dreams, which were common among the peasants in remote districts five-and-twenty years ago, have vanished, simply from the spread (by the grace of God, as I hold) of an inductive habit of mind; of the habit of looking coolly, boldly, carefully, at facts; till now, even among the most ignorant peasantry, the woman who says that she has seen a ghost is likely not to be complimented on her assertion. But it does not follow that that woman's grandmother, when she said that she saw a ghost, was a consciously dishonest person; on the contrary, so complex and contradictory is human nature, she would have been, probably, a person of more than average intellect and earnestness; and her instinct of the invisible and the infinite (which is that which raises man above the brutes) would have been, because misinformed, the honourable cause of her error. And thus we may believe of the good hermits, of whom prodigies are recorded.

As to the truth of the prodigies themselves, there are several ways of looking at them.

First, we may neither believe nor disbelieve them; but talk of them as "devout fairy tales," religious romances, and allegories; and so save ourselves the trouble of judging whether they were true. That is at least an easy and pleasant method; very fashionable in a careless, unbelieving age like this: but in following it we shall be somewhat cowardly; for there is hardly any matter a clear judgment on which is more important just now than these same saints' miracles.

Next, we may believe them utterly and all; and that is also an easy and pleasant method. But if we follow it, we shall be forced to believe, among other facts, that St. Paphnutius was carried miraculously across a river, because he was too modest to undress himself and wade; that St. Helenus rode a savage crocodile across a river, and then commanded it to die; and that it died accordingly upon the spot; and that St. Goar, entering the palace of the Archbishop of Treves, hung his cape on a sunbeam, mistaking it for a peg. And many other like things we shall be forced to believe, with which this book has no concern.

Or, again, we may believe as much as we can, because we should like, if we could, to believe all. But as we have not—no man has as yet- -any criterion by which we can judge how much of these stories we ought to believe and how much not, which actually happened and which did not, therefore we shall end (as not only the most earnest and pious, but the most clear and logical persons, who have taken up this view, have ended already) by believing all: which is an end not to be desired.

Or we may believe as few as possible of them, because we should like, if we could, to believe none. And this method, for the reason aforesaid (namely, that there is no criterion by which we can settle what to believe and what not), usually ends in believing none at all.

This, of believing none at all, is the last method; and this, I confess fairly, I am inclined to think is the right one; and that these good hermits worked no real miracles and saw no real visions whatsoever.

I confess that this is a very serious assertion. For there is as much evidence in favour of these hermits' miracles and visions as there is, with most men, of the existence of China; and much more than there, with most men, is of the earth's going round the sun.

But the truth is, that evidence, in most matters of importance, is worth very little. Very few people decide a question on its facts, but on their own prejudices as to what they would like to have happened. Very few people are judges of evidence; not even of their own eyes and ears. Very few persons, when they see a thing, know what they have seen, and what not. They tell you quite honestly, not what they saw, but what they think they ought to have seen, or should like to have seen. It is a fact too often conveniently forgotten, that in every human crowd the majority will be more or less bad, or at least foolish; the slaves of anger, spite, conceit, vanity, sordid hope, and sordid fear. But let them be as honest and as virtuous as they may, pleasure, terror, and the desire of seeming to have seen or heard more than their neighbours, and all about it, make them exaggerate. If you take apart five honest men, who all stood by and saw the same man do anything strange, offensive, or even exciting, no two of them will give you quite the same account of it. If you leave them together, while excited, an hour before you question them, they will have compared notes and made up one story, which will contain all their mistakes combined; and it will require the skill of a practised barrister to pick the grain of wheat out of the chaff.

Moreover, when people are crowded together under any excitement, there is nothing which they will not make each other believe. They will make each other believe in spirit-rapping, table-turning, the mesmeric fluid, electro-biology; that they saw the lion on Northumberland House wagging his tail; {203} that witches have been seen riding in the air; that the Jews had poisoned the wells; that— but why go further into the sad catalogue of human absurdities, and the crimes which have followed them? Every one is ashamed of not seeing what every one else sees, and persuades himself against his own eye sight for fear of seeming stupid or ill-conditioned; and therefore in all evidence, the fewer witnesses, the more truth, because the evidence of ten men is worth more than that of a hundred together; and the evidence of a thousand men together is worth still less.

Now, if people are savage and ignorant, diseased and poverty-stricken; even if they are merely excited and credulous, and quite sure that something wonderful must happen, then they will be also quite certain that something wonderful has happened; and their evidence will be worth nothing at all.

Moreover, suppose that something really wonderful has happened; suppose, for instance, that some nervous or paralytic person has been suddenly restored to strength by the command of a saint or of some other remarkable man. This is quite possible, I may say common; and it is owing neither to physical nor to so-called spiritual causes, but simply to the power which a strong mind has over a weak one, to make it exert itself, and cure itself by its own will, though but for a time.

When this good news comes to be told, and to pass from mouth to mouth, it ends of quite a different shape from that in which it began. It has been added to, taken from, twisted in every direction according to the fancy or the carelessness of each teller, till what really happened in the first case no one will be able to say; {204} and this is, therefore, what actually happened, in the case of these reported wonders. Moreover (and this is the most important consideration of all) for men to be fair judges of what really happens, they must have somewhat sound minds in somewhat sound bodies; which no man can have (however honest and virtuous) who gives himself up, as did these old hermits, to fasting and vigils. That continued sleeplessness produces delusions, and at last actual madness, every physician knows; and they know also, as many a poor sailor has known when starving on a wreck, and many a poor soldier in such a retreat as that of Napoleon from Moscow, that extreme hunger and thirst produce delusions also, very similar to (and caused much in the same way as) those produced by ardent spirits; so that many a wretched creature ere now has been taken up for drunkenness, who has been simply starving to death.

Whence it follows that these good hermits, by continual fasts and vigils, must have put themselves (and their histories prove that they did put themselves) into a state of mental disease, in which their evidence was worth nothing; a state in which the mind cannot distinguish between facts and dreams; in which life itself is one dream; in which (as in the case of madness, or of a feverish child) the brain cannot distinguish between the objects which are outside it and the imaginations which are inside it. And it is plain, that the more earnest and pious, and therefore the more ascetic, one of these good men was, the more utterly would his brain be in a state of chronic disease. God forbid that we should scorn them, therefore, or think the worse of them in any way. They were animated by a truly noble purpose, the resolution to be good according to their light; they carried out that purpose with heroical endurance, and they have their reward: but this we must say, if we be rational people, that on their method of holiness, the more holy any one of them was, the less trustworthy was his account of any matter whatsoever; and that the hermit's peculiar temptations (quite unknown to the hundreds of unmarried persons who lead quiet and virtuous, because rational and healthy, lives) are to be attributed, not as they thought, to a daemon, but to a more or less unhealthy nervous system.

It must be remembered, moreover, in justice to these old hermits, that they did not invent the belief that the air was full of daemons. All the Eastern nations had believed in Genii (Jinns), Fairies (Peris), and Devas, Divs, or devils. The Devas of the early Hindus were beneficent beings: to the eyes of the old Persians (in their hatred of idolatry and polytheism), they appeared evil beings, Divs, or Devils. And even so the genii and daemons of the Roman Empire became, in the eyes of the early Christians, wicked and cruel spirits.

And they had their reasons, and on the whole sound ones, for so regarding them. The educated classes had given up any honest and literal worship of the old gods. They were trying to excuse themselves for their lingering half belief in them, by turning them into allegories, powers of nature, metaphysical abstractions, as did Porphyry and Iamblichus, Plotinus and Proclus, and the rest of the Neo-Platonist school of aristocratic philosophers and fine ladies: but the lower classes still, in every region, kept up their own local beliefs and worships, generally of the most foul and brutal kind. The animal worship of Egypt among the lower classes was sufficiently detestable in the time of Herodotus. It had certainly not improved in that of Juvenal and Persius; and was still less likely to have improved afterwards. This is a subject so shocking that it can be only hinted at. But as a single instance—what wonder if the early hermits of Egypt looked on the crocodile as something diabolic, after seeing it, for generations untold, petted and worshipped in many a city, simply because it was the incarnate symbol of brute strength, cruelty, and cunning? We must remember, also, that earlier generations (the old Norsemen and Germans just as much as the old Egyptians) were wont to look on animals as more miraculous than we do; as more akin, in many cases, to human beings; as guided, not by a mere blind instinct, but by an intellect which was allied to, and often surpassed man's intellect. "The bear," said the old Norsemen, "had ten men's strength, and eleven men's wit; "and in some such light must the old hermits have looked on the hyaena, "bellua," the monster par excellence; or on the crocodile, the hippopotamus, and the poisonous snakes, which have been objects of terror and adoration in every country where they have been formidable. Whether the hyaenas were daemons, or were merely sent by the daemons, St. Antony and St. Athanasius do not clearly define, for they did not know. It was enough for them that the beasts prowled at night in those desert cities, which were, according to the opinions, not only of the Easterns, but of the Romans, the special haunt of ghouls, witches, and all uncanny things. Their fiendish laughter—which, when heard even in a modern menagerie, excites and shakes most person's nerves—rang through hearts and brains which had no help or comfort, save in God alone. The beast tore up the dead from their graves; devoured alike the belated child and the foulest offal; and was in all things a type and incarnation of that which man ought not to be. Why should not he, so like the worst of men, have some bond or kindred with the evil beings who were not men? Why should not the graceful and deadly cobra, the horrid cerastes, the huge throttling python, and even more, the loathly puff-adder, undistinguishable from the gravel among which he lay coiled, till he leaped furiously and unswerving, as if shot from a bow, upon his prey—why should not they too be kindred to that evil power who had been, in the holiest and most ancient books, personified by the name of the Serpent? Before we have a right to say that the hermits' view of these deadly animals was not the most rational, as well as the most natural, which they could possibly have taken up, we must put ourselves in their places; and look at nature as they had learnt to look at it, not from Scripture and Christianity, so much as from the immemorial traditions of their heathen ancestors.

If it be argued, that they ought to have been well enough acquainted with these beasts to be aware of their merely animal nature, the answer is—that they were probably not well acquainted with the beasts of the desert. They had never, perhaps, before their "conversion," left the narrow valley, well tilled and well inhabited, which holds the Nile. A climb from it into the barren mountains and deserts east and west was a journey out of the world into chaos, and the region of the unknown and the horrible, which demanded high courage from the unarmed and effeminate Egyptian, who knew not what monster he might meet ere sundown. Moreover, it is very probable that during these centuries of decadence, in Egypt, as in other parts of the Roman Empire, "the wild beasts of the field had increased" on the population, and were reappearing in the more cultivated grounds.

But these old hermits appear perpetually in another, and a more humane, if not more human aspect, as the miraculous tamers of savage beasts. Those who wish to know all which can be alleged in favour of their having possessed such a power, should read M. de Montalembert's chapter, "Les Moines et la Nature." {209} All that learning and eloquence can say in favour of the theory is said there; and with a candour which demands from no man full belief of many beautiful but impossible stories, "travesties of historic verity," which have probably grown up from ever-varying tradition in the course of ages. M. de Montalembert himself points out a probable explanation of many of them:—An ingenious scholar of our times{210} (he says) has pointed out their true and legitimate origin—at least in Ancient Gaul. According to him, after the gradual disappearance of the Gallo-Roman population, the oxen, the horses, the dogs had returned to the wild state; and it was in the forest that the Breton missionaries had to seek these animals, to employ them anew for domestic use. The miracle was, to restore to man the command and the enjoyment of those creatures, which God had given him as instruments.

This theory is probable enough, and will explain, doubtless, many stories. It may even explain those of tamed wolves, who may have been only feral dogs, i.e. dogs run wild. But it will not explain those in which (in Ireland as well as in Gaul) the stag appears as obeying the hermit's commands. The twelve huge stags who come out of the forest to draw the ploughs for St. Leonor and his monks, or those who drew to his grave the corpse of the Irish hermit Kellac, or those who came out of the forest to supply the place of St. Colodoc's cattle, which the seigneur had carried off in revenge for his having given sanctuary to a hunted deer, must have been wild from the beginning; and many another tale must remain without any explanation whatsoever—save the simplest of all. Neither can any such theory apply to the marvels vouched for by St. Athanasius, St. Jerome, and other contemporaries, which "show us (to quote M. de Montalembert) the most ferocious animals at the feet of such men as Antony, Pachomius, Macarius, and Hilarion, and those who copied them. At every page one sees wild asses, crocodiles, hippopotami, hyaenas, and, above all, lions, transformed into respectful companions and docile servants of these prodigies of sanctity; and one concludes thence, not that these beasts had reasonable souls, but that God knew how to glorify those who devoted themselves to his glory, and thus show how all Nature obeyed man before he was excluded from Paradise by his disobedience."

This is, on the whole, the cause which the contemporary biographers assign for these wonders. The hermits were believed to have returned, by celibacy and penitence, to "the life of angels;" to that state of perfect innocence which was attributed to our first parents in Eden: and therefore of them our Lord's words were true: "He that believeth in me, greater things than these (which I do) shall he do."

But those who are of a different opinion will seek for different causes. They will, the more they know of these stories, admire often their gracefulness, often their pathos, often their deep moral significance; they will feel the general truth of M. de Montalembert's words: "There is not one of them which does not honour and profit human nature, and which does not express a victory of weakness over force, and of good over evil." But if they look on physical facts as sacred things, as the voice of God revealed in the phenomena of matter, their first question will be, "Are they true?"

Some of them must be denied utterly, like that of St. Helenus, riding and then slaying the crocodile. It did not happen. Abbot Ammon {212a} did not make two dragons guard his cell against robbers. St. Gerasimus {212b} did not set the lion, out of whose foot he had taken a thorn, to guard his ass; and when the ass was stolen by an Arabian camel-driver, he did not (fancying that the lion had eaten the ass) make him carry water in the ass's stead. Neither did the lion, when next he met the thief and the ass, bring them up, in his own justification, {212c} to St. Gerasimus. St. Costinian did not put a pack-saddle on a bear, and make him carry a great stone. A lioness did not bring her five blind whelps to a hermit, that he might give them sight. {212d} And, though Sulpicius Severus says that he saw it with his own eyes, {212e} it is hard to believe the latter part of the graceful story which he tells—of an old hermit whom he found dwelling alone twelve miles from the Nile, by a well of vast depth. One ox he had, whose whole work was to raise the water by a wheel. Around him was a garden of herbs, kept rich and green amid the burning sand, where neither seed nor root could live. The old man and the ox fed together on the produce of their common toil; but two miles off there was a single palm-tree, to which, after supper, the hermit takes his guests. Beneath the palm they find a lioness; but instead of attacking them, she moves "modestly" away at the old man's command, and sits down to wait for her share of dates. She feeds out of his hand, like a household animal, and goes her way, leaving her guests trembling, "and confessing how great was the virtue of the hermit's faith, and how great their own infirmity."

This last story, which one would gladly believe, were it possible, I have inserted as one of those which hang on the verge of credibility. In the very next page, Sulpicius Severus tells a story quite credible, of a she-wolf, which he saw with his own eyes as tame as any dog. There can be no more reason to doubt that fact than to ascribe it to a miracle. We may even believe that the wolf, having gnawed to pieces the palm basket which the good old man was weaving, went off, knowing that she had done wrong, and after a week came back, begged pardon like a rational soul, and was caressed, and given a double share of bread. Many of these stories which tell of the taming of wild beasts may be true, and yet contain no miracle. They are very few in number, after all, in proportion to the number of monks; they are to be counted at most by tens, while the monks are counted by tens of thousands. And among many great companies of monks, there may have been one individual, as there is, for instance, in many a country parish a bee-taker or a horse-tamer, of quiet temper and strong nerve, and quick and sympathetic intellect, whose power over animals is so extraordinary, as to be attributed by the superstitious and uneducated to some hereditary secret, or some fairy gift. Very powerful to attract wild animals must have been the good hermits' habit of sitting motionless for hours, till (as with St. Guthlac) the swallows sat and sang upon his knee; and of moving slowly and gently at his work, till (as with St. Karilef, while he pruned his vines) the robin came and built in his hood as it hung upon a tree: very powerful his freedom from anger, and, yet more important, from fear, which always calls out rage in wild beasts, while a calm and bold front awes them: and most powerful of all, the kindliness of heart, the love of companionship, which brought the wild bison to feed by St. Karilef's side as he prayed upon the lawn; and the hind to nourish St. Giles with her milk in the jungles of the Bouches du Rhone. There was no miracle; save the moral miracle that, in ages of cruelty and slaughter, these men had learned (surely by the inspiration of God) how —

"He prayeth well who loveth well Both man and bird and beast; He prayeth best who loveth best All things, both great and small; For the dear God who loveth us, He made and loveth all."

After all, let these old Lives of the Fathers tell their own tale. By their own merits let them stand or fall; and stand they will in one sense: for whatsoever else they are not, this they are—the histories of good men. Their physical science and their daemonology may have been on a par with those of the world around them: but they possessed what the world did not possess, faith in the utterly good and self-sacrificing God, and an ideal of virtue and purity such as had never been seen since the first Whitsuntide. And they set themselves to realize that ideal with a simplicity, an energy, an endurance, which were altogether heroic. How far they were right in "giving up the world" depends entirely on what the world was then like, and whether there was any hope of reforming it. It was their opinion that there was no such hope; and those who know best the facts which surrounded them, its utter frivolity, its utter viciousness, the deadness which had fallen on art, science, philosophy, human life, whether family, social, or political; the prevalence of slavery, in forms altogether hideous and unmentionable; the insecurity of life and property, whether from military and fiscal tyranny, or from perpetual inroads of the so- called "Barbarians:" those, I say, who know these facts best will be most inclined to believe that the old hermits were wise in their generation; that the world was past salvation; that it was not a wise or humane thing to marry and bring children into the world; that in such a state of society, an honest and virtuous man could not exist, and that those who wished to remain honest and virtuous must flee into the desert, and be alone with God and their fellows.

The question which had to be settled then and there, at that particular crisis of the human race, was not—Are certain wonders true or false? but—Is man a mere mortal animal, or an immortal soul? Is his flesh meant to serve his spirit, or his spirit his flesh? Is pleasure, or virtue, the end and aim of his existence?

The hermits set themselves to answer that question, not by arguing or writing about it, but by the only way in which any question can be settled—by experiment. They resolved to try whether their immortal souls could not grow better and better, while their mortal bodies were utterly neglected; to make their flesh serve their spirit; to make virtue their only end and aim; and utterly to relinquish the very notion of pleasure. To do this one thing, and nothing else, they devoted their lives; and they succeeded. From their time it has been a received opinion, not merely among a few philosophers or a few Pharisees, but among the lowest, the poorest, the most ignorant, who have known aught of Christianity, that man is an immortal soul; that the spirit, and not the flesh, ought to be master and guide; that virtue is the highest good; and that purity is a virtue, impurity a sin. These men were, it has been well said, the very fathers of purity. And if, in that and in other matters, they pushed their purpose to an extreme— if, by devoting themselves utterly to it alone, they suffered, not merely in wideness of mind or in power of judging evidence, but even in brain, till they became some of them at times insane from over-wrought nerves—it is not for us to blame the soldier for the wounds which have crippled him, or the physician for the disease which he has caught himself while trying to heal others. Let us not speak ill of the bridge which carries us over, nor mock at those who did the work for us as seemed to them best, and perhaps in the only way in which it could be done in those evil days. As a matter of fact, through these men's teaching and example we have learnt what morality, purity, and Christianity we possess; and if any answer that we have learnt them from the Scriptures, who but these men preserved the Scriptures to us? Who taught us to look on them as sacred and inspired? Who taught us to apply them to our own daily lives, and find comfort and teaching in every age, in words written ages ago by another race in a foreign land? The Scriptures were the book, generally the only book, which they read and meditated, not merely from morn till night, but, as far as fainting nature would allow, from night to morn again: and their method of interpreting them (as far as I can discover) differed in nothing from that common to all Christians now, save that they interpreted literally certain precepts of our Lord and of St. Paul which we consider to have applied only to the "temporary necessity" of a decayed, dying, and hopeless age such as that in which they lived. And therefore, because they knew the Scripture well, and learned in it lessons of true virtue and true philosophy, though unable to save civilization in the East, they were able at least to save it in the West. The European hermits, and the monastic communities which they originated, were indeed a seed of life, not merely to the conquered Roman population of Gaul or Spain or Britain, but to the heathen and Arian barbarians who conquered them. Among those fierce and armed savages, the unarmed hermits stood, strong only by justice, purity, and faith in God, defying the oppressor, succouring the oppressed, and awing and softening the new aristocracy of the middle age, which was founded on mere brute force and pride of race; because the monk took his stand upon mere humanity; because he told the wild conqueror, Goth or Sueve, Frank or Burgund, Saxon or Norseman, that all men were equal in the sight of God; because he told them (to quote Athanasius's own words concerning Antony) that "virtue is not beyond human nature;" that the highest moral excellence was possible to the most low-born and unlettered peasant whom they trampled under their horses' hoofs, if he were only renewed and sanctified by the Spirit of God. They accepted the lowest and commonest facts of that peasant's wretched life; they outdid him in helplessness, loneliness, hunger, dirt, and slavery; and then said, "Among all these I can yet be a man of God, wise, virtuous, pure, free, and noble in the sight of God, though not in the sight of Caesars, counts, and knights." They went on, it is true, to glorify the means above the end; to consecrate childlessness, self-torture, dirt, ignorance, as if they were things pleasing to God and holy in themselves. But in spite of those errors they wrought throughout Europe a work which, as far as we can judge, could have been done in no other way; done only by men who gave up all that makes life worth having for the sake of being good themselves and making others good.

THE HERMITS OF EUROPE

Most readers will recollect what an important part in the old ballads and romances is played by the hermit.

He stands in strongest contrast to the knight. He fills up, as it were, by his gentleness and self-sacrifice, what is wanting in the manhood of the knight, the slave too often of his own fierceness and self-assertion. The hermit rebukes him when he sins, heals him when he is wounded, stays his hand in some mad murderous duel, such as was too common in days when any two armed horsemen meeting on road or lawn ran blindly at each other in the mere lust of fighting, as boars or stags might run. Sometimes he interferes to protect the oppressed serf; sometimes to rescue the hunted deer which has taken sanctuary at his feet. Sometimes, again, his influence is that of intellectual superiority; of worldly experience; of the travelled man who has seen many lands and many nations. Sometimes, again, that of sympathy; for he has been a knight himself, and fought and sinned, and drank of the cup of vanity and vexation of spirit, like the fierce warrior who kneels at his feet.

All who have read (and all ought to have read) Spenser's Fairy Queen, must recollect his charming description of the hermit with whom Prince Arthur leaves Serena and the squire after they have been wounded by "the blatant beast" of Slander; when—

"Toward night they came unto a plain By which a little hermitage there lay Far from all neighbourhood, the which annoy it may.

"And nigh thereto a little chapel stood, Which being all with ivy overspread Decked all the roof, and shadowing the rood, Seemed like a grove fair branched overhead; Therein the hermit which his here led In straight observance of religious vow, Was wont his hours and holy things to bed; And therein he likewise was praying now, When as these knights arrived, they wist not where nor how.

"They stayed not there, but straightway in did pass: Who when the hermit present saw in place, From his devotions straight he troubled was; Which breaking off, he toward them did pace With staid steps and grave beseeming grace: For well it seemed that whilom he had been Some goodly person, and of gentle race, That could his good to all, and well did ween How each to entertain with courtesy beseen.

The Hermits

* * * * *

"He thence them led into his hermitage, Letting their steeds to graze upon the green: Small was his house, and like a little cage, For his own term, yet inly neat and clean, Decked with green boughs, and flowers gay beseen Therein he them full fair did entertain, Not with such forged shews, as fitter been For courting fools that courtesies would feign, But with entire affection and appearance plain.

* * * * *

How be that careful hermit did his best With many kinds of medicines meet to tame The poisonous humour that did most infest Their reakling wounds, and every day them duly dressed.

"For he right well in leech's craft was seen; And through the long experience of his days, Which had in many fortunes tossed been, And passed through many perilous assays: He knew the divers want of mortal ways, And in the minds of men had great insight; Which with sage counsel, when they went astray, He could inform and them reduce aright; And all the passions heal which wound the weaker sprite.

"For whilome he had been a doughty knight, As any one that lived in his days, And proved oft in many a perilous fight, In which he grace and glory won always, And in all battles bore away the bays: But being now attached with timely age, And weary of this world's unquiet ways, He took himself unto this hermitage, In which he lived alone like careless bird in cage."

This picture is not poetry alone: it is history. Such men actually lived, and such work they actually did, from the southernmost point of Italy to the northernmost point of Scotland, during centuries in which there was no one else to do the work. The regular clergy could not have done it. Bishops and priests were entangled in the affairs of this world, striving to be statesmen, striving to be landowners, striving to pass Church lands on from father to son, and to establish themselves as an hereditary caste of priests. The chaplain or house-priest who was to be found in every nobleman's, almost every knight's castle, was apt to become a mere upper servant, who said mass every morning in return for the good cheer which he got every evening, and fetched and carried at the bidding of his master and mistress. But the hermit who dwelt alone in the forest glen, occupied, like an old Hebrew prophet, a superior and an independent position. He needed nought from any man save the scrap of land which the lord was only too glad to allow him in return for his counsels and his prayers. And to him, as to a mysterious and supernatural personage, the lord went privately for advice in his quarrels with the neighbouring barons, or with his own kin. To him the lady took her children when they were sick, to be healed, as she fancied, by his prayers and blessings; or poured into his ears a hundred secret sorrows and anxieties which she dare not tell to her fierce lord, who hunted and fought the livelong day, and drank too much liquor every night.

This class of men sprang up rapidly, by natural causes, and yet by a Divine necessity, as soon as the Western Empire was conquered by the German tribes; and those two young officers whom we saw turning monks at Treves, in the time of St. Augustine, may, if they lived to be old men, have given sage counsel again and again to fierce German knights and kinglets, who had dispossessed the rich and effeminate landowners of their estates, and sold them, their wives, and children, in gangs by the side of their own slaves. Only the Roman who had turned monk would probably escape that fearful ruin; and he would remain behind, while the rest of his race was enslaved or swept away, as a seed of Christianity and of civilization, destined to grow and spread, and bring the wild conquerors in due time into the kingdom of God.

For the first century or two after the invasion of the barbarians, the names of the hermits and saints are almost exclusively Latin. Their biographies represent them in almost every case as born of noble Roman parents. As time goes on, German names appear, and at last entirely supersede the Latin ones; showing that the conquering race had learned from the conquered to become hermits and monks like them.

ST. SEVERINUS, THE APOSTLE OF NORICUM

Of all these saintly civilizers, St. Severinus of Vienna is perhaps the most interesting, and his story the most historically instructive. {224}

A common time, the middle of the fifth century, the province of Noricum (Austria, as we should now call it) was the very highway of invading barbarians, the centre of the human Maelstrom in which Huns, Alemanni, Rugi, and a dozen wild tribes more, wrestled up and down and round the starving and beleaguered towns of what had once been a happy and fertile province, each tribe striving to trample the other under foot, and to march southward over their corpses to plunder what was still left of the already plundered wealth of Italy and Rome. The difference of race, in tongue, and in manners, between the conquered and their conquerors, was made more painful by difference in creed. The conquering Germans and Huns were either Arians or heathens. The conquered race (though probably of very mixed blood), who called themselves Romans, because they spoke Latin and lived under the Roman law, were orthodox Catholics; and the miseries of religious persecution were too often added to the usual miseries of invasion.

It was about the year 455-60. Attila, the great King of the Huns, who called himself—and who was—"the Scourge of God," was just dead. His empire had broken up. The whole centre of Europe was in a state of anarchy and war; and the hapless Romans along the Danube were in the last extremity of terror, not knowing by what fresh invader their crops would be swept off up to the very gates of the walled towers which were their only defence: when there appeared among them, coming out of the East, a man of God.

Who he was, he would not tell. His speech showed him to be an African Roman—a fellow-countryman of St. Augustine—probably from the neighbourhood of Carthage. He had certainly at one time gone to some desert in the East, zealous to learn "the more perfect life." Severinus, he said, was his name; a name which indicated high rank, as did the manners and the scholarship of him who bore it. But more than his name he would not tell. "If you take me for a runaway slave," he said, smiling, "get ready money to redeem me with when my master demands me back." For he believed that they would have need of him; that God had sent him into that land that he might be of use to its wretched people. And certainly he could have come into the neighbourhood of Vienna at that moment for no other purpose than to do good, unless he came to deal in slaves.

He settled first at a town called by his biographer Casturis; and, lodging with the warden of the church, lived quietly the hermit life. Meanwhile the German tribes were prowling round the town; and Severinus, going one day into the church, began to warn the priests and clergy and all the people that a destruction was coming on them which they could only avert by prayer and fasting and the works of mercy. They laughed him to scorn, confiding in their lofty Roman walls, which the invaders—wild horsemen, who had no military engines—were unable either to scale or batter down. Severinus left the town at once, prophesying, it was said, the very day and hour of its fall. He went on to the next town, which was then closely garrisoned by a barbarian force, and repeated his warning there: but while the people were listening to him, there came an old man to the gate, and told them how Casturis had been already sacked, as the man of God had foretold; and, going into the church, threw himself at the feet of St. Severinus, and said that he had been saved by his merits from being destroyed with his fellow-townsmen.

Then the dwellers in the town hearkened to the man of God, and gave themselves up to fasting and almsgiving and prayer for three whole days.

And on the third day, when the solemnity of the evening sacrifice was fulfilled, a sudden earthquake happened, and the barbarians, seized with panic fear, and probably hating and dreading—like all those wild tribes—confinement between four stone walls instead of the free open life of the tent and the stockade, forced the Romans to open their gates to them, rushed out into the night, and in their madness slew each other.

In those days a famine fell upon the people of Vienna; and they, as their sole remedy, thought good to send for the man of God from the neighbouring town. He went, and preached to them, too, repentance and almsgiving. The rich, it seems, had hidden up their stores of corn, and left the poor to starve. At least St. Severinus discovered (by Divine revelation, it was supposed), that a widow named Procula had done as much. He called her out into the midst of the people, and asked her why she, a noble woman and free-born, had made herself a slave to avarice, which is idolatry. If she would not give her corn to Christ's poor, let her throw it into the Danube to feed the fish, for any gain from it she would not have. Procula was abashed, and served out her hoards thereupon willingly to the poor; and a little while afterwards, to the astonishment of all, vessels came down the Danube, laden with every kind of merchandise. They had been frozen up for many days near Passau, in the thick ice of the river Enns. But the prayers of God's servant (so men believed) had opened the ice-gates, and let them down the stream before the usual time.

Then the wild German horsemen swept around the walls, and carried off human beings and cattle, as many as they could find. Severinus, like some old Hebrew prophet, did not shrink from advising hard blows, where hard blows could avail. Mamertinus, the tribune, or officer in command, told him that he had so few soldiers, and those so ill-armed, that he dare not face the enemy. Severinus answered, that they should get weapons from the barbarians themselves; the Lord would fight for them, and they should hold their peace: only if they took any captives they should bring them safe to him. At the second milestone from the city they came upon the plunderers, who fled at once, leaving their arms behind. Thus was the prophecy of the man of God fulfilled. The Romans brought the captives back to him unharmed. He loosed their bonds, gave them food and drink, and let them go. But they were to tell their comrades that, if ever they came near that spot again, celestial vengeance would fall on them, for the God of the Christians fought from heaven in his servants' cause.

So the barbarians trembled, and went away. And the fear of St. Severinus fell on all the Goths, heretic Arians though they were; and on the Rugii, who held the north bank of the Danube in those evil days. St. Severinus, meanwhile, went out of Vienna, and built himself a cell at a place called "At the Vineyards." But some benevolent impulse—Divine revelation, his biographer calls it— prompted him to return, and build himself a cell on a hill close to Vienna, round which other cells soon grew up, tenanted by his disciples. "There," says his biographer, "he longed to escape the crowds of men who were wont to come to him, and cling closer to God in continual prayer: but the more he longed to dwell in solitude, the more often he was warned by revelations not to deny his presence to the afflicted people." He fasted continually; he went barefoot even in the midst of winter, which was so severe, the story continues, in those days around Vienna, that wagons crossed the Danube on the solid ice: and yet, instead of being puffed-up by his own virtues, he set an example of humility to all, and bade them with tears to pray for him, that the Saviour's gifts to him might not heap condemnation on his head.

Over the wild Rugii St. Severinus seems to have acquired unbounded influence. Their king, Flaccitheus, used to pour out his sorrows to him, and tell him how the princes of the Goths would surely slay him; for when he had asked leave of him to pass on into Italy, he would not let him go. But St. Severinus prophesied to him that the Goths would do him no harm. Only one warning he must take: "Let it not grieve him to ask peace even for the least of men."

The friendship which had thus begun between the barbarian king and the cultivated saint was carried on by his son Feva: but his "deadly and noxious wife" Gisa, who appears to have been a fierce Arian, always, says his biographer, kept him back from clemency. One story of Gisa's misdeeds is so characteristic both of the manners of the time and of the style in which the original biography is written, that I shall take leave to insert it at length.

"The King Feletheus (who is also Feva), the son of the aforementioned Flaccitheus, following his father's devotion, began, at the commencement of his reign, often to visit the holy man. His deadly and noxious wife, named Gisa, always kept him back from the remedies of clemency. For she, among the other plague-spots of her iniquity, even tried to have certain Catholics re-baptized: but when her husband did not consent, on account of his reverence for St. Severinus, she gave up immediately her sacrilegious intention, burdening the Romans, nevertheless, with hard conditions, and commanding some of them to be exiled to the Danube. For when one day, she, having come to the village next to Vienna, had ordered some of them to be sent over the Danube, and condemned to the most menial offices of slavery, the man of God sent to her, and begged that they might be let go. But she, blazing up in a flame of fury, ordered the harshest of answers to be returned. 'I pray thee,' she said, 'servant of God, hiding there within thy cell, allow us to settle what we choose about our own slaves.' But the man of God hearing this, 'I trust,' he said, 'in my Lord Jesus Christ, that she will be forced by necessity to fulfil that which in her wicked will she has despised.' And forthwith a swift rebuke followed, and brought low the soul of the arrogant woman. For she had confined in close custody certain barbarian goldsmiths, that they might make regal ornaments. To them the son of the aforesaid king, Frederic by name, still a little boy, had gone in, in childish levity, on the very day on which the queen had despised the servant of God. The goldsmiths put a sword to the child's breast, saying, that if any one attempted to enter without giving them an oath that they should be protected, he should die; and that they would slay the king's child first, and themselves afterwards, seeing that they had no hope of life left, being worn out with long prison. When she heard that, the cruel and impious queen, rending her garments for grief, cried out, 'O servant of God, Severinus, are the injuries which I did thee thus avenged? Hast thou obtained by the earnest prayer thou hast poured out this punishment for my contempt, that thou shouldst avenge it on my own flesh and blood?' Then, running up and down with manifold contrition and miserable lamentation, she confessed that for the act of contempt which she had committed against the servant of God she was struck by the vengeance of the present blow; and forthwith she sent knights to ask for forgiveness, and sent across the river the Romans his prayers for whom she had despised. The goldsmiths, having received immediately a promise of safety, and giving up the child, were in like manner let go.

"The most reverend Severinus, when he heard this, gave boundless thanks to the Creator, who sometimes puts off the prayers of suppliants for this end, that as faith, hope, and charity grow, while lesser things are sought, He may concede greater things. Lastly, this did the mercy of the Omnipotent Saviour work, that while it brought to slavery a woman free, but cruel overmuch, she was forced to restore to liberty those who were enslaved. This having been marvellously gained, the queen hastened with her husband to the servant of God, and showed him her son, who, she confessed, had been freed from the verge of death by his prayers, and promised that she would never go against his commands."

To this period of Severinus's life belongs the once famous story of his interview with Odoacer, the first barbarian king of Italy, and brother of the great Onulph or Wolf, who was the founder of the family of the Guelphs, Counts of Altorf, and the direct ancestors of Victoria, Queen of England. Their father was AEdecon, secretary at one time of Attila, and chief of the little tribe of Turklings, who, though German, had clung faithfully to Attila's sons, and came to ruin at the great battle of Netad, when the empire of the Huns broke up once and for ever. Then Odoacer and his brother started over the Alps to seek their fortunes in Italy, and take service, after the fashion of young German adventurers, with the Romans; and they came to St. Severinus's cell, and went in, heathens as they probably were, to ask a blessing of the holy man; and Odoacer had to stoop and to stand stooping, so huge he was. The saint saw that he was no common lad, and said, "Go to Italy, clothed though thou be in ragged sheepskins: thou shalt soon give greater gifts to thy friends." So Odoacer went on into Italy, deposed the last of the Caesars, a paltry boy, Romulus Augustulus by name, and found himself, to his own astonishment, and that of all the world, the first German king of Italy; and, when he was at the height of his power, he remembered the prophecy of Severinus, and sent to him, offering him any boon he chose to ask. But all that the saint asked was, that he should forgive some Romans whom he had banished. St. Severinus meanwhile foresaw that Odoacer's kingdom would not last, as he seems to have foreseen many things, by no miraculous revelation, but simply as a far-sighted man of the world. For when certain German knights were boasting before him of the power and glory of Odoacer, he said that it would last some thirteen, or at most fourteen years; and the prophecy (so all men said in those days) came exactly true.

There is no need to follow the details of St. Severinus's labours through some five-and-twenty years of perpetual self-sacrifice—and, as far as this world was concerned, perpetual disaster. Eugippius's chapters are little save a catalogue of towns sacked one after the other, from Passau to Vienna, till the miserable survivors of the war seemed to have concentrated themselves under St. Severinus's guardianship in the latter city. We find, too, tales of famine, of locust-swarms, of little victories over the barbarians, which do not arrest wholesale defeat: but we find through all St. Severinus labouring like a true man of God, conciliating the invading chiefs, redeeming captives, procuring for the cities which were still standing supplies of clothes for the fugitives, persuading the husbandmen, seemingly through large districts, to give even in time of dearth a tithe of their produce to the poor;—a tale of noble work which one regrets to see defaced by silly little prodigies, more important seemingly in the eyes of the monk Eugippius than the great events which were passing round him. But this is a fault too common with monk chroniclers. The only historians of the early middle age, they have left us a miserably imperfect record of it, because they were looking always rather for the preternatural than for the natural. Many of the saints' lives, as they have come down to us, are mere catalogues of wonders which never happened, from among which the antiquary must pick, out of passing hints and obscure allusions, the really important facts of the time,—changes political and social, geography, physical history, the manners, speech, and look of nations now extinct, and even the characters and passions of the actors in the story. How much can be found among such a list of wonders, by an antiquary who has not merely learning but intellectual insight, is proved by the admirable notes which Dr. Reeves has appended to Adamnan's life of St. Columba: but one feels, while studying his work, that, had Adamnan thought more of facts and less of prodigies, he might have saved Dr. Reeves the greater part of his labour, and preserved to us a mass of knowledge now lost for ever.

And so with Eugippius's life of St. Severinus. The reader finds how the man who had secretly celebrated a heathen sacrifice was discovered by St. Severinus, because, while the tapers of the rest of the congregation were lighted miraculously from heaven, his taper alone would not light; and passes on impatiently, with regret that the biographer omits to mention what the heathen sacrifice was like. He reads how the Danube dared not rise above the mark of the cross which St. Severinus had cut upon the posts of a timber chapel; how a poor man, going out to drive the locusts off his little patch of corn instead of staying in the church all day to pray, found the next morning that his crop alone had been eaten, while all the fields around remained untouched. Even the well-known story, which has a certain awfulness about it, how St. Severinus watched all night by the bier of the dead priest Silvinus, and ere the morning dawned bade him in the name of God speak to his brethren; and how the dead man opened his eyes, and Severinus asked him whether he wished to return to life, and he answered complainingly, "Keep me no longer here; nor cheat me of that perpetual rest which I had already found," and so, closing his eyes once more, was still for ever:— even such a story as this, were it true, would be of little value in comparison with the wisdom, faith, charity, sympathy, industry, utter self-sacrifice, which formed the true greatness of such a man as Severinus.

At last the noble life wore itself out. For two years Severinus had foretold that his end was near; and foretold, too, that the people for whom he had spent himself should go forth in safety, as Israel out of Egypt, and find a refuge in some other Roman province, leaving behind them so utter a solitude, that the barbarians, in their search for the hidden treasures of the civilization which they had exterminated, should dig up the very graves of the dead. Only, when the Lord willed that people to deliver them, they must carry away his bones with them, as the children of Israel carried the bones of Joseph.

Then Severinus sent for Feva, the Rugian king, and Gisa, his cruel wife; and when he had warned them how they must render an account to God for the people committed to their charge, he stretched his hand out to the bosom of the king. "Gisa," he asked, "dost thou love most the soul within that breast, or gold and silver?" She answered that she loved her husband above all. "Cease then," he said, "to oppress the innocent: lest their affliction be the ruin of your power."

Severinus' presage was strangely fulfilled. Feva had handed over the city of Vienna to his brother Frederic,—"poor and impious," says Eugippius. Severinus, who knew him well, sent for him, and warned him that he himself was going to the Lord; and that if, after his death, Frederic dared touch aught of the substance of the poor and the captive, the wrath of God would fall on him. In vain the barbarian pretended indignant innocence; Severinus sent him away with fresh warnings.

"Then on the nones of January he was smitten slightly with a pain in the side. And when that had continued for three days, at midnight he bade the brethren come to him." He renewed his talk about the coming emigration, and entreated again that his bones might not be left behind; and having bidden all in turn come near and kiss him, and having received the sacrament of communion, he forbade them to weep for him, and commanded them to sing a psalm. They hesitated, weeping. He himself gave out the psalm, "Praise the Lord in his saints, and let all that hath breath praise the Lord;" and so went to rest in the Lord.

No sooner was he dead than Frederic seized on the garments kept in the monastery for the use of the poor, and even commanded his men to carry off the vessels of the altar. Then followed a scene characteristic of the time. The steward sent to do the deed shrank from the crime of sacrilege. A knight, Anicianus by name, went in his stead, and took the vessels of the altar. But his conscience was too strong for him. Trembling and delirium fell on him, and he fled away to a lonely island, and became a hermit there. Frederic, impenitent, swept away all in the monastery, leaving nought but the bare walls, "which he could not carry over the Danube." But on him, too, vengeance fell. Within a month he was slain by his own nephew.

Then Odoacer attacked the Rugii, and carried off Feva and Gisa captive to Rome. And then the long-promised emigration came. Odoacer, whether from mere policy (for he was trying to establish a half-Roman kingdom in Italy), or for love of St. Severinus himself, sent his brother Onulf to fetch away into Italy the miserable remnant of the Danubian provincials, to be distributed among the wasted and unpeopled farms of Italy. And with them went forth the corpse of St. Severinus, undecayed, though he had been six years dead, and giving forth exceeding fragrance, though (says Eugippius) no embalmer's hand had touched it. In a coffin, which had been long prepared for it, it was laid on a wagon, and went over the Alps into Italy, working (according to Eugippius) the usual miracles on the way, till it found a resting-place near Naples, in that very villa of Lucullus at Misenum, to which Odoacer had sent the last Emperor of Rome to dream his ignoble life away in helpless luxury.

So ends this tragic story. Of its substantial truth there can be no doubt. The miracles recorded in it are fewer and less strange than those of the average legends—as is usually the case when an eye-witness writes. And that Eugippius was an eye-witness of much which he tells, no one accustomed to judge of the authenticity of documents can doubt, if he studies the tale as it stands in Pez. {238} As he studies, too, he will perhaps wish with me that some great dramatist may hereafter take Eugippius's quaint and rough legend, and shape it into immortal verse. For tragic, in the very nighest sense, the story is throughout. M. Ozanam has well said of that death-bed scene between the saint and the barbarian king and queen—"The history of invasions has many a pathetic scene: but I know none more instructive than the dying agony of that old Roman expiring between two barbarians, and less touched with the ruin of the empire than with the peril of their souls." But even more instructive, and more tragic also, is the strange coincidence that the wonder-working corpse of the starved and barefooted hermit should rest beside the last Emperor of Rome. It is the symbol of a new era. The kings of this world have been judged and cast out. The empire of the flesh is to perish, and the empire of the spirit to conquer thenceforth for evermore.

But if St. Severinus's labours in Austria were in vain, there were other hermits, in Gaul and elsewhere, whose work endured and prospered, and developed to a size of which they had never dreamed. The stories of these good men may be read at length in the Bollandists and Surius: in a more accessible and more graceful form in M. de Montalembert's charming pages. I can only sketch, in a few words, the history of a few of the more famous. Pushing continually northward and westward from the shores of the Mediterranean, fresh hermits settled in the mountains and forests, collected disciples round them, and founded monasteries, which, during the sanguinary and savage era of the Merovingian kings, were the only retreats for learning, piety, and civilization. St. Martin (the young soldier who may be seen in old pictures cutting his cloak in two with a sword, to share it with a beggar) left, after twenty campaigns, the army into which he had been enrolled against his will, a conscript of fifteen years old, to become a hermit, monk, and missionary. In the desert isle of Gallinaria, near Genoa, he lived on roots, to train himself for the monastic life; and then went north-west, to Poitiers, to found Liguge (said to be the most ancient monastery in France), to become Bishop of Tours, and to overthrow throughout his diocese, often at the risk of his life, the sacred oaks and Druid stones of the Gauls, and the temples and idols of the Romans. But he—like many more—longed for the peace of the hermit's cell; and near Tours, between the river Loire and lofty cliffs, he hid himself in a hut of branches, while his eighty disciples dwelt in caves of the rocks above, clothed only in skins of camels. He died in A.D. 397, at the age of eighty-one, leaving behind him, not merely that famous monastery of Marmontier (Martini Monasterium), which endured till the Revolution of 1793, but, what is infinitely more to his glory, his solemn and indignant protest against the first persecution by the Catholic Church—the torture and execution of those unhappy Priscillianist fanatics, whom the Spanish Bishops (the spiritual forefathers of the Inquisition) had condemned in the name of the God of love. Martin wept over the fate of the Priscillianists. Happily he was no prophet, or his head would have become (like Jeremiah's) a fount of tears, could he have foreseen that the isolated atrocity of those Spanish Bishops would have become the example and the rule, legalized and formulized and commanded by Pope after Pope, for every country in Christendom.

Sulpicius Severus, again (whose Lives of the Desert Fathers I have already quoted), carried the example of these fathers into his own estates in Aquitaine. Selling his lands, he dwelt among his now manumitted slaves, sleeping on straw, and feeding on the coarsest bread and herbs; till the hapless neophytes found that life was not so easily sustained in France as in Egypt; and complained to him that it was in vain to try "to make them live like angels, when they were only Gauls."

Another centre of piety and civilization was the rocky isle of Lerins, off the port of Toulon. Covered with the ruins of an ancient Roman city, and swarming with serpents, it was colonized again, in A.D. 410, by a young man of rank named Honoratus, who gathered round him a crowd of disciples, converted the desert isle into a garden of flowers and herbs, and made the sea-girt sanctuary of Lerins one of the most important spots of the then world.

"The West," says M. de Montalembert, "had thenceforth nothing to envy the East; and soon that retreat, destined by its founder to renew on the shores of Provence the austerities of the Thebaid, became a celebrated school of Christian theology and philosophy, a citadel inaccessible to the waves of the barbarian invasion, an asylum for the letters and sciences which were fleeing from Italy, then overrun by the Goths; and, lastly, a nursery of bishops and saints, who spread through Gaul the knowledge of the Gospel and the glory of Lerins. We shall soon see the rays of his light flash even into Ireland and England, by the blessed hands of Patrick and Augustine."

In the year 425, Romanus, a young monk from the neighbourhood of Lyons, had gone up into the forests of the Jura, carrying with him the "Lives of the Hermits," and a few seeds and tools; and had settled beneath an enormous pine; shut out from mankind by precipices, torrents, and the tangled trunks of primaeval trees, which had fallen and rotted on each other age after age. His brother Lupicinus joined him; then crowds of disciples; then his sister, and a multitude of women. The forests were cleared, the slopes planted; a manufacture of box-wood articles—chairs among the rest—was begun; and within the next fifty years the Abbey of Condat, or St. Claude, as it was afterwards called, had become, not merely an agricultural colony, or even merely a minster for the perpetual worship of God, but the first school of that part of Gaul; in which the works of Greek as well as Latin orators were taught, not only to the young monks, but to young laymen likewise.

Meanwhile the volcanic peaks of the Auvergne were hiding from their Arian invaders the ruined gentry of Central France. Effeminate and luxurious slave-holders, as they are painted by Sidonius Appolineris, bishop of Clermont, in that same Auvergne, nothing was left for them when their wealth was gone but to become monks:

and monks they became. The lava grottoes held hermits, who saw visions and daemons, as St. Antony had seen them in Egypt; while near Treves, on the Moselle, a young hermit named Wolflaich tried to imitate St. Simeon Stylites' penance on the pillar; till his bishop, foreseeing that in that severe climate he would only kill himself, wheedled him away from his station, pulled down the pillar in his absence, and bade him be a wiser man. Another figure, and a more interesting one, is the famous St. Goar; a Gaul, seemingly (from the recorded names of his parents) of noble Roman blood, who took his station on the Rhine, under the cliffs of that Lurlei so famous in legend and ballad as haunted by some fair fiend, whose treacherous song lured the boatmen into the whirlpool at their foot. To rescue the shipwrecked boatmen, to lodge, feed, and if need be clothe, the travellers along the Rhine bank, was St. Goar's especial work; and Wandelbert, the monk of Prum, in the Eifel, who wrote his life at considerable length, tells us how St. Goar was accused to the Archbishop of Treves as a hypocrite and a glutton, because he ate freely with his guests; and how his calumniators took him through the forest to Treves; and how he performed divers miracles, both on the road and in the palace of the Archbishop, notably the famous one of hanging his cape upon a sunbeam, mistaking it for a peg. And other miracles of his there are, some of them not altogether edifying: but no reader is bound to believe them, as Wandelbert is evidently writing in the interests of the Abbey of Prum as against those of the Prince-Bishops of Treves; and with a monk's or regular's usual jealousy of the secular or parochial clergy and their bishops.

A more important personage than any of these is the famous St. Benedict, father of the Benedictine order, and "father of all monks," as he was afterwards called, who, beginning himself as a hermit, caused the hermit life to fall, not into disrepute, but into comparative disuse; while the coenobitic life—that is, life, not in separate cells, but in corporate bodies, with common property, and under one common rule—was accepted as the general form of the religious life in the West. As the author of this organization, and of the Benedictine order, to whose learning, as well as to whose piety, the world has owed so much, his life belongs rather to a history of the monastic orders than to that of the early hermits. But it must be always remembered that it was as a hermit that his genius was trained; that in solitude he conceived his vast plans; in solitude he elaborated the really wise and noble rules of his, which he afterwards carried out as far as he could during his lifetime in the busy world; and which endured for centuries, a solid piece of practical good work. For the existence of monks was an admitted fact; even an admitted necessity: St. Benedict's work was to tell them, if they chose to be monks, what sort of persons they ought to be, and how they ought to live, in order to fulfil their own ideal. In the solitude of the hills of Subiaco, above the ruined palace of Nero, above, too, the town of Nurscia, of whose lords he was the last remaining scion, he fled to the mountain grotto, to live the outward life of a wild beast, and, as he conceived, the inward life of an angel. How he founded twelve monasteries; how he fled with some of his younger disciples, to withdraw them from the disgusting persecutions and temptations of the neighbouring secular clergy; how he settled himself on the still famous Monte Cassino, which looks down upon the Gulf of Gaeta, and founded there the "Archi-Monasterium of Europe," whose abbot was in due time first premier baron of the kingdom of Naples,—which counted among its dependencies {245} four bishoprics, two principalities, twenty earldoms, two hundred and fifty castles, four hundred and forty towns or villages, three hundred and thirty-six manors, twenty-three seaports, three isles, two hundred mills, three hundred territories, sixteen hundred and sixty-two churches, and at the end of the sixteenth century an annual revenue of 1,500,000 ducats,—are matters which hardly belong to this volume, which deals merely with the lives of hermits.

THE CELTIC HERMITS

It is not necessary to enter into the vexed question whether any Christianity ever existed in these islands of an earlier and purer type than that which was professed and practised by the saintly disciples of St. Antony. It is at least certain that the earliest historic figures which emerge from the haze of barbarous antiquity in both the Britains and in Ireland, are those of hermits, who, in celibacy and poverty, gather round them disciples, found a convent, convert and baptize the heathen, and often, like Antony and Hilarion, escape from the bustle and toil of the world into their beloved desert. They work the same miracles, see the same visions, and live in the same intimacy with the wild animals, as the hermits of Egypt, or of Roman Gaul: but their history, owing to the wild imagination and (as the legends themselves prove) the gross barbarism of the tribes among whom they dwell, are so involved in fable and legend, that it is all but impossible to separate fact from fiction; all but impossible, often, to fix the time at which they lived.

Their mode of life, it must always be remembered, is said to be copied from that of the Roman hermits of Gaul. St. Patrick, the apostle of Ireland, seems to have been of Roman or Roman British lineage. In his famous "Confession" (which many learned antiquaries consider as genuine) he calls his father, Calphurnius a deacon; his grandfather, Potitus a priest—both of these names being Roman. He is said to have visited, at some period of his life, the monastery of St. Martin at Tours; to have studied with St. Germanus at Auxerre; and to have gone to one of the islands of the Tuscan sea, probably Lerins itself; and, whether or not we believe the story that he was consecrated bishop by Pope Celestine at Rome, we can hardly doubt that he was a member of that great spiritual succession of ascetics who counted St. Antony as their father.

Such another must that Palladius have been, who was sent, says Prosper of Aquitaine, by Pope Celestine to convert the Irish Scots, and who (according to another story) was cast on shore on the north-east coast of Scotland, founded the church of Fordun, in Kincardineshire, and became a great saint among the Pictish folk.

Another primaeval figure, almost as shadowy as St. Patrick, is St. Ninian, a monk of North Wales, who (according to Bede) first attempted the conversion of the Southern Picts, and built himself, at Whithorn in Galloway, the Candida Casa, or White House, a little church of stone,—a wonder in those days of "creel houses" and wooden stockades. He too, according to Bede, who lived some 250 years after his time, went to Rome; and he is said to have visited and corresponded with St. Martin of Tours.

Dubricius, again, whom legend makes the contemporary both of St. Patrick and of King Arthur, appears in Wales, as bishop and abbot of Llandaff. He too is ordained by a Roman bishop, St. Germanus of Auxerre; and he too ends his career, according to tradition, as a hermit, while his disciples spread away into Armorica (Brittany) and Ireland.

We need not, therefore, be surprised to find Ireland, Wales, Cornwall, Scotland, and Brittany, during the next three centuries, swarming with saints, who kept up, whether in company or alone, the old hermit-life of the Thebaid; or to find them wandering, whether on missionary work, or in search of solitude, or escaping, like St. Cadoc the Wise, from the Saxon invaders. Their frequent journeys to Rome, and even to Jerusalem, may perhaps be set down as a fable, invented in after years by monks who were anxious to prove their complete dependence on the Holy See, and their perfect communion with the older and more civilized Christianity of the Roman Empire.

It is probable enough, also, that Romans from Gaul, as well as from Britain, often men of rank and education, who had fled before the invading Goths and Franks, and had devoted themselves (as we have seen that they often did) to the monastic life, should have escaped into those parts of these islands which had not already fallen into the hands of the Saxon invaders. Ireland, as the most remote situation, would be especially inviting to the fugitives; and we can thus understand the story which is found in the Acts of St. Senanus, how fifty monks, "Romans born," sailed to Ireland to learn the Scriptures, and to lead a stricter life; and were distributed between St. Senan, St. Finnian, St. Brendan, St. Barry, and St. Kieran. By such immigrations as this, it may be, Ireland became—as she certainly was for a while—the refuge of what ecclesiastical civilization, learning, and art the barbarian invaders had spared; a sanctuary from whence, in after centuries, evangelists and teachers went forth once more, not only to Scotland and England, but to France and Germany. Very fantastic, and often very beautiful, are the stories of these men; and sometimes tragical enough, like that of the Welsh St. Iltut, cousin of the mythic Arthur, and founder of the great

monastery of Bangor, on the banks of the Dee, which was said—
though we are not bound to believe the fact—to have held more than
two thousand monks at the time of the Saxon invasion. The wild
warrior was converted, says this legend, by seeing the earth open
and swallow up his comrades, who had extorted bread, beer, and a
fat pig from St. Cadoc of Llancarvan, a princely hermit and abbot,
who had persuaded his father and mother to embrace the hermit life
as the regular, if not the only, way of saving their souls. In a
paroxysm of terror he fled from his fair young wife into the forest;
would not allow her to share with him even his hut of branches; and
devoted himself to the labour of making an immense dyke of mud
and stones to keep out the inundations of a neighbouring river. His
poor wife went in search of him once more, and found him in the
bottom of a dyke, no longer a gay knight, but poorly dressed, and
covered with mud. She went away, and never saw him more;
"fearing to displease God and one so beloved by God." Iltut dwelt
afterwards for four years in a cave, sleeping on the bare rock, and
seems at last to have crossed over to Brittany, and died at Dol.

We must not forget—though he is not strictly a hermit—St. David,
the popular saint of the Welsh, son of a nephew of the mythic
Arthur, and educated by one Paulinus, a disciple, it is said, of St.
Germanus of Auxerre. He is at once monk and bishop: he gathers
round him young monks in the wilderness, makes them till the
ground, drawing the plough by their own strength, for he allows
them not to own even an ox. He does battle against "satraps" and
"magicians"— probably heathen chieftains and Druids; he goes to
the Holy Land, and is made archbishop by the Patriarch of
Jerusalem: he introduces, it would seem, into this island the right of
sanctuary for criminals in any field consecrated to himself. He
restores the church of Glastonbury over the tomb of his cousin, King
Arthur, and dies at 100 years of age, "the head of the whole British
nation, and honour of his fatherland." He is buried in one of his own
monasteries at St. David's, near the headland whence St. Patrick had
seen, in a vision, all Ireland stretched out before him, waiting to be
converted to Christ; and the Celtic people go on pilgrimage to his
tomb, even from Brittany and Ireland: and, canonized in 1120, he
becomes the patron saint of Wales.

From that same point, in what year is not said, an old monk of St.
David's monastery, named Modonnoc, set sail for Ireland, after a
long life of labour and virtue. A swarm of bees settled upon the bow
of his boat, and would not be driven away. He took them, whether

he would or not, with him into Ireland, and introduced there, says the legend, the culture of bees and the use of honey.

Ireland was then the "Isle of Saints." Three orders of them were counted by later historians: the bishops (who seem not to have had necessarily territorial dioceses), with St. Patrick at their head, shining like the sun; the second, of priests, under St. Columba, shining like the moon; and the third, of bishops, priests, and hermits, under Colman and Aidan, shining like the stars. Their legends, full of Irish poetry and tenderness, and not without touches here and there of genuine Irish humour, lie buried now, to all save antiquaries, in the folios of the Bollandists and Colgan: but the memory of their virtue and beneficence, as well as of their miracles, shadowy and distorted by the lapse of centuries, is rooted in the heart and brain of the Irish peasantry; and who shall say altogether for evil? For with the tradition of their miracles has been entwined the tradition of their virtues, as an enduring heirloom for the whole Irish race, through the sad centuries which part the era of saints from the present time. We see the Irish women kneeling beside some well, whose waters were hallowed, ages since, by the fancied miracle of some mythic saint, and hanging gaudy rags (just as do the half savage Buddhists of the Himalayas) upon the bushes round. We see them upon holy days crawling on bare and bleeding knees around St. Patrick's cell, on the top of Croagh Patrick, the grandest mountain, perhaps, with the grandest outlook, in these British Isles, where stands still, I believe, an ancient wooden image, said to have belonged to St. Patrick himself; and where, too, hung till late years (it is now preserved in Dublin) an ancient bell; such a strange little oblong bell as the Irish saints carried with them to keep off daemons; one of those magic bells which appear, so far as I am aware, in no country save Ireland and Scotland till we come to Tartary and the Buddhists: such a bell as came down from heaven to St. Senan: such a bell as St. Fursey sent flying through the air to greet St. Cuandy at his devotions when he could not come himself: such a bell as another saint, wandering in the woods, rang till a stag came out of the covert, and carried it for him on his horns. On that peak, so legends tell, St. Patrick stood once, in the spirit and power of Elias—after whom the mountain was long named; fasting, like Elias, forty days and forty nights, and wrestling with the daemons of the storm, and the snakes of the fen, and the Peishta-More, the gigantic monster of the lakes, till he smote the evil things with the golden rod of Jesus, and they rolled over the cliff in hideous rout, and perished in the Atlantic far below. We know that these tales are but the dreams of children: but shall we sneer at the devotion of those poor Irish? Not if we remember (what is an undoubted fact) that the memory of these same saints has kept up in their minds an ideal of nobleness and purity, devotion and beneficence, which, down-trodden slaves as they have been, they would otherwise have inevitably lost; that it has helped to preserve them from mere brutality, and mere ferocity; and that the thought that these men were of their own race and their own kin has given them a pride in their own race, a sense of national unity and of national dignity, which has endured—and surely for their benefit, for reverence for ancestors and the self-respect which springs from it is a benefit to every human being—through all the miseries, deserved or undeserved, which have fallen upon the Irish since Pope Adrian IV. (the true author of all the woes of Ireland), in the year 1155, commissioned Henry II. to conquer Ireland and destroy its primaeval Church, on consideration of receiving his share of the booty in the shape of Peter's Pence.

Among these Irish saints, two names stand out as especially interesting: that of St. Brendan, and that of St. Columba—the former as the representative of the sailor monks of the early period, the other as the great missionary who, leaving his monastery at Durrow, in Ireland, for the famous island of Hy, Iona, or Icolumbkill, off the western point of Mull, became the apostle of Scotland and the north of England. I shall first speak of St. Brendan, and at some length. His name has become lately familiar to many, through the medium of two very beautiful poems, one by Mr. Matthew Arnold, and the other by Mr. Sebastian Evans; and it may interest those who have read their versions of the story to see the oldest form in which the story now exists.

The Celts, it must be remembered, are not, in general, a sea-going folk. They have always neglected the rich fisheries of their coasts; and in Ireland every seaport owes its existence, not to the natives, but to Norse colonists. Even now, the Irishman or Western Highlander, who emigrates to escape the "Saxons," sails in a ship built and manned by those very "Saxons," to lands which the Saxons have discovered and civilized. But in the seventh and eighth centuries, and perhaps earlier, many Celts were voyagers and emigrants, not to discover new worlds, but to flee from the old one. There were deserts in the sea, as well as on land; in them they hoped to escape from men, and, yet more, from women.

They went against their carnal will. They had no liking for the salt water. They were horribly frightened, and often wept bitterly, as they themselves confess. And they had reason for fear; for their vessels were, for the most part, only "curachs" (coracles) of wattled twigs, covered with tanned hides. They needed continual exhortation and comfort from the holy man who was their captain; and needed often miracles likewise for their preservation. Tempests had to be changed into calm, and contrary winds into fair ones, by the prayers of a saint; and the spirit of prophecy was needed, to predict that a whale would be met between Iona and Tiree, who appeared accordingly, to the extreme terror of St. Berach's crew, swimming with open jaws, and (intent on eating, not monks, but herrings) nearly upsetting them by the swell which he raised. And when St. Baithenius met the same whale on the same day, it was necessary for him to rise, and bless, with outspread hands, the sea and the whale, in order to make him sink again, after having risen to breathe. But they sailed forth, nevertheless, not knowing whither they went; true to their great principle, that the spirit must conquer the flesh: and so showed themselves actually braver men than the Norse pirates, who sailed afterwards over the same seas without fear, and without the need of miracles, and who found everywhere on desert islands, on sea-washed stacks and skerries, round Orkney, Shetland, and the Faroes, even to Iceland, the cells of these "Papas" or Popes; and named them after the old hermits, whose memory still lingers in the names of Papa Strona and Papa Westra, in the Orkneys, and in that of Papey, off the coast of Iceland, where the first Norse settlers found Irish books, bells, and crosiers, the relics of old hermits who had long since fasted and prayed their last, and migrated to the Lord.

Adanman, in his life of St. Columba, tells of more than one such voyage. He tells how one Baitanus, with the saint's blessing, sailed forth to find "a desert" in the sea; and how when he was gone, the saint prophesied that he should be buried, not in a desert isle, but where a woman should drive sheep over his grave, the which came true in the oak-wood of Calgaich, now Londonderry, whither he came back again. He tells, again, of one Cormac, "a knight of Christ," who three times sailed forth in a coracle to find some desert isle, and three times failed of his purpose; and how, in his last voyage, he was driven northward by the wind fourteen days' sail, till he came where the summer sea was full of foul little stinging creatures, of the size of frogs, which beat against the sides of the frail boat, till all expected them to be stove in. They clung, moreover, to the oar blades; {256} and Cormac was in some danger of never seeing land again, had not St. Columba, at home in Iona far away, seen him in a vision, him and his fellows, praying and "watering their cheeks with floods of tears," in the midst of "perturbations monstrous, horrific, never seen before, and almost unspeakable." Calling together his monks, he bade them pray for a north wind, which came accordingly, and blew Cormac safe back to Iona, to tempt the waves no more. "Let the reader therefore perpend how great and what manner of man this same blessed personage was, who, having so great prophetic knowledge, could command, by invoking the name of Christ, the winds and ocean."

Even as late as the year 891, says the Anglo-Saxon Chronicle: "Three Scots came to King Alfred, in a boat without any oars, from Ireland, whence they had stolen away, because for the love of God they desired to be on pilgrimage, they recked not where. The boat in which they came was made of two hides and a half; and they took with them provisions for seven days; and about the seventh day they came on shore in Cornwall, and soon after went to King Alfred. Thus they were named, Dubslane, and Macbeth, and Maelinmun."

Out of such wild feats as these; out of dim reports of fairy islands in the west; of the Canaries and Azores; of that Vinland, with its wild corn and wild grapes which Leif, the son of Eirek Rauda, had found beyond the ocean a thousand years and one after the birth of Christ; of icebergs and floes sailing in the far northern sea, upon the edge of the six-months' night; out of Edda stories of the Midgard snake, which is coiled round the world; out of reports, it may be, of Indian fakirs and Buddhist shamans; out of scraps of Greek and Arab myth, from the Odyssey or the Arabian Nights, brought home by "Jorsala Farar," vikings who had been for pilgrimage and plunder up the Straits of Gibraltar into the far East;—out of all these materials were made up, as years rolled on, the famous legend of St. Brendan and his seven years' voyage in search of the "land promised to the saints."

This tale was so popular in the middle age, that it appears, in different shapes, in almost every early European language. {257} It was not only the delight of monks, but it stirred up to wild voyages many a secular man in search of St. Brendan's Isle, "which is not found when it is sought," but was said to be visible at times, from Palma in the Canaries. The myth must have been well known to Columbus, and may have helped to send him forth in search of

"Cathay." Thither (so the Spanish peasants believed) Don Roderic had retired from the Moorish invaders. There (so the Portuguese fancied) King Sebastian was hidden from men, after his reported death in the battle of Alcazar. The West Indies, when they were first seen, were surely St. Brendan's Isle: and the Mississippi may have been, in the eyes of such old adventurers as Don Ferdinando da Soto, when he sought for the Fountain of Perpetual Youth, the very river which St. Brendan found parting in two the Land of Promise. From the year 1526 (says M. Jubinal), till as late as 1721, armaments went forth from time to time into the Atlantic, and went forth in vain.

For the whole tale, from whatever dim reports of fact they may have sprung, is truly (as M. Jubinal calls it) a monkish Odyssey, and nothing more. It is a dream of the hermit's cell. No woman, no city, nor nation, are ever seen during the seven years' voyage. Ideal monasteries and ideal hermits people the "deserts of the ocean." All beings therein (save daemons and Cyclops) are Christians, even to the very birds, and keep the festivals of the Church as eternal laws of nature. The voyage succeeds, not by seamanship, or geographic knowledge, nor even by chance: but by the miraculous prescience of the saint, or of those whom he meets; and the wanderings of Ulysses, or of Sinbad, are rational and human in comparison with those of St. Brendan.

Yet there are in them, as was to be expected, elements in which the Greek or the Arab legends are altogether deficient; perfect innocence, patience, and justice; utter faith in a God who prospers the innocent and punishes the guilty; ennobling obedience to the saint, who stands out a truly heroic figure above his trembling crew; and even more valuable still, the belief in, the craving for, an ideal, even though that ideal be that of a mere earthly Paradise; the "divine discontent," as it has been well called, which is the root of all true progress; which leaves (thank God) no man at peace save him who has said, "Let us eat and drink, for to-morrow we die."

And therefore I have written at some length the story of St. Brendan; because, though it be but a monk-ideal, it is an ideal still: and therefore profitable for all who are not content with this world, and its paltry ways.

Saint Brendan, we read, the son of Finnloga, and great grandson of Alta, son of Ogaman, of the race of Ciar son of Fergus, was born at Tralee, and founded, in 559, the Abbey of Clonfert, {260a} and was a man famous for his great abstinence and virtues, and the father of nearly 3,000 monks. {260b} And while he was "in his warfare," there came to him one evening a holy hermit named "Barintus," of the royal race of Neill; and when he was questioned, he did nought but cast himself on the ground, and weep and pray. And when St. Brendan asked him to make better cheer for him and his monks, he told him a strange tale. How a nephew of his had fled away to be a solitary, and found a delicious island, and established a monastery therein; and how he himself had gone to see his nephew, and sailed with him to the eastward to an island, which was called "the land of promise of the saints," wide and grassy, and bearing all manner of fruits; wherein was no night, for the Lord Jesus Christ was the light thereof; and how they abode there for a long while without eating and drinking; and when they returned to his nephew's monastery, the brethren knew well where they had been, for the fragrance of Paradise lingered on their garments for nearly forty days.

So Barintus told his story, and went back to his cell. But St. Brendan called together his most loving fellow-warriors, as he called them, and told them how he had set his heart on seeking that Promised Land. And he went up to the top of the hill in Kerry, which is still called Mount Brendan, with fourteen chosen monks; and there, at the utmost corner of the world, he built him a coracle of wattle, and covered it with hides tanned in oak-bark and softened with butter, and set up in it a mast and a sail, and took forty days' provision, and commanded his monks to enter the boat, in the name of the Holy Trinity. And as he stood alone, praying on the shore, three more monks from his monastery came up, and fell at his feet, and begged to go too, or they would die in that place of hunger and thirst; for they were determined to wander with him all the days of their life. So he gave them leave. But two of them, he prophesied, would come to harm and to judgment. So they sailed away toward the summer solstice, with a fair wind, and had no need to row. But after twelve days the wind fell to a calm, and they had only light airs at night, till forty days were past, and all their victual spent. Then they saw toward the north a lofty island, walled round with cliffs, and went about it three days ere they could find a harbour. And when they landed, a dog came fawning on them, and they followed it up to a great hall with beds and seats, and water to wash their feet. But St. Brendan said, "Beware, lest Satan bring you into temptation. For I see him busy with one of those three who followed us." Now the hall was hung all round with vessels of divers metals, and bits and horns overlaid with silver. Then St. Brendan told his servant to bring the meal which God had prepared; and at once a table was laid with napkins, and loaves wondrous white, and fishes. Then they blessed God, and ate, and took likewise drink as much as they would, and lay down to sleep. Then St. Brendan saw the devil's work; namely, a little black boy holding a silver bit, and calling the brother aforementioned. So they rested three days and three nights. But when they went to the ship, St. Brendan charged them with theft, and told what was stolen, and who had stolen it. Then the brother cast out of his bosom a silver bit, and prayed for mercy. And when he was forgiven and raised up from the ground, behold, a little black boy flew out of his bosom, howling aloud, and crying, "Why, O man of God, dost thou drive me from my habitation, where I have dwelt for seven years?"

Then the brother received the Holy Eucharist, and died straightway, and was buried in that isle, and the brethren saw the angels carry his soul aloft, for St. Brendan had told him that so it should be: but that the brother who came with him should have his sepulchre in hell. And as they went on board, a youth met them with a basket of loaves and a bottle of water, and told them that it would not fail till Pentecost.

Then they sailed again many days, till they came to an isle full of great streams and fountains swarming with fish; and sheep there all white, as big as oxen, so many that they hid the face of the earth. And they stayed there till Easter Eve, and took one of the sheep (which followed them as if it had been tame) to eat for the Paschal feast. Then came a man with loaves baked in the ashes, and other victual, and fell down before St. Brendan and cried, "How have I merited this, O pearl of God, that thou shouldest be fed at this holy tide from the labours of my hand?"

And they learned from that man that the sheep grew there so big because they were never milked, nor pinched with winter, but they fed in those pastures all the year round. Moreover, he told them that they must keep Easter in an isle hard by, opposite a shore to the west, which some called the Paradise of Birds.

So to the nearest island they sailed. It had no harbour, nor sandy shore, and there was no turf on it, and very little wood. Now the Saint knew what manner of isle it was, but he would not tell the brethren, lest they should be terrified. So he bade them make the boat fast stem and stern, and when morning came he bade those who were priests to celebrate each a mass, and then to take the lamb's fleece on shore and cook it in the caldron with salt, while St. Brendan remained in the boat.

But when the fire blazed up, and the pot began to boil, that island began to move like water. Then the brethren ran to the boat imploring St. Brendan's aid; and he helped them each in by the hand, and cast off. After which the island sank in the ocean. And when they could see their fire burning more than two miles off, St. Brendan told them how that God had revealed to him that night the mystery; that this was no isle, but the biggest of all fishes which swam in the ocean, always it tries to make its head and its tail meet, but cannot, by reason of its length; and its name is Jasconius.

Then, across a narrow strait, they saw another isle, very grassy and wooded, and full of flowers. And they found a little stream, and towed the boat up it (for the stream was of the same width as the boat), with St. Brendan sitting on board, till they came to the fountain thereof. Then said the holy father, "See, brethren, the Lord has given us a place wherein to celebrate his holy Resurrection. And if we had nought else, this fountain, I think, would serve for food as well as drink." For the fountain was too admirable. Over it was a huge tree of wonderful breadth, but no great height, covered with snow-white birds, so that its leaves and boughs could scarce be seen.

And when the man of God saw that, he was so desirous to know the cause of that assemblage of birds, that he besought God upon his knees, with tears, saying, "God, who knowest the unknown, and revealest the hidden, thou knowest the anxiety of my heart. . . . Deign of thy great mercy to reveal to me thy secret. . . . But not for the merit of my own dignity, but regarding thy clemency, do I presume to ask."

Then one of those birds flew from off the tree, and his wings sounded like bells over the boat. And he sat on the prow, and spread his wings joyfully, and looked quietly on St. Brendan. And when the man of God questioned that bird, it told how they were of the spirits which fell in the great ruin of the old enemy; not by sin or by consent, but predestined by the piety of God to fall with those with whom they were created. But they suffered no punishment; only they could not, in part, behold the presence of God. They wandered about this world, like other spirits of the air, and firmament, and earth. But on holy days they took those shapes of birds, and praised their Creator in that place.

Then the bird told him, how he and his monks had wandered one year already, and should wander for six more; and every year should celebrate their Easter in that place, and after find the Land of Promise; and so flew back to its tree.

And when the eventide was come, the birds began all with one voice to sing, and clap their wings, crying, "Thou, O God, art praised in Zion, and unto Thee shall the vow be performed in Jerusalem." And always they repeated that verse for an hour, and their melody and the clapping of their wings was like music which drew tears by its sweetness.

And when the man of God wakened his monks at the third watch of the night with the verse, "Thou shalt open my lips, O Lord," all the birds answered, "Praise the Lord, all his angels; praise him, all his virtues." And when the dawn shone, they sang again, "The splendour of the Lord God is over us;" and at the third hour, "Sing psalms to our God, sing; sing to our King, sing with wisdom." And at the sixth, "The Lord hath lifted up the light of his countenance upon us, and had mercy on us." And at the ninth, "Behold how good and pleasant it is for brethren to dwell in unity." So day and night those birds gave praise to God. St. Brendan, therefore, seeing these things, gave thanks to God for all his marvels, and the brethren were refreshed with that spiritual food till the octave of Easter.

After which, St. Brendan advised to take of the water of the fountain; for till then they had only used it to wash their feet and hands. But there came to him the same man who had been with them three days before Easter, and with his boat full of meat and drink, and said, "My brothers, here you have enough to last till Pentecost: but do not drink of that fountain. For its nature is, that whosoever drinks will sleep for four-and-twenty hours." So they stayed till Pentecost, and rejoiced in the song of the birds. And after mass at Pentecost, the man brought them food again, and bade them take of the water of the fountain and depart. Then the birds came again, and sat upon the prow, and told them how they must, every year, celebrate Easter in the Isle of Birds, and Easter Eve upon the back of the fish Jasconius; and how, after eight months, they should come to the isle called Ailbey, and keep their Christmas there.

After which they were on the ocean for eight months, out of sight of land, and only eating after every two or three days, till they came to an island, along which they sailed for forty days, and found no harbour. Then they wept and prayed, for they were almost worn out with weariness; and after they had fasted and prayed for three days, they saw a narrow harbour, and two fountains, one foul, one clear. But when the brethren hurried to draw water, St. Brendan (as he had done once before) forbade them, saying that they must take nought without leave from the elders who were in that isle.

And of the wonders which they saw in that isle it were too long to tell: how there met them an exceeding old man, with snow-white hair, who fell at St. Brendan's feet three times, and led him in silence up to a monastery of four-and-twenty silent monks, who washed their feet, and fed them with bread and water, and roots of wonderful sweetness; and then at last, opening his mouth, told them how that bread was sent them perpetually, they knew not from whence; and how they had been there eighty years, since the times of St. Patrick, and how their father Ailbey and Christ had nourished them; and how they grew no older, nor ever fell sick, nor were overcome by cold or heat; and how brother never spoke to brother, but all things were done by signs; and how he led them to a square chapel, with three candles before the mid-altar, and two before each of the side altars; and how they, and the chalices and patens, and all the other vessels, were of crystal; and how the candles were lighted always by a fiery arrow, which came in through the window, and returned; and how St. Brendan kept his Christmas there, and then sailed away till Lent, and came to a fruitful island where he found fish; and how when certain brethren drank too much of the charmed water they slept, some three days, and some one; and how they sailed north, and then east, till they came back to the Isle of Sheep at Easter, and found on the shore their caldron, which they had lost on Jasconius's back; and how, sailing away, they were chased by a mighty fish which spouted foam, but was slain by another fish which spouted fire; and how they took enough of its flesh to last them three months; and how they came to an island flat as the sea, without trees, or aught that waved in the wind; and how on that island were three troops of monks (as the holy man had foretold), standing a stone's throw from each other: the first of boys, robed in snow-white; the second of young men, dressed in hyacinthine; the third of old men, in purple dalmatics, singing alternately their psalms, all day and night: and how when they stopped singing, a cloud of wondrous brightness overshadowed the isle; and how two of the young men, ere they sailed away, brought baskets of grapes, and asked that one of the monks (as had been prophesied) should remain with them, in the Isle of Strong Men; and how St. Brendan let him go, saying, "In a good hour did thy mother conceive thee, because thou hast merited to dwell with such a congregation;" and how those grapes were so big, that a pound of juice ran out of each of them, and an ounce thereof fed each brother for a whole day, and was as sweet as honey; and how a magnificent bird dropped into the ship the bough of an unknown tree, with a bunch of grapes thereon; and how they came to a land where the trees were all bowed down with vines, and their odour as the odour of a house full of pomegranates; and how they fed forty days on those grapes, and strange herbs and roots; and how they saw flying against them the bird which is called gryphon; and how that bird who had brought the bough tore out the gryphon's eyes, and slew him; and how they looked down into the clear sea, and saw all the fishes sailing round and round, head to tail, innumerable as flocks in the pastures, and were terrified, and would have had the man of God celebrate mass in silence, lest the fish should hear, and attack them; and how the man of God laughed at their folly; and how they came to a column of clear crystal in the sea, with a canopy round it of the colour of silver, harder than marble, and sailed in through an opening, and found it all light within; {269} and how they found in that hall a chalice of the same stuff as the canopy, and a paten of that of the column, and took them, that they might make many believe; and how they sailed out again, and past a treeless island, covered with slag and forges; and how a great hairy man, fiery and smutty, came down and shouted after them; and how when they made the sign of the Cross and sailed away, he and his fellows brought down huge lumps of burning slag in tongs, and hurled them after the ship; and how they went back, and blew their forges up, till the whole island flared, and the sea boiled, and the howling and stench followed them, even when they were out of sight of that evil isle; and how St. Brendan bade them strengthen themselves in faith and spiritual arms, for they were now on the confines of hell, therefore they must watch, and play the man. All this must needs be hastened over, that we may come to the famous legend of Judas Iscariot.

They saw a great and high mountain toward the north, with smoke about its peak. And the wind blew them close under the cliffs, which were of immense height, so that they could hardly see their top, upright as walls, and black as coal. {270} Then he who remained of the three brethren who had followed St. Brendan sprang out of the ship, and waded to the cliff foot, groaning, and crying, "Woe to me, father, for I am carried away from you; and cannot turn back." Then the brethren backed the ship, and cried to the Lord for mercy. But the blessed Father Brendan saw how that wretch was carried off by a multitude of devils, and all on fire among them. Then a fair wind blew them away southward; and when they looked back they saw the peak of the isle uncovered, and flame spouting from it up to heaven, and sinking back again, till the whole mountain seemed one burning pile.

After that terrible vision they sailed seven days to the south, till Father Brendan saw a dense cloud; when they neared it, a form as of a man sitting, and before him a veil, as big as a sack, hanging between two iron tongs, and rocking on the waves like a boat in a whirlwind. Which when the brethren saw some thought was a bird, and some a boat; but the man of God bade them give over arguing, and row thither. And when they got near, the waves were still, as if they had been frozen; and they found a man sitting on a rough and shapeless rock, and the waves beating over his head; and when they fell back, the bare rock appeared on which that wretch was sitting. And the cloth which hung before him the wind moved, and beat him with it on the eyes and brow. But when the blessed man asked him who he was, and how he had earned that doom, he said, "I am that most wretched Judas, who made the worst of all bargains. But I hold not this place for any merit of my own, but for the ineffable mercy of Christ. I expect no place of repentance: but for the indulgence and mercy of the Redeemer of the world, and for the honour of His holy resurrection, I have this refreshment; for it is the Lord's-day now, and as I sit here I seem to myself in a paradise of delight, by reason of the pains which will be mine this evening; for when I am in my pains I burn day and night like lead melted in a pot. But in the midst of that mountain which you saw, is Leviathan with his satellites, and I was there when he swallowed your brother; and therefore the king of hell rejoiced, and sent forth huge flames, as he doth always when he devours the souls of the impious." Then he told them how he had his refreshings there every Lord's-day from even to even, and from Christmas to Epiphany, and from Easter to Pentecost, and from the Purification of the Blessed Virgin to her Assumption: but the rest of his time he was tormented with Herod and Pilate, Annas and Caiaphas; and so adjured them to intercede for him with the Lord that he might be there at least till sunrise in the morn. To whom the man of God said, "The will of the Lord be done. Thou shalt not be carried off by the daemons till to-morrow." Then he asked him of that clothing, and he told how he had given it to a leper when he was the Lord's chamberlain; "but because it was no more mine than it was the Lord's and the other brethren's, therefore it is of no comfort to me, but rather a hurt. And these forks I gave to the priests to hang their caldrons on. And this stone on which I always sit I took off the road, and threw it into a ditch for a stepping-stone, before I was a disciple of the Lord." {272}

But when the evening hour had covered the face of Thetis," behold a multitude of daemons shouting in a ring, and bidding the man of God depart, for else they could not approach; and they dared not behold their prince's face unless they brought back their prey. But the man of God bade them depart. And in the morning an infinite multitude of devils covered the face of the abyss, and cursed the man of God for coming thither; for their prince had scourged them cruelly that night for not bringing back the captive. But the man of God returned their curses on their own heads, saying that "cursed was he whom they blest, and blessed he whom they cursed;" and when they threatened Judas with double torments because he had not come back, the man of God rebuked them.

"Art thou, then, Lord of all," they asked, "that we should obey thee?" "I am the servant," said he, "of the Lord of all; and whatsoever I command in his name is done; and I have no ministry save what he concedes to me."

So they blasphemed him till he left Judas, and then returned, and carried off that wretched soul with great rushing and howling.

After which they saw a little isle; and the holy man told them that now seven years were nigh past; and that in that isle they should soon see a hermit, named Paul the Spiritual, who had lived for sixty years without any corporeal food, but for thirty years before that he had received food from a certain beast.

The isle was very small, about a furlong round; a bare rock, so steep that they could find no landing-place. But at last they found a creek, into which they thrust the boat's bow, and then discovered a very difficult ascent. Up that the man of God climbed, bidding them wait for him, for they must not enter the isle without the hermit's leave; and when he came to the top he saw two caves, with their mouths opposite each other, and a very small round well before the cave mouth, whose waters, as fast as they ran out, were sucked in again by the rock. {274} As he went to one entrance, the old man came out of the other, saying, "Behold how good and pleasant it is, brethren, to dwell together in unity," and bade him call up the brethren from the boat; and when they came, he kissed them, and called them each by his name. Whereat they marvelled, not only at his spirit of prophecy, but also at his attire; for he was all covered with his locks and beard, and with the other hair of his body, down to his feet. His hair was white as snow for age, and none other covering had he. When St. Brendan saw that, he sighed again and again, and said within himself, "Woe is me, sinner that I am, who wear a monk's habit, and have many monks under me, when I see a man of angelic dignity sitting in a cell, still in the flesh, and unhurt by the vices of the flesh." To whom the man of God answered, "Venerable father, what great and many wonders God hath showed thee, which he hath manifested to none of the fathers, and thou sayest in thy heart that thou art not worthy to wear a monk's habit. I tell thee, father, that thou art greater than a monk; for a monk is fed and clothed by the work of his own hands: but God has fed and clothed thee and thy family for seven years with his secret things, while wretched I sit here on this rock like a bird, naked save the hair of my body."

Then St. Brendan asked him how and whence he came thither; and he told how he was nourished in St. Patrick's monastery for fifty years, and took care of the cemetery; and how when the dean had bidden him dig a grave, an old man, whom he knew not, appeared to him, and forbade him, for that grave was another man's. And how he revealed to him that he was St. Patrick, his own abbot, who had died the day before, and bade him bury that brother elsewhere, and go down to the sea and find a boat, which would take him to the place where he should wait for the day of his death; and how he landed on that rock, and thrust the boat off with his foot, and it went swiftly back to its own land; and how, on the very first day, a beast came to him, walking on its hind paws, and between its fore paws a fish, and grass to make a fire, and laid them at his feet; and so every third day for twenty years; and every Lord's day a little water came out of the rock, so that he could drink and wash his hands; and how after thirty years he had found these caves and that fountain, and had fed for the last sixty years on nought but the water thereof. For all the years of his life were 150, and henceforth he awaited the day of his judgment in that his flesh.

Then they took of that water, and received his blessing, and kissed each other in the peace of Christ, and sailed southward: but their food was the water from the isle of the man of God. Then (as Paul the Hermit had foretold) they came back on Easter Eve to the Isle of Sheep, and to him who used to give them victuals; and then went on to the fish Jasconius, and sang praises on his back all night, and mass at morn. After which the fish carried them on his back to the Paradise of Birds, and there they stayed till Pentecost. Then the man who always tended them, bade them fill their skins from the fountain, and he would lead them to the land promised to the saints. And all the birds wished them a prosperous voyage in God's name; and they sailed away, with forty days' provision, the man being their guide, till after forty days they came at evening to a great darkness which lay round the Promised Land. But after they had sailed through it for an hour, a great light shone round them, and the boat stopped at a shore. And when they landed they saw a spacious land, full of trees bearing fruit as in autumn time. And they walked about that land for forty days, eating of the fruit and drinking of the fountains, and found no end thereof. And there was no night there, but the light shone like the light of the sun. At last they came to a great river, which they could not cross, so that they could not find out the extent of that land. And as they were pondering over this, a youth, with shining face and fair to look upon, met them, and kissed them with great joy, calling them each by his name, and said, "Brethren, peace be with you, and with all that follow the peace of Christ." And after that, "Blessed are they who dwell in thy house, O Lord; they shall be for ever praising thee."

Then he told St. Brendan that that was the land which he had been seeking for seven years, and that he must now return to his own country, taking of the fruits of that land, and of its precious gems, as much as his ship could carry; for the days of his departure were at hand, when he should sleep in peace with his holy brethren. But after many days that land should be revealed to his successors, and should be a refuge for Christians in persecution. As for the river that they saw, it parted that island; and the light shone there for ever, because Christ was the light thereof.

Then St. Brendan asked if that land would ever be revealed to men: and the youth answered, that when the most high Creator should have put all nations under his feet, then that land should be manifested to all his elect.

After which St. Brendan, when the youth had blessed him, took of the fruits and of the gems, and sailed back through the darkness, and returned to his monastery; whom when the brethren saw, they glorified God for the miracles which he had heard and seen. After which he ended his life in peace. Amen.

Here ends (says the French version) concerning St. Brendan, and the marvels which he found in the sea of Ireland.

ST. MALO

Intermingled, fantastically and inconsistently, with the story of St. Brendan, is that of St. Maclovius or Machutus, who has given his name to the seaport of St. Malo, in Brittany. His life, written by Sigebert, a monk of Gembloux, about the year 1100, tells us how he was a Breton, who sailed with St. Brendan in search of the fairest of all islands, in which the citizens of heaven were said to dwell. With St. Brendan St. Malo celebrated Easter on the whale's back, and with St. Brendan he returned. But another old hagiographer, Johannes a Bosco, tells a different story, making St. Malo an Irishman brought up by St. Brendan, and preserved by his prayers from a wave of the sea. He gives, moreover, to the Isle of Paradise the name of Inga, and says that St. Brendan and his companions never reached it after all, but came home after sailing round the Orkneys and other Northern isles. The fact is, that the same saints reappear so often on both sides of the British and the Irish Channels, that we must take the existence of many of them as mere legend, which has been carried from land to land by monks in their migrations, and taken root upon each fresh soil which it has reached. One incident in St. Malo's voyage is so fantastic, and so grand likewise, that it must not be omitted. The monks come to an island whereon they find the barrow of some giant of old time. St. Malo, seized with pity for the lost soul of the heathen, opens the mound and raises the dead to life. Then follows a strange conversation between the giant and the saint. He was slain, he says, by his kinsmen, and ever since has been tormented in the other world. In that nether pit they know (he says) of the Holy Trinity: but that knowledge is rather harm than gain to them, because they did not choose to know it when alive on earth. Therefore he begs to be baptized, and so delivered from his pain. He is therefore instructed, catechised, and in due time baptized, and admitted to the Holy Communion. For fifteen days more he remains alive: and then, dying once more, is again placed in his sepulchre, and left in peace.

From fragmentary recollections of such tales as these (it may be observed in passing) may have sprung the strange fancy of the modern Cornishmen, which identifies these very Celtic saints of their own race with the giants who, according to Geoffrey of Monmouth, inhabited the land before Brutus and his Trojans founded the Arthuric dynasty. St. Just, for instance, who is one of the guardian saints of the Land's End, and St. Kevern, one of the guardian saints of the Lizard, are both giants; and Cornishmen a few years since would tell how St. Just came from his hermitage by Cape Cornwall to visit St. Kevern in his cave on the east side of Goonhilly Downs; and how they took the Holy Communion together; and how St. Just, tempted by the beauty of St. Kevern's paten and chalice, arose in the night and fled away with the holy vessels, wading first the Looe Pool, and then Mount's Bay itself; and how St. Kevern pursued him, and hurled after him three great boulders of porphyry, two of which lie on the slates and granites to this day; till St. Just, terrified at the might of his saintly brother, tossed the stolen vessels ashore opposite St. Michael's Mount, and, fleeing back to his own hermitage, never appeared again in the neighbourhood of St. Kevern.

But to return. St. Malo, coming home with St. Brendan, craves for peace, and solitude, and the hermit's cell, and goes down to the sea-shore, to find a vessel which may carry him out once more into the infinite unknown. Then there comes by a boat with no one in it but a little boy, who takes him on board, and carries him to the isle of the hermit Aaron, near the town of Aletha, which men call St. Malo now; and then the little boy vanishes away, and St. Malo knows that he was Christ himself. There he lives with Aaron, till the Bretons of the neighbourhood make him their bishop. He converts the idolaters around, and performs the usual miracles of hermit saints. He changes water into wine, and restores to life not only a dead man, but a dead sow likewise, over whose motherless litter a wretched slave, who has by accident killed the sow with a stone, is weeping and wringing his hands in dread of his master's fury. While St. Malo is pruning vines, he lays his cape upon the ground, and a redbreast comes and lays an egg on it. He leaves it there, for the bird's sake, till the young are hatched, knowing, says his biographer, that without God the Father not a sparrow falls to the ground. Hailoch, the prince of Brittany, destroys his church, and is struck blind. Restored to sight by the saint, he bestows large lands on the Church. "The impious generation," who, with their children after them, have lost their property by Hailoch's gift, rise against St. Malo. They steal his horses, and in mockery leave him only a mare. They beat his baker, tie his feet under the horse's body, and leave him on the sand to be drowned by the rising tide. The sea by a miracle stops a mile off, and the baker is saved.

St. Malo, weary of the wicked Bretons, flees to Saintonge in Aquitaine, where he performs yet more miracles. Meanwhile, a dire famine falls on the Bretons, and a thousand horrible diseases.

The Hermits

Penitent, they send for St. Malo, who delivers them and their flocks. But, at the command of an angel, he returns to Saintonge and dies there, and Saintonge has his relics, and the innumerable miracles which they work, even to the days of Sigebert, of Gembloux.

ST. COLUMBA

The famous St. Columba cannot perhaps be numbered among the hermits: but as the spiritual father of many hermits, as well as many monks, and as one whose influence upon the Christianity of these islands is notorious and extensive, he must needs have some notice in these pages. Those who wish to study his life and works at length will of course read Dr. Reeves's invaluable edition of Adamnan. The more general reader will find all that he need know in Mr. Hill Burton's excellent "History of Scotland," chapters vii. and viii.; and also in Mr. Maclear's "History of Christian Missions during the Middle Ages"—a book which should be in every Sunday library.

St. Columba, like St. David and St. Cadoc of Wales, and like many great Irish saints, is a prince and a statesman as well as a monk. He is mixed up in quarrels between rival tribes. He is concerned, according to antiquaries, in three great battles, one of which sprang, according to some, from Columba's own misdeeds. He copies by stealth the Psalter of St. Finnian. St. Finnian demands the copy, saying it was his as much as the original. The matter is referred to King Dermod, who pronounces, in high court at Tara, the famous decision which has become a proverb in Ireland, that "to every cow belongs her own calf." {283} St. Columba, who does not seem at this time to have possessed the dove-like temper which his name, according to his disciples, indicates, threatens to avenge upon the king his unjust decision. The son of the king's steward and the son of the King of Connaught, a hostage at Dermod's court, are playing hurley on the green before Dermod's palace. The young prince strikes the other boy, kills him, and flies for protection to Columba. He is nevertheless dragged away, and slain upon the spot. Columba leaves the palace in a rage, goes to his native mountains of Donegal, and returns at the head of an army of northern and western Irish to fight the great battle of Cooldrevny in Sligo. But after a while public opinion turns against him; and at the Synod of Teltown, in Meath, it is proclaimed that Columba, the man of blood, shall quit Ireland, and win for Christ out of heathendom as many souls as have perished in that great fight. Then Columba, with twelve comrades, sails in a coracle for the coast of Argyleshire; and on the eve of Pentecost, A.D. 563, lands upon that island which, it may be, will be famous to all times as Iona, Hy, or Icolumkill,—Hy of Columb of the Cells.

Thus had Columba, if the tale be true, undertaken a noble penance; and he performed it like a noble man. If, according to the fashion of those times, he bewailed his sins with tears, he was no morbid or selfish recluse, but a man of practical power, and of wide humanity. Like one of Homer's old heroes, St. Columba could turn his hand to every kind of work. He could turn the hand-mill, work on the farm, heal the sick, and command as a practised sailor the little fleet of coracles which lay hauled up on the strand of Iona, ready to carry him and his monks on their missionary voyages to the mainland or the isles. Tall, powerful, handsome, with a face which, as Adamnan said, made all who saw him glad, and a voice so stentorian that it could be heard at times a full mile off, and coming too of royal race, it is no wonder if he was regarded as a sort of demigod, not only by his own monks, but by the Pictish chiefs to whom he preached the Cross. We hear of him at Craig Phadrick, near Inverness; at Skye, at Tiree, and other islands; we hear of him receiving visits from his old monks of Derry and Durrow; returning to Ireland to decide between rival chiefs; and at last dying at the age of seventy-seven, kneeling before the altar in his little chapel of Iona—a death as beautiful as had been the last thirty-four years of his life; and leaving behind him disciples destined to spread the light of Christianity over the whole of Scotland and the northern parts of England.

St. Columba, at one period or other of his life, is said to have visited a missionary hermit, whose name still lingers in Scotland as St. Kentigern, or more commonly St. Mungo, the patron saint of Glasgow. The two men, it is said (but the story belongs to the twelfth century, and can hardly be depended on), exchanged their crooked staves or crosiers in token of Christian brotherhood, and that which St. Columba is said to have given to St. Kentigern was preserved in Ripon Cathedral to the beginning of the fifteenth century. But who St. Kentigern was, or what he really did, is hard to say; for all his legends, like most of these early ones, are as tangled as a dream. He dies in the year 601: and yet he is the disciple of the famous St. Servanus or St. Serf, who lived in the times of St. Palladius and St. Patrick, 180 years before. This St. Serf is a hermit of the true old type; and even if his story be, as Dr. Reeves thinks, a fabrication throughout, it is at least a very early one, and true to the ideal which had originated with St. Antony. He is brought up in a monastery at Culross: he is tempted by the devil in a cave in the parish of Dysart (the Desert), in Fifeshire, which still retains that name. The daemon, fleeing from him, enters an unfortunate man, who is forthwith plagued with a wolfish appetite. St. Serf cures him by putting his thumb into his mouth. A man is accused of stealing and eating a lamb, and denies the theft. St. Serf, however, makes the lamb bleat in the robber's stomach, and so substantiates the charge beyond all doubt. He works other wonders; among them the slaying of a great dragon in the place called "Dunyne;" sails for the Orkneys, and converts the people there; and vanishes thenceforth into the dreamland from which he sprung.

Two great disciples he has, St. Ternan and St. Kentigern; mystery and miracle hang round the boyhood of the latter. His father is unknown. His mother is condemned to be cast from the rock of "Dunpelder," but is saved and absolved by a miracle. Before the eyes of the astonished Picts, she floats gently down through the air, and arrives at the cliff foot unhurt. St. Kentigern is thenceforth believed to be virgin-born, and is reverenced as a miraculous being from his infancy. He goes to school to the mythic St. Serf, who calls him Mungo, or the Beloved; which name he bears in Glasgow until this day. His fellow-scholars envy his virtue and learning, and try to ruin him with their master. St. Serf has a pet robin, which is wont to sit and sing upon his shoulder. The boys pull off its head, and lay the blame upon Kentigern. The saint comes in wrathful, tawse in hand, and Kentigern is for the moment in serious danger; but, equal to the occasion then as afterwards, he puts the robin's head on again, sets it singing, and amply vindicates his innocence. To this day the robin figures in the arms of the good city of Glasgow, with the tree which St. Kentigern, when his enemies had put out his fire, brought in from the frozen forest and lighted with his breath, and the salmon in whose mouth a ring which had been cast into the Clyde had been found again by St. Kentigern's prophetic spirit.

The envy of his fellow-scholars, however, is too much for St. Kentigern's peace of mind. He wanders away to the spot where Glasgow city now stands, lives in a rock hollowed out into a tomb, is ordained by an Irish bishop (according to a Celtic custom, of which antiquaries have written learnedly and dubiously likewise), and has ecclesiastical authority over all the Picts from the Frith of Forth to the Roman Wall. But all these stories, as I said before, are tangled as a dream; for the twelfth century monks, in their loyal devotion to the see of Rome, are apt to introduce again and again ecclesiastical customs which belonged to their own time, and try to represent these primaeval saints as regular and well- disciplined servants of the Pope.

It may be remarked that St. Serf is said to have come into a "dysart" or desert. So did many monks of the school of St. Columba and his disciples, who wished for a severer and a more meditative life than could be found in the busy society of a convent. "There was a 'disert,'" says Dr. Reeves, "for such men to retire to, besides the monastery of Derry, and another at Iona itself, situate near the shore in the low ground, north of the Cathedral, as may be inferred from Portandisiart, the name of a little bay in this situation." A similar "disert" or collection of hermit cells was endowed at Cashel in 1101; and a "disert columkill," with two townland mills and a vegetable garden, was endowed at Kells, at a somewhat earlier period, for the use of "devout pilgrims," as those were called who left the society of men to worship God in solitude.

The Venerable Bede speaks of as many as three personages, Saxons by their names, who in the Isle of Ireland led the "Pilgrim" or anchoritic life, to obtain a country in heaven; and tells of a Drycthelm of the monastery at Melrose, who went into a secret dwelling therein to give himself more utterly to prayer, and who used to stand for hours in the cold waters of the Tweed, as St. Godric did centuries afterwards in those of the Wear. Solitaries, "recluses," are met with again and again in these old records, who more than once became Abbots of Iona itself. But there is no need to linger on over instances which are only quoted to show that some of the noblest spirits of the Celtic Church kept up wherever they could the hermit's ideal, the longing for solitude, for passive contemplation, for silence and perpetual prayer, which they had inherited from St. Antony and the Fathers of the Egyptian Desert.

The same ideal was carried by them over the Border into England. Off its extreme northern coast, for instance, nearly half-way between Berwick and Bamborough Castle, lies, as travellers northward may have seen for themselves, the "Holy Island," called in old times Lindisfarne. A monk's chapel on that island was the mother of all the churches between Tyne and Tweed, as well as of many between Tyne and Humber. The Northumbrians had been nominally converted, according to Bede, A.D. 627, under their King Edwin, by Paulinus, one of the Roman monks who had followed in the steps of St. Augustine, the apostle of Kent. Evil times had fallen on them. Penda, at the head of the idolatrous Mercians (the people of Mid-England), and Ceadwalla, at the head of the Western Britons, had ravaged the country north of Tweed with savage cruelty, slain King Edwin, at Hatfield, near Doncaster, and exterminated Christianity; while Paulinus had fled to Kent, and become Bishop of Rochester. The invaders had been driven out, seemingly by Oswald, who knew enough of Christianity to set up, ere he engaged the enemy, a cross of wood on the "Heavenfield," near Hexham. That cross stood till the time of Bede, some 150 years after; and had become, like Moses' brazen serpent, an object of veneration. For if chips cut off from it were put into water, that water cured men or cattle of their diseases.

Oswald, believing that it was through the mercy of him whom that cross symbolized he had conquered the Mercians and the Britons, would needs reconvert his people to the true faith. He had been in exile during Edwin's lifetime among the Scots, and had learned from them something of Christianity. So out of Iona a monk was sent to him, Aidan by name, to be a bishop over the Northumbrians; and he settled himself upon the isle of Lindisfarne, and began to convert it into another Iona. "A man he was," says Bede, "of singular sweetness, piety, and moderation; zealous in the cause of God, though not altogether according to knowledge, for he was wont to keep Easter after the fashion of his country;" i.e. of the Picts and Northern Scots. . . . "From that time forth many Scots came daily into Britain, and with great devotion preached the word to these provinces of the English over whom King Oswald reigned. . . . Churches were built, money and lands were given of the king's bounty to build monasteries; the English, great and small, were by their Scottish masters instructed in the rules and observance of regular discipline; for most of those who came to preach were monks." {290}

So says the Venerable Bede, the monk of Jarrow, and the father (as he has been well called) of English history. He tells us too, how Aidan, wishing, it may be supposed, for greater solitude, went away and lived on the rocky isle of Farne, some two miles out at sea, off Bamborough Castle; and how, when he saw Penda and his Mercians, in a second invasion of Northumbria, trying to burn down the walls of Bamborough—which were probably mere stockades of timber— he cried to God, from off his rock, to "behold the mischief:" whereon the wind changed suddenly, and blew the flames back on the besiegers, discomfiting them, and saving the town.

Bede tells us, too, how Aidan wandered, preaching from place to place, haunting King Oswald's court, but owning nothing of his own save his church, and a few fields about it; and how, when death came upon him, they set up a tent for him close by the wall at the west end of the church, so that it befell that he gave up the ghost leaning against a post, which stood outside to strengthen the wall.

A few years after, Penda came again and burned the village, with the church; and yet neither could that fire, nor one which happened soon after, destroy that post. Wherefore the post was put inside the church, as a holy thing, and chips of it, like those of the Cross of Heaven Field, healed many folk of their distempers.

. . . A tale at which we may look in two different humours. We may pass it by with a sneer, and a hypothesis (which will be probably true) that the post was of old heart-of-oak, which is burnt with extreme difficulty; or we may pause a moment in reverence before the noble figure of the good old man, ending a life of unselfish toil without a roof beneath which to lay his head; penniless and comfortless in this world: but sure of his reward in the world to come.

A few years after Aidan's death another hermit betook him to the rocks of Farne, who rose to far higher glory; who became, in fact, the tutelar saint of the fierce Northern men; who was to them, up to the time even of the Tudor monarchs, what Pallas Athene was to Athens, or Diana to the Ephesians. St. Cuthbert's shrine, in Durham Cathedral (where his biographer Bede also lay in honour), was their rallying point, not merely for ecclesiastical jurisdiction or for miraculous cures, but for political movements. Above his shrine rose the noble pile of Durham. The bishop, who ruled in his name, was a Count Palatine, and an almost independent prince. His sacred banner went out to battle before the Northern levies, or drove back again and again the flames which consumed the wooden houses of Durham. His relics wrought innumerable miracles; and often he himself appeared with long countenance, ripened by abstinence, his head sprinkled with grey hairs, his casule of cloth of gold, his mitre of glittering crystal, his face brighter than the sun, his eyes mild as the stars of heaven, the gems upon his hand and robes rattling against his pastoral staff beset with pearls. {292} Thus glorious the demigod of the Northern men appeared to his votaries, and steered with his pastoral staff, as with a rudder, the sinking ship in safety to Lindisfarne; received from the hands of St. Brendan, as from a saint of inferior powers, the innocent yeoman, laden with fetters, whom he had delivered out of the dungeon of Brancepeth, and, smiting asunder the massive Norman walls, led him into the forest, and bade him flee to sanctuary in Durham, and be safe; or visited the little timber vine-clad chapel of Lixtune, on the Cheshire shore, to heal the sick who watched all night before his altar, or to forgive the lad who had robbed the nest which his sacred raven had built upon the roof, and, falling with the decayed timber, had broken his bones, and maimed his sacrilegious hand.

Originally, says Bede, a monk at Melrose, and afterward abbot of the same place, he used to wander weeks together out of his monastery, seemingly into Ettrick and the Lammermuirs, and preach in such villages as "being seated high up among craggy, uncouth mountains, were frightful to others even to look at, and whose poverty and barbarity rendered them inaccessible to other teachers." "So skilful an orator was he, so fond of enforcing his subject, and such a brightness appeared in his angelic face, that no man presumed to conceal from him the most hidden secrets of their hearts, but all openly confessed what they had done."

So he laboured for many years, till his old abbot Eata, who had become bishop and abbot at Lindisfarne, sent for him thither, and made him prior of the monks for several years. But at last he longed, like so many before him, for solitude. He considered (so he said afterwards to the brethren) that the life of the disciplined and obedient monk was higher than that of the lonely and independent hermit: but yet he longed to be alone; longed, it may be, to recall at least upon some sea-girt rock thoughts which had come to him in those long wanderings on the heather moors, with no sound to distract him save the hum of the bee and the wail of the curlew; and so he went away to that same rock of Farne, where Aidan had taken refuge some ten or fifteen years before, and there, with the deep sea rolling at his feet and the gulls wailing about his head, he built himself one of those "Picts' Houses," the walls of which remain still in many parts of Scotland—a circular hut of turf and rough stone— and dug out the interior to a depth of some feet, and thatched it with sticks and grass; and made, it seems, two rooms within; one for an oratory, one for a dwelling-place: and so lived alone, and worshipped God. He grew his scanty crops of barley on the rock (men said, of course, by miracle): he had tried wheat, but, as was to be expected, it failed. He found (men said, of course, by miracle) a spring upon the rock. Now and then brethren came to visit him. And what did man need more, save a clear conscience and the presence of his Creator? Certainly not Cuthbert. When he asked the brethren to bring him a beam that he might prop up his cabin where the sea had eaten out the floor, and when they forgot the commission, the sea itself washed one up in the very cove where it was needed: when the choughs from the cliff stole his barley and the straw from the roof of his little hospice, he had only to reprove them, and they never offended again; on one occasion, indeed, they atoned for their offence by bringing him a lump of suet, wherewith he greased his shoes for many a day. We are not bound to believe this story; it is one of many which hang about the memory of St. Cuthbert, and which have sprung out of that love of the wild birds which may have grown up in the good man during his long wanderings through woods and over moors. He bequeathed (so it was believed) as a sacred legacy to the wild-fowl of the Farne islands, "St. Cuthbert's peace;" above all to the eider-ducks, which swarmed there in his days, but are now, alas! growing rarer and rarer, from the intrusion of vulgar sportsmen who never heard St. Cuthbert's name, or learnt from him to spare God's creatures when they need them not. On Farne, in Reginald's time, they bred under your very bed, got out of your way if you made a sign to them, let you take up them or their young ones, and nestled silently in your bosom, and croaked joyfully with fluttering wings when stroked. "Not to nature, but to grace; not to hereditary tendency, but only to the piety and compassion of the blessed St. Cuthbert," says Reginald, "is so great a miracle to be ascribed. For the Lord who made all things in heaven and earth has subjected them to the nod of his saints, and prostrated them under the feet of obedience." Insufficient induction (the cause of endless mistakes, and therefore of endless follies and crimes) kept Reginald unaware of the now notorious fact that the female eider, during the breeding season, is just as tame, allowing for a little exaggeration, as St. Cuthbert's own ducks are, while the male eider is just as wild and wary as any other sea-bird: a mistake altogether excusable in one who had probably never seen or heard of eider-ducks in any other spot. It may be, nevertheless, that St. Cuthbert's special affection for the eider may have been called out by another strange and well-known fact about them of which Reginald oddly enough takes no note— namely, that they line their nests with down plucked from their own bosom; thus realizing the fable which has made the pelican for so many centuries the type of the Church. It is a question, indeed, whether the pelican, which is always represented in mediaeval paintings and sculptures with a short bill, instead of the enormous bill and pouch which is the especial mark of the "Onocrotalus" of the ancients, now miscalled pelican, be not actually the eider-duck itself, confounded with the true pelecanus, which was the mediaeval, and is still the scientific, name of the cormorant. Be that as it may, ill befell any one who dare touch one of St. Cuthbert's birds, as was proved in the case of Liveing, servant to AElric, who was a hermit in Farne after the time of St. Cuthbert. For he, tired it may be of barley and dried fish, killed and ate an eider-duck in his master's absence, scattering the bones and feathers over the cliffs. But when the hermit came back, what should he find but those same bones and feathers rolled into a lump and laid inside the door of the little chapel; the very sea, says Reginald, not having dared to swallow them up. Whereby the hapless Liveing being betrayed, was soundly flogged, and put on bread and water for many a day; the which story Liveing himself told to Reginald.

Not only the eider, but all birds in Farne, were protected by St. Cuthbert's peace. Bartholomew, who was a famous hermit there in after years, had a tame bird, says the chronicler, who ate from his hand, and hopped about the table among him and his guests, till some thought it a miracle; and some, finding, no doubt, the rocks of Farne weary enough, derived continual amusement from the bird. But when he one day went off to another island, and left his bird to keep the house, a hawk came in and ate it up. Cuthbert, who could not save the bird, at least could punish the murderer. The hawk flew round and round the island, imprisoned, so it was thought, by some mysterious power, till, terrified and worn out, it flew into the chapel, and lay, cowering and half dead, in a corner by the altar. Bartholomew came back, found his bird's feathers, and the tired hawk. But even the hawk must profit by St. Cuthbert's peace. He took it up, carried it to the harbour, and there bade it depart in St. Cuthbert's name, whereon it flew off free, and was no more seen. Such tales as these may be explained, even to their most minute details, by simply natural causes: and yet, in this age of wanton destruction of wild birds, one is tempted at moments to wish for the return of some such graceful and humane superstition which could keep down, at least in the name of mercy and humanity, the needless cruelty of man.

But to return. After St. Cuthbert, says Bede, had served God in the solitude of Farne for many years, the mound which encompassed his habitation being so high that he could see nothing from thence but heaven, to which he so ardently aspired, he was compelled by tears and entreaties—King Egfrid himself coming to the island, with bishops and religious and great men—to become himself bishop in Holy Island. There, as elsewhere, he did his duty. But after two years he went again to Farne, knowing that his end was near. For when, in his episcopal labours, he had gone across to Lugubalia—old Penrith, in Cumberland—there came across to him a holy hermit, Herebert by name, who dwelt upon an island in Derwentwater, and talked with him a long while on heavenly things; and Cuthbert bade him ask him then all the questions which he wished to have resolved, for they should see each other no more in this world. Herebert, who seems to have been one of his old friends, fell at Cuthbert's feet, and bade him remember that whenever he had done wrong he had submitted himself to him utterly, and always tried to live according to his rules; and all he wished for now was that, as they had served God together upon earth, they might depart for ever to see his bliss in heaven: the which befell; for a few months afterwards, that is, on the 20th of March, their souls quitted their mortal bodies on the same day, and they were re-united in spirit.

St. Cuthbert wished to have been buried on his rock in Farne: but the brethren had persuaded him to allow his corpse to be removed to Holy Island. He begged them, said Bede, should they be forced to leave that place, to carry his bones along with them; and so they were forced to do at last; for in the year 875; whilst the Danes were struggling with Alfred in Wessex, an army of them, with Halfdene at their head, went up into Northumbria, burning towns, destroying churches, tossing children on their pike-points, and committing all those horrors which made the Norsemen terrible and infamous for so many years. Then the monks fled from the monastery, bearing the shrine of St. Cuthbert, and all their treasures, and followed by their retainers, men, women, and children, and their sheep and oxen: and behold! the hour of their flight was that of an exceedingly high spring tide. The Danes were landing from their ships in their rear; in their front was some two miles of sea. Escape seemed hopeless; when, says the legend, the water retreated before the holy relics as they advanced; and became, as to the children of Israel of old, a wall on their right hand and on their left; and so St. Cuthbert came safe to shore, and wandered in the woods, borne upon his servants' shoulders, and dwelling in tents for seven years, and found rest at last in Durham, till at the Reformation his shrine, and that of the Venerable Bede, were robbed of their gold and jewels; and no trace of them (as far as I know) is left, save that huge slab, whereon is written the monkish rhyme: —

Hic jacet in fossa Bedae Venerabilis ossa. {299}

The Hermits

ST. GUTHLAC

Hermits dwelling in the wilderness, as far as I am aware, were to be seen only in the northern and western parts of the island, where not only did the forest afford concealment, but the crags and caves shelter. The southern and eastern English seldom possess the vivid imagination of the Briton, the Northumbrian, and the Scot; while the rich lowlands of central, southern, and eastern England, well peopled and well tilled, offered few spots lonely enough for the hermit's cell.

One district only was desolate enough to attract those who wished to be free from the world,—namely, the great fens north of Cambridge; and there, accordingly, as early as the seventh century, hermits settled in morasses now so utterly transformed that it is difficult to restore in one's imagination the original scenery.

The fens in the seventh century were probably very like the forests at the mouth of the Mississippi, or the swampy shores of the Carolinas. Their vast plain is now, in summer, one sea of golden corn; in winter, a black dreary fallow, cut into squares by stagnant dykes, and broken only by unsightly pumping mills and doleful lines of poplar-trees. Of old it was a labyrinth of black wandering streams; broad lagoons; morasses submerged every spring-tide; vast beds of reed and sedge and fern; vast copses of willow, alder, and grey poplar, rooted in the floating peat, which was swallowing up slowly, all-devouring, yet all-preserving, the forests of fir and oak, ash and poplar, hazel and yew, which had once grown on that low, rank soil, sinking slowly (so geologists assure us) beneath the sea from age to age. Trees, torn down by flood and storm, floated and lodged in rafts, damming the waters back upon the land. Streams, bewildered in the flats, changed their channels, mingling silt and sand with the peat moss. Nature, left to herself, ran into wild riot and chaos more and more, till the whole fen became one "Dismal Swamp," in which, at the time of the Norman Conquest, the "Last of the English," like Dred in Mrs. Stowe's tale, took refuge from their tyrants, and lived, like him, a free and joyous life awhile.

For there are islands in the sea which have escaped the destroying deluge of peat-moss,—outcrops of firm and fertile land, which in the early Middle Age were so many natural parks, covered with richest grass and stateliest trees, swarming with deer and roe, goat and boar, as the streams around swarmed with otter and beaver, and with fowl of every feather, and fish of every scale.

Beautiful after their kind were those far isles in the eyes of the monks who were the first settlers in the wilderness. The author of the "History of Ramsey" grows enthusiastic, and somewhat bombastic also, as he describes the lovely isle, which got its name from the solitary ram who had wandered thither, either in extreme drought or over the winter ice, and, never able to return, was found feeding among the wild deer, fat beyond the wont of rams. He tells of the stately ashes, most of them cut in his time, to furnish mighty beams for the church roof; of the rich pastures painted with all gay flowers in spring; of the "green crown" of reed and alder which encircled the isle; of the fair wide mere (now drained) with its "sandy beach" along the forest side; "a delight," he says, "to all who look thereon."

In like humour William of Malmesbury, writing in the first half of the twelfth century, speaks of Thorney Abbey and its isle. "It represents," says he, "a very paradise; for that in pleasure and delight it resembles heaven itself. These marshes abound in trees, whose length, without a knot, doth emulate the stars. The plain there is as level as the sea, alluring the eye with its green grass, and so smooth that there is nought to trip the foot of him who runs through it. Neither is there any waste place; for in some parts are apples, in others vines, which are either spread on the ground, or raised on poles. A mutual strife there is between Nature and Art; so that what one produces not the other supplies. What shall I say of those fair buildings, which 'tis so wonderful to see the ground among those fens upbear?"

So wrote William of Malmesbury, after the industry and wisdom of the monks, for more than four centuries, had been at work to civilize and cultivate the wilderness. Yet even then there was another side to the picture; and Thorney, Ramsey, or Crowland would have seemed, for nine months every year, sad places enough to us comfortable folk of the nineteenth century. But men lived hard in those days, even the most high-born and luxurious nobles and ladies; under dark skies, in houses which we should think, from darkness, draught, and want of space, unfit for felons' cells. Hardly they lived; and easily were they pleased; and thanked God for the least gleam of sunshine, the least patch of green, after the terrible and long winters of the Middle Ages. And ugly enough those winters must have been, what with snow and darkness, flood and ice, ague and rheumatism; while through the dreary winter's night the whistle of the wind and the wild cries of the waterfowl were translated into the howls of witches and daemons; and (as in St. Guthlac's case), the delirious fancies of marsh fever made those fiends take hideous shapes before the inner eye, and act fantastic horrors round the fen-man's bed of sedge.

Concerning this St. Guthlac full details remain, both in Latin and Anglo-Saxon; the author of the original document professing to be one Felix, a monk of Ramsey near by, who wrote possibly as early as the eighth century. {303}

There we may read how the young warrior-noble Guthlac ("The Battle- Play," the "Sport of War"), tired of slaying and sinning, bethought him to fulfil the prodigies seen at his birth; how he wandered into the fen, where one Tatwin (who after became a saint likewise) took him in his canoe to a spot so lonely as to be almost unknown, buried in reeds and alders, and how he found among the trees nought but an old "law," as the Scots still call a mound, which men of old had broken into seeking for treasure, and a little pond; and how he built himself a hermit's cell thereon, and saw visions and wrought miracles; and how men came to him, as to a fakir or shaman of the East; notably one Beccel, who acted as his servant; and how as Beccel was shaving the saint one day there fell on him a great temptation: Why should he not cut St. Guthlac's throat, and instal himself in his cell, that he might have the honour and glory of sainthood? But St. Guthlac perceived the inward temptation (which is told with the naive honesty of those half-savage times), and rebuked the offender into confession, and all went well to the end.

There we may read, too, a detailed account of the Fauna now happily extinct in the fens; of the creatures who used to hale St. Guthlac out of his hut, drag him through the bogs, carry him aloft through frost and fire—"Develen and luther gostes"—such as tormented in like wise St. Botolph (from whom Botulfston = Boston, has its name), and who were supposed to haunt the meres and fens, and to have an especial fondness for old heathen barrows with their fancied treasure-hoards: how they "filled the house with their coming, and poured in on every side, from above, and from beneath, and everywhere. They were in countenance horrible, and they had great heads, and a long neck, and a lean visage; they were filthy and squalid in their beards, and they had rough ears, and crooked 'nebs,' and fierce eyes, and foul mouths; and their teeth were like horses' tusks; and their throats were filled with flame, and they were grating in their voice; they had crooked shanks, and knees big and great behind, and distorted toes, and cried hoarsely with their voices; and they came with immoderate noise and immense horror, that he thought that all between, heaven and earth resounded with their voices. . . . And they tugged and led him out of the cot, and led him to the swart fen, and threw and sunk him in the muddy waters. After that they brought him into the wild places of the wilderness, among the thick beds of brambles, that all his body was torn. . . . After that they took him and beat him with iron whips, and after that they brought him on their creaking wings between the cold regions of the air."

But there are gentler and more human touches in that old legend. You may read in it how all the wild birds of the fen came to St. Guthlac, and he fed them after their kind; how the ravens tormented him, stealing letters, gloves, and what not, from his visitors; and then, seized with compunction at his reproofs, brought them back, or hanged them on the reeds; and how, as Wilfrid, a holy visitant, was sitting with him, discoursing of the contemplative life, two swallows came flying in, and lifted up their song, sitting now on the saint's hand, now on his shoulder, now on his knee; and how, when Wilfrid wondered thereat, Guthlac made answer, "Know you not that he who hath led his life according to God's will, to him the wild beasts and the wild birds draw the more near?"

After fifteen years of such a life, in fever, ague, and starvation, no wonder if St. Guthlac died. They buried him in a leaden coffin (a grand and expensive luxury in the seventh century) which had been sent to him during his life by a Saxon princess; and then, over his sacred and wonder-working corpse, as over that of a Buddhist saint, there arose a chapel, with a community of monks, companies of pilgrims who came to worship, sick who came to be healed; till at last, founded on great piles driven into the bog, arose the lofty wooden Abbey of Crowland; in "sanctuary of the four rivers," with its dykes, parks, vineyards, orchards, rich ploughlands, from which, in time of famine, the monks of Crowland fed all people of the neighbouring fens; with its tower with seven bells, which had not their like in England; its twelve altars rich with the gifts of Danish vikings and princes, and even with twelve white bear-skins, the gift of Canute's self; while all around were the cottages of the corrodiers, or folk who, for a corrody, or life pittance from the abbey, had given away their lands, to the wrong and detriment of their heirs.

But within those four rivers, at least, were neither tyranny nor slavery. Those who took refuge in St Guthlac's place from cruel lords must keep his peace toward each other, and earn their living like honest men, safe while they so did: for between those four rivers St. Guthlac and his abbot were the only lords; and neither summoner, nor sheriff of the king, nor armed force of knight or earl, could enter—"the inheritance of the Lord, the soil of St. Mary and St. Bartholomew, the most holy sanctuary of St. Guthlac and his monks; the minister free from worldly servitude; the special almshouse of most illustrious kings; the sole refuge of any one in worldly tribulation; the perpetual abode of the saints; the possession of religious men, specially set apart by the common council of the realm; by reason of the frequent miracles of the holy confessor St. Guthlac, an ever-fruitful mother of camphire in the vineyards of Engedi; and, by reason of the privileges granted by the kings, a city of grace and safety to all who repent."

Does not all this sound like a voice from another planet? It is all gone; and it was good and right that it should go when it had done its work, and that the civilization of the fen should be taken up and carried out by men like the good knight, Richard of Rulos, who, two generations after the Conquest, marrying Hereward's grand-daughter, and becoming Lord of Deeping (the deep meadow), thought that he could do the same work from the hall of Bourne as the monks did from their cloisters; got permission from the Crowland monks, for twenty marks of silver, to drain as much as he could of the common marshes; and then shut out the Welland by strong dykes, built cottages, marked out gardens, and tilled fields, till "out of slough and bogs accursed he made a garden of pleasure."

Yet one lasting work those monks of Crowland seem to have done, besides those firm dykes and rich corn-lands of the Porsand, which endure unto this day. For within two generations of the Norman conquest, while the old wooden abbey, destroyed by fire, was being replaced by that noble pile of stone whose ruins are still standing, the French abbot of Crowland (so runs the legend) sent French monks to open a school under the new French donjon, in the little Roman town of Grante-brigge; whereby—so does all earnest work, however mistaken, grow and spread in this world, infinitely and for ever— St. Guthlac, by his canoe-voyage into Crowland Island, became the spiritual father of the University of Cambridge in the old world; and therefore of her noble daughter, the University of Cambridge, in the new world which fen-men sailing from Boston deeps colonized and Christianized 800 years after St. Guthlac's death.

ST. GODRIC OF FINCHALE

A personage quite as interesting, though not as famous, as Cuthbert or Guthlac, is St. Godric; the hermit around whose cell rose the Priory of Finchale. In a loop of the river Wear, near Durham, there settled in the days of Bishop Flambard, between 1099 and 1128, a man whose parentage and history was for many years unknown to the good folks of the neighbourhood. He had come, it seems, from a hermitage in Eskdale, in the parish of Whitby, whence he had been driven by the Percys, lords of the soil. He had gone to Durham, become the doorkeeper of St. Giles's church, and gradually learnt by heart (he was no scholar) the whole Psalter. Then he had gone to St. Mary's church, where (as was the fashion of the times) there was a children's school; and, listening to the little ones at their lessons, picked up such hymns and prayers as he thought would suffice his spiritual wants. And then, by leave of the bishop, he had gone away into the woods, and devoted himself to the solitary life in Finchale. Buried in the woods and crags of the "Royal Park," as it was then called, which swarmed with every kind of game, there was a little flat meadow, rough with sweet-gale and bramble and willow, beside a teeming salmon-pool. Great wolves haunted the woods; but Godric cared nought for them; and the shingles swarmed with snakes,— probably only the harmless collared snakes of wet meadows, but reputed, as all snakes are by the vulgar, venomous: but he did not object to become "the companion of serpents and poisonous asps." He handled them, caressed them, let them lie by the fire in swarms on winter nights, in the little cave which he had hollowed in the ground and thatched with turf. Men told soon how the snakes obeyed him; how two especially huge ones used to lie twined about his legs; till after many years, annoyed by their importunity, he turned them all gently out of doors, with solemn adjurations never to return, and they, of course, obeyed.

His austerities knew no bounds. He lived on roots and berries, flowers and leaves; and when the good folk found him out, and put gifts of food near his cell, he carried them up to the crags above, and, offering them solemnly up to the God who feeds the ravens when they call on him, left them there for the wild birds. He watched, fasted, and scourged himself, and wore always a hair shirt and an iron cuirass. He sat, night after night, even in mid-winter, in the cold Wear, the waters of which had hollowed out a rock near by into a natural bath, and afterwards in a barrel sunk in the floor of a little chapel of wattle, which he built and dedicated to the blessed Virgin

Mary. He tilled a scrap of ground, and ate the grain from it, mingled with ashes. He kept his food till it was decayed before he tasted it; and led a life the records of which fill the reader with astonishment, not only at the man's iron strength of will, but at the iron strength of the constitution which could support such hardships, in such a climate, for a single year.

A strong and healthy man must Godric have been, to judge from the accounts (there are two, both written by eye-witnesses) of his personal appearance—a man of great breadth of chest and strength of arm; black-haired, hook-nosed, deep-browed, with flashing grey eyes; altogether a personable and able man, who might have done much work and made his way in many lands. But what his former life had been he would not tell. Mother-wit he had in plenty, and showed insight into men and things which the monks of Durham were ready enough to call the spirit of prophecy. After awhile it was whispered that he wrought miraculous cures: that even a bit of the bread which he was wont to eat had healed a sick woman; that he fought with daemons in visible shape; that he had seen (just as one of the old Egyptian hermits had seen) a little black boy running about between two monks who had quarrelled and come to hard blows and bleeding faces because one of them had made mistakes in the evening service: and, in short, there were attributed to him, during his lifetime, and by those who knew him well, a host of wonders which would be startling and important were they not exactly the same as those which appear in the life of every hermit since St. Antony. It is impossible to read the pages of Reginald of Durham (for he, the biographer of St. Cuthbert, is also the biographer of St. Godric) without feeling how difficult it is to obtain anything like the truth, even from eye- witnesses, if only men are (as they were in those days) in a state of religious excitement, at a period of spiritual revivals. The ignorant populace were ready to believe, and to report, anything of the Fakeer of Finchale. The monks of Durham were glad enough to have a wonder-working man belonging to them; for Ralph Flambard, in honour of Godric, had made over to them the hermitage of Finchale, with its fields and fisheries. The lad who, in after years, waited on the hermit, would have been ready enough to testify that his master saw daemons and other spiritual beings; for he began to see them on his own account; {312} fell asleep in the forest coming home from Durham with some bottles; was led in a vision by St. John the Baptist to the top of a hill, and shown by him wonders unspeakable; saw, on another occasion, a daemon in St. Godric's cell, hung all over with bottles of different liquors, offering them to the saint, who bade the lad drive him out of the little chapel, with a holy water sprinkle, but not go outside it himself. But the lad, in the fury of successful pursuit, overstepped the threshold; whereon the daemon, turning in self-defence, threw a single drop of one of his liquors into the lad's mouth, and vanished with a laugh of scorn. The boy's face and throat swelled horribly for three days; and he took care thenceforth to obey the holy man more strictly: a story which I have repeated, like the one before it, only to show the real worth of the evidence on which Reginald has composed his book. Ailred, Abbot of Rievaux (for Reginald's book, though dedicated to Hugh Pudsey, his bishop, was prompted by Ailred) was capable (as his horrible story of the nun of Watton proves) of believing anything and everything which fell in with his fanatical, though pious and gentle, temper.

And here a few words must be said to persons with whose difficulties I deeply sympathise, but from whose conclusions I differ utterly: those, namely, who say that if we reject the miracles of these saints' lives, we must reject also the miracles of the New Testament. The answer is, as I believe, that the Apostles and Evangelists were sane men: men in their right minds, wise, calm; conducting themselves (save in the matter of committing sins) like other human beings, as befitted the disciples of that Son of Man who came eating and drinking, and was therefore called by the ascetics of his time a gluttonous man, and a wine-bibber: whereas these monks were not (as I have said elsewhere) in their right minds at all.

This is, or ought to be, patent to any one who will compare the style of the Apostles and Evangelists with that of the monkish hagiologists. The calm, the simplicity, the brevity, the true grandeur of the former is sufficient evidence of their healthy- mindedness and their trustworthiness. The affectation, the self- consciousness, the bombast, the false grandeur of the latter is sufficient evidence that they are neither healthy-minded or trustworthy. Let students compare any passage of St. Luke or St. John, however surprising the miracle which it relates, with St. Jerome's life of Paul the First Hermit, or with that famous letter of his to Eustochium, which (although historically important) is unfit for the eyes of pure-minded readers and does not appear in this volume; and let them judge for themselves. Let them compare, again, the opening sentences of the Four Gospels, or of the Acts of the Apostles, with the words with which Reginald begins this life of St. Godric. "By the touch of the Holy Spirit's finger the chord of the harmonic human heart resounds melodiously. For when the vein of the heart is touched by the grace of the Holy Spirit, forthwith, by the permirific sweetness of the harmony, an exceeding operation of sacred virtue is perceived more manifestly to spring forth. With this sweetness of spirit, Godric, the man of God, was filled from the very time of his boyhood, and grew famous for many admirable works of holy work (sic), because the harmonic teaching of the Holy Spirit fired the secrets of his very bosom with a wondrous contact of spiritual grace:"—and let them say, after the comparison, if the difference between the two styles is not that which exists between one of God's lilies, fresh from the field, and a tawdry bunch of artificial flowers?

But to return. Godric himself took part in the history of his own miracles and life. It may be that he so overworked his brain that he believed that he was visited by St. Peter, and taught a hymn by the blessed Virgin Mary, and that he had taken part in a hundred other prodigies; but the Prologue to the Harleian manuscript (which the learned Editor, Mr. Stevenson, believes to be an early edition of Reginald's own composition) confesses that Reginald, compelled by Ailred of Rievaux, tried in vain for a long while to get the hermit's story from him.

"You wish to write my life?" he said. "Know then that Godric's life is such as this:—Godric, at first a gross rustic, an unclean liver, an usurer, a cheat, a perjurer, a flatterer, a wanderer, pilfering and greedy; now a dead flea, a decayed dog, a vile worm, not a hermit, but a hypocrite; not a solitary, but a gad-about in mind; a devourer of alms, dainty over good things, greedy and negligent, lazy and snoring, ambitious and prodigal, one who is not worthy to serve others, and yet every day beats and scolds those who serve him: this, and worse than this, you may write of Godric." "Then he was silent as one indignant," says Reginald, "and I went off in some confusion," and the grand old man was left to himself and to his God.

The ecclesiastical Boswell dared not mention the subject again to his hero for several years, though he came after from Durham to visit him, and celebrate mass for him in his little chapel. After some years, however, he approached the matter again; and whether a pardonable vanity had crept over Godric, or whether he had begun at last to believe in his miracles, or whether the old man had that upon his mind of which he longed to unburthen himself, he began to answer questions, and Reginald delighted to listen and note down till he had finished, he says, that book of his life and miracles; {316} and after a while brought it to the saint, and falling on his knees, begged him to bless, in the name of God, and for the benefit of the faithful, the deeds of a certain religious man, who had suffered much for God in this life which he (Reginald) had composed accurately. The old man perceived that he himself was the subject, blessed the book with solemn words (what was written therein he does not seem to have read), and bade Reginald conceal it till his death, warning him that a time would come when he should suffer rough and bitter things on account of that book, from those who envied him. That prophecy, says Reginald, came to pass; but how, or why, he does not tell. There may have been, among those shrewd Northumbrian heads, even then, incredulous men, who used their common sense.

But the story which Godric told was wild and beautiful; and though we must not depend too much on the accuracy of the old man's recollections, or on the honesty of Reginald's report, who would naturally omit all incidents which made against his hero's perfection, it is worth listening to, as a vivid sketch of the doings of a real human being, in that misty distance of the Early Middle Age.

He was born, he said, at Walpole, in Norfolk, on the old Roman sea-bank, between the Wash and the deep Fens. His father's name was AEilward; his mother's, AEdwen—"the Keeper of Blessedness," and "the Friend of Blessedness," as Reginald translates them—poor and pious folk; and, being a sharp boy, he did not take to field-work, but preferred wandering the fens as a pedlar, first round the villages, then, as he grew older, to castles and to towns, buying and selling—what, Reginald does not tell us: but we should be glad to know.

One day he had a great deliverance, which Reginald thinks a miracle. Wandering along the great tide-flats near Spalding and the old Well- stream, in search of waifs, and strays, of wreck or eatables, he saw three porpoises stranded far out upon the banks. Two were alive, and the boy took pity on them (so he said) and let them be: but one was dead, and off it (in those days poor folks ate anything) he cut as much flesh and blubber as he could carry, and toiled back towards the high-tide mark. But whether he lost his way among the banks, or whether he delayed too long, the tide came in on him up to his knees, his waist, his chin, and at last, at times, over his head. The boy made the sign of the cross (as all men in danger did then) and struggled on valiantly a full mile through the sea, like a brave lad never loosening his hold of his precious porpoise-meat till he reached the shore at the very spot from which he had set out.

As he grew, his pedlar journeys became longer. Repeating to himself, as he walked, the Creeds and the Lord's Prayer—his only lore—he walked for four years through Lindsey; then went to St. Andrew's in Scotland; after that, for the first time, to Rome. Then the love of a wandering sea life came on him, and he sailed with his wares round the east coasts; not merely as a pedlar, but as a sailor himself, he went to Denmark and to Flanders, buying and selling, till he owned (in what port we are not told, but probably in Lynn or Wisbeach) half one merchant ship and the quarter of another. A crafty steersman he was, a wise weather-prophet, a shipman stout in body and in heart, probably such a one as Chaucer tells us of 350 years after:—

"—A dagger hanging by a las hadde hee About his nekke under his arm adoun. The hote summer hadde made his hewe al broun. And certainly he was a good felaw; Full many a draught of wine he hadde draw, From Burdeaux ward, while that the chapmen slepe, Of nice conscience took he no kepe. If that he fought, and hadde the higher hand, By water he sent hem home to every land. But of his craft to recken wel his tides, His stremes and his strandes him besides, His herberwe, his mone, and his lode manage, There was none swiche, from Hull unto Carthage. Hardy he was, and wise, I undertake: With many a tempest hadde his berd be shake. He knew wel alle the havens, as they were, From Gotland to the Cape de Finisterre, And every creke in Bretagne and in Spain."

But gradually there grew on the stout merchantman the thought that there was something more to be done in the world than making money. He became a pious man after the fashion of those days. He worshipped at the famous shrine of St. Andrew. He worshipped, too, at St. Cuthbert's hermitage at Farne, and there, he said afterwards, he longed for the first time for the rest and solitude of the hermitage. He had been sixteen years a seaman now, with a seaman's temptations—it may be (as he told Reginald plainly) with some of a seaman's vices. He may have done things which lay heavy on his conscience. But it was getting time to think about his soul. He took the cross, and went off to Jerusalem, as many a man did then, under difficulties incredible, dying, too often, on the way. But Godric not only got safe thither, but went out of his way home by Spain to visit the sanctuary of St. James of Compostella, a see which Pope Calixtus II. had just raised to metropolitan dignity.

Then he appears as steward to a rich man in the Fens, whose sons and young retainers, after the lawless fashion of those Anglo-Norman times, rode out into the country round to steal the peasants' sheep and cattle, skin them on the spot, and pass them off to the master of the house as venison taken in hunting. They ate and drank, roystered and rioted, like most other young Normans; and vexed the staid soul of Godric, whose nose told him plainly enough, whenever he entered the kitchen, that what was roasting had never come off a deer. In vain he protested and warned them, getting only insults for his pains. At last he told his lord. The lord, as was to be expected, cared nought about the matter. Let the lads rob the English villains: for what other end had their grandfathers conquered the land? Godric punished himself, as he could not punish them, for the unwilling share which he had had in the wrong. It may be that he, too, had eaten of that stolen food. So away he went into France, and down the Rhone, on pilgrimage to the hermitage of St. Giles, the patron saint of the wild deer; and then on to Rome a second time, and back to his poor parents in the Fens.

And now follows a strange and beautiful story. All love of seafaring and merchandise had left the deep-hearted sailor. The heavenly and the eternal, the salvation of his sinful soul, had become all in all to him; and yet he could not rest in the little dreary village on the Roman bank. He would go on pilgrimage again. Then his mother would go likewise, and see St. Peter's church, and the Pope, and all the wonders of Rome, and have her share in all the spiritual blessings which were to be obtained (so men thought then) at Rome alone. So off they set on foot; and when they came to ford or ditch, Godric carried his mother on his back, until they came to London town. And there AEdwen took off her shoes, and vowed out of devotion to the holy apostles Peter and Paul (who, so she thought, would be well pleased at such an act) to walk barefoot to Rome and barefoot back again.

Now just as they went out of London, on the Dover Road, there met them in the way the loveliest maiden they had ever seen, and asked to bear them company in their pilgrimage. And when they agreed, she walked with them, sat with them, and talked with them with superhuman courtesy and grace; and when they turned into an inn, she ministered to them herself, and washed and kissed their feet, and then lay down with them to sleep, after the simple fashion of those days. But a holy awe of her, as of some saint and goddess, fell on the wild seafarer; and he never, so he used to aver, treated her for a moment save as a sister. Never did either ask the other who they were, and whence they came; and Godric reported (but this was long after the event) that no one of the company of pilgrims could see that fair maid, save he and his mother alone. So they came safe to Rome, and back to London town; and when they were at the place outside Southwark, where the fair maid had met them first, she asked permission to leave them, for she "must go to her own land, where she had a tabernacle of rest, and dwelt in the house of her God." And then, bidding them bless God, who had brought them safe over the Alps, and across the sea, and all along that weary road, she went on her way, and they saw her no more.

Then with this fair mysterious face clinging to his memory, and it may be never leaving it, Godric took his mother safe home, and delivered her to his father, and bade them both after awhile farewell, and wandered across England to Penrith, and hung about the churches there, till some kinsmen of his recognised him, and gave him a psalter (he must have taught himself to read upon his travels), which he learnt by heart. Then, wandering ever in search of solitude, he went into the woods and found a cave, and passed his time therein in prayer, living on green herbs and wild honey, acorns and crabs; and when he went about to gather food, he fell down on his knees every few yards and said a prayer, and rose and went on.

After awhile he wandered on again, until at Wolsingham, in Durham, he met with another holy hermit, who had been a monk at Durham, living in a cave in forests in which no man dare dwell, so did they swarm with packs of wolves; and there the two good men dwelt together till the old hermit fell sick, and was like to die. Godric nursed him, and sat by him, to watch for his last breath. For the same longing had come over him which came over Marguerite d'Angouleme when she sat by the dying bed of her favourite maid of honour—to see if the spirit, when it left the body, were visible, and what kind of thing it was: whether, for instance, it was really like the little naked babe which is seen in mediaeval illuminations flying out of the mouths of dying men. But, worn out with watching, Godric could not keep from sleep. All but despairing of his desire, he turned to the dying man, and spoke, says Reginald, some such words as these:—"O spirit! who art diffused in that body in the likeness of God, and art still inside that breast, I adjure thee by the Highest, that thou leave not the prison of this thine habitation while I am overcome by sleep, and know not of it." And so he fell asleep: but when he woke, the old hermit lay motionless and breathless. Poor Godric wept, called on the dead man, called on God; his simple heart was set on seeing this one thing. And, behold, he was consoled in a wondrous fashion. For about the third hour of the day the breath returned. Godric hung over him, watching his lips. Three heavy sighs he drew, then a shudder, another sigh: {323} and then (so Godric was believed to have said in after years) he saw the spirit flit.

What it was like, he did not like to say, for the most obvious reason—that he saw nothing, and was an honest man. A monk teased him much to impart to him this great discovery, which seemed to the simple untaught sailor a great spiritual mystery, and which was, like some other mediaeval mysteries which were miscalled spiritual (transubstantiation above all), altogether material and gross imaginations. Godric answered wisely enough, that "no man could perceive the substance of the spiritual soul."

But the monk insisting, and giving him no rest, he answered,— whether he wished to answer a fool according to his folly, or whether he tried to fancy (as men will who are somewhat vain—and if a saint was not vain, it was no fault of the monks who beset him) that he had really seen something. He told how it was like a dry, hot wind rolled into a sphere, and shining like the clearest glass, but that what it was really like no one could express. Thus much, at least, may be gathered from the involved bombast of Reginald.

Another pilgrimage to the Holy Sepulchre did Godric make before he went to the hermitage in Eskdale, and settled finally at Finchale. And there about the hills of Judaea he found, says Reginald, hermits dwelling in rock-caves, as they had dwelt since the time of St. Jerome. He washed himself, and his hair shirt and little cross, in the sacred waters of the Jordan, and returned, after incredible suffering, to become the saint of Finchale.

His hermitage became, in due time, a stately priory, with its community of monks, who looked up to the memory of their holy father Godric as to that of a demigod. The place is all ruinate now; the memory of St. Godric gone; and not one in ten thousand, perhaps, who visit those crumbling walls beside the rushing Wear, has heard of the sailor-saint, and his mother, and that fair maid who tended them on their pilgrimage.

Meanwhile there were hermits for many years in that same hermitage in Eskdale, from which a Percy expelled St. Godric, possibly because he interfered with the prior claim of some protege of their own; for they had, a few years before Godric's time, granted that hermitage to the monks of Whitby, who were not likely to allow a stranger to establish himself on their ground.

About that hermitage hung one of those stories so common in the Middle Ages, in which the hermit appears as the protector of the hunted wild beast; a story, too, which was probably authentic, as the curious custom which was said to perpetuate its memory lasted at least till the year 1753. I quote it at length from Burton's "Monasticon Eboracense," p. 78, knowing no other authority.

"In the fifth year of the reign of King Henry II. after the conquest of England by William, duke of Normandy, the Lord of Uglebardby, then called William de Bruce, and the Lord of Sneton, called Ralph de Perci, with a gentleman and a freeholder called Allatson, did on the 16th day of October appoint to meet and hunt the wild boar, in a certain wood or desert place belonging to the abbot of the monastery of Whitby; the place's name is Eskdale-side; the abbot's name was Sedman. Then these gentlemen being met, with their hounds and boar- staves, in the place before-named, and there having found a great wild boar, the hounds ran him well near about the chapel and hermitage of Eskdale-side, where was a monk of Whitby, who was a hermit. The boar being very sore, and very hotly pursued, and dead run, took in at the chapel door, and there died: whereupon the hermit shut the hounds out of the chapel, and kept himself within at his meditations and prayers, the hounds standing at bay without. The gentlemen in the thick of the wood, being put behind their game, followed the cry of their hounds, and so came to the hermitage, calling on the hermit, who opened the door and came forth, and within they found the boar lying dead, for which the gentlemen in very great fury (because their hounds were put from their game) did most violently and cruelly run at the hermit with their boar-staves, whereby he died soon after: thereupon the gentlemen, perceiving and knowing that they were in peril of death, took sanctuary at Scarborough. But at that time the abbot, being in very great favour with King Henry, removed them out of the sanctuary, whereby they came in danger of the law, and not to be privileged, but likely to have the severity of the law, which was death. But the hermit, being a holy and devout man, at the point of death sent for the abbot, and desired him to send for the gentlemen who had wounded him: the abbot so doing, the gentlemen came, and the hermit, being very sick and weak, said unto them, 'I am sure to die of those wounds you have given me.' The abbot answered, 'They shall as surely die for the same;' but the hermit answered, 'Not so, for I will freely forgive them my death, if they will be contented to be enjoined this penance for the safeguard of their souls.' The gentlemen being present, and terrified with the fear of death, bade him enjoin what penance he would, so that he would but save their lives. Then said the hermit, 'You and yours shall hold your lands of the Abbot of Whitby and his successors in this manner: That upon Ascension Eve, you or some of you shall come to the woods of the Strag Heads, which is in Eskdale-side, the same day at sun-rising, and there shall the abbot's officer blow his horn, to the intent that you may know how to find him; and he shall deliver unto you, William de Bruce, ten stakes, eleven strut-towers, and eleven yethers, to be cut by you or some for you, with a knife of one penny price; and you, Ralph de Perci, shall take twenty and one of each sort, to be cut in the same manner; and you, Allatson, shall take nine of each sort, to be cut as aforesaid, and to be taken on your backs, and carried to the town of Whitby, and to be there before nine of the clock the same day before-mentioned; at the same hour of nine of the clock (if it be full sea) your labour or service shall cease; but if it be not full sea, each of you shall set your stakes at the brim, each stake one yard from the other, and so yether them on each side of your yethers, and so stake on each side with your strut-towers, that they may stand three tides without removing by the force thereof: each of you shall do, make, and execute the said service at that very hour every year, except it shall be full sea at that hour: but when it shall so fall out, this service shall cease. You shall faithfully do this in remembrance that you did most cruelly slay me; and that you may the better call to God for mercy, repent unfeignedly for your sins, and do good works, the officers of Eskdale-side shall blow, Out on you, out on you, out on you, for this heinous crime. If you or your successors shall refuse this service, so long as it shall not be full sea at the aforesaid hour, you or yours shall forfeit your lands to the Abbot of Whitby, or his successors. This I intreat, and earnestly beg that you may have lives and goods preserved for this service; and I request of you to promise by your parts in heaven that it shall be done by you and your successors, as it is aforesaid requested, and I will confirm it by the faith of an honest man.' Then the hermit said: 'My soul longeth for the Lord, and I do as freely forgive these men my death as Christ forgave the thieves upon the cross;' and in the presence of the abbot and the rest he said, moreover, these words: 'Into thy hands, O Lord, I commend my spirit, for from the bonds of death Thou hast redeemed me, O Lord of truth. Amen.' So he yielded up the ghost the eighth day of December, A.D. 1160, upon whose soul God have mercy. Amen."

ANCHORITES, STRICTLY SO CALLED

The fertile and peaceable lowlands of England, as I have just said, offered few spots sufficiently wild and lonely for the habitation of a hermit; those, therefore, who wished to retire from the world into a more strict and solitary life than that which the monastery afforded were in the habit of immuring themselves, as anchorites, or in old English "Ankers," in little cells of stone, built usually against the wall of a church. There is nothing new under the sun; and similar anchorites might have been seen in Egypt, 500 years before the time of St. Antony, immured in cells in the temples of Isis or Serapis. It is only recently that antiquaries have discovered how common this practice was in England, and how frequently the traces of these cells are to be found about our parish churches. They were so common in the Diocese of Lincoln in the thirteenth century, that in 1233 the archdeacon is ordered to inquire whether any Anchorites' cells had been built without the Bishop's leave; and in many of our parish churches may be seen, either on the north or the south side of the chancel, a narrow slit in the wall, or one of the lights of a window prolonged downwards, the prolongation, if not now walled up, being closed with a shutter. Through these apertures the "incluse," or anker, watched the celebration of mass, and partook of the Holy Communion. Similar cells were to be found in Ireland, at least in the diocese of Ossory; and doubtless in Scotland also. Ducange, in his Glossary, on the word "inclusi," lays down rules for the size of the anker's cell, which must be twelve feet square, with three windows, one opening into the church, one for taking in his food, and one for light; and the "Salisbury Manual" as well as the "Pontifical" of Lacy, bishop of Exeter, in the first half of the fifteenth century, contains a regular "service" for the walling in of an anchorite. {330} There exists too a most singular and painful book, well known to antiquaries, but to them alone, "The Ancren Riwle," addressed to three young ladies who had immured themselves (seemingly about the beginning of the thirteenth century) at Kingston Tarrant, in Dorsetshire.

For women as well as men entered these living tombs; and there spent their days in dirt and starvation, and such prayer and meditation doubtless as the stupified and worn-out intellect could compass; their only recreation being the gossip of the neighbouring women, who came to peep in through the little window—a recreation in which (if we are to believe the author of "The Ancren Riwle") they were tempted to indulge only too freely; till the window of the recluse's cell, he says, became what the smith's forge or the alehouse has become since—the place where all the gossip and scandal of the village passed from one ear to another. But we must not believe such scandals of all. Only too much in earnest must those seven young maidens have been, whom St. Gilbert of Sempringham persuaded to immure themselves, as a sacrifice acceptable to God, in a den along the north wall of his church; or that St. Hutta, or Huetta, in the beginning of the thirteenth century, who after ministering to lepers, and longing and even trying to become a leper herself, immured herself for life in a cell against the church of Huy near Liege.

Fearful must have been the fate of these incluses if any evil had befallen the building of which (one may say) they had become a part. More than one in the stormy Middle Age may have suffered the fate of the poor women immured beside St. Mary's church at Mantes, who, when town and church were burnt by William the Conqueror, unable to escape (or, according to William of Malmesbury, thinking it unlawful to quit their cells even in that extremity), perished in the flames; and so consummated once and for all their long martyrdom.

How long the practice of the hermit life was common in these islands is more than my learning enables me to say. Hermits seem, from the old Chartularies, {331} to have been not unfrequent in Scotland and the North of England during the whole Middle Age. We have seen that they were frequent in the times of Malcolm Canmore and the old Celtic Church; and the Latin Church, which was introduced by St. Margaret, seems to have kept up the fashion. In the middle of the thirteenth century, David de Haigh conveyed to the monks of Cupar the hermitage which Gilmichael the Hermit once held, with three acres of land. In 1329 the Convent of Durham made a grant of a hermitage to Roger Eller at Norham on the Tweed, in order that he might have a "fit place to fight with the old enemy and bewail his sins, apart from the turmoil of men." In 1445 James the Second, king of Scots, granted to John Smith the hermitage in the forest of Kilgur, "which formerly belonged in heritage to Hugh Cominch the Hermit, and was resigned by him, with the croft and the green belonging to it, and three acres of arable land."

I have quoted these few instances, to show how long the custom lingered; and doubtless hermits were to be found in the remoter parts of these realms when the sudden tempest of the Reformation swept away alike the palace of the rich abbot and the cell of the poor recluse, and exterminated throughout England the ascetic life. The two last hermits whom I have come across in history are both figures which exemplify very well those times of corruption and of change. At Loretto (not in Italy, but in Musselburgh, near Edinburgh) there lived a hermit who pretended to work miracles, and who it seems had charge of some image of "Our Lady of Loretto." The scandals which ensued from the visits of young folks to this hermit roused the wrath of that terrible scourge of monks, Sir David Lindsay of the Mount: yet as late as 1536, James the Fifth of Scotland made a pilgrimage from Stirling to the shrine, in order to procure a propitious passage to France in search of a wife. But in 1543, Lord Hertford, during his destructive voyage to the Forth, destroyed, with other objects of greater consequence, the chapel of the "Lady of Lorett," which was not likely in those days to be rebuilt; and so the hermit of Musselburgh vanishes from history.

A few years before, in 1537, says Mr. Froude, {333} while the harbours, piers, and fortresses were rising in Dover, "an ancient hermit tottered night after night from his cell to a chapel on the cliff, and the tapers on the altar before which he knelt in his lonely orisons made a familiar beacon far over the rolling waters. The men of the rising world cared little for the sentiment of the past. The anchorite was told sternly by the workmen that his light was a signal to the King's enemies" (a Spanish invasion from Flanders was expected), "and must burn no more; and, when it was next seen, three of them waylaid the old man on his way home, threw him down and beat him cruelly."

So ended, in an undignified way, as worn-out institutions are wont to end, the hermit life in the British Isles. Will it ever reappear? Who can tell? To an age of luxury and unbelief has succeeded, more than once in history, an age of remorse and superstition. Gay gentlemen and gay ladies may renounce the world, as they did in the time of St Jerome, when the world is ready to renounce them. We have already our nunneries, our monasteries, of more creeds than one; and the mountains of Kerry, or the pine forests of the Highlands, may some day once more hold hermits, persuading themselves to believe, and at last succeeding in believing, the teaching of St. Antony, instead of that of our Lord Jesus Christ, and of that Father of the spirits of all flesh, who made love, and marriage, and little children, sunshine and flowers, the wings of butterflies and the song of birds; who rejoices in his own works, and bids all who truly reverence him rejoice in them with him. The fancy may seem impossible. It is not more impossible than many religious phenomena seemed forty years ago, which are now no fancies, but powerful facts.

The following books should be consulted by those who wish to follow out this curious subject in detail:—

The "Vitae Patrum Eremiticorum."

The "Acta Sanctorum." The Bollandists are, of course, almost exhaustive of any subject on which they treat. But as they are difficult to find, save in a few public libraries, the "Acta Sanctorum" of Surius, or of Aloysius Lipommasius, may be profitably consulted. Butler's "Lives of the Saints" is a book common enough, but of no great value.

M. de Montalembert's "Moines d'Occident," and Ozanam's "Etudes Germaniques," may be read with much profit.

Dr. Reeves' edition of Adamnan's "Life of St. Columba," published by the Irish Archaeological and Celtic Society, is a treasury of learning, which needs no praise of mine.

The lives of St. Cuthbert and St. Godric may be found among the publications of the Surtees Society.

Footnotes:

{12} About A.D. 368. See the details in Ammianus Marcellinus, lib. xxviii.

{15} In the Celtic Irish Church, there seems to have been no other pattern. The hermits who became abbots, with their monks, were the only teachers of the people—one had almost said, the only Christians. Whence, as early as the sixth century, if not the fifth, they, and their disciples of Iona and Scotland, derived their peculiar tonsure, their use of bells, their Eastern mode of keeping the Paschal feast, and other peculiarities, seemingly without the intervention of Rome, is a mystery still unsolved.

{17a} A book which, from its bearing on present problems, well deserves translation.

{17b} "Vitae Patrum." Published at Antwerp, 1628.

{23} He is addressing our Lord.

{24} "Agentes in rebus." On the Emperor's staff?

{27} St. Augustine says, that Potitianus's adventure at Treves happened "I know not when." His own conversation with Potitianus must have happened about A.D. 385, for he was baptized April 25, A.D. 387. He does not mention the name of Potitianus's emperor: but as Gratian was Augustus from A.D. 367 to A.D. 375, and actual Emperor of the West till A.D. 383, and as Treves was his usual residence, he is most probably the person meant: but if not, then his father Valentinian.

{29} See the excellent article on Gratian in Smith's Dictionary, by Mr. Means.

{30} I cannot explain this fact: but I have seen it with my own eyes.

{32} I use throughout the text published by Heschelius, in 1611.

{33} He is said to have been born at Coma, near Heracleia, in Middle Egypt, A.D. 251.

{34} Seemingly the Greek language and literature.

{35} I have thought it more honest to translate [Greek text] by "training," which is now, as then, its true equivalent; being a metaphor drawn from the Greek games by St. Paul, 1 Tim. iv. 8.

{41} I give this passage as it stands in the Greek version. In the Latin, attributed to Evagrius, it is even more extravagant and rhetorical.

{42} Surely the imagery painted on the inner walls of Egyptian tombs, and probably believed by Antony and his compeers to be connected with devil-worship, explain these visions. In the "Words of the Elders" a monk complains of being troubled with "pictures, old and new." Probably, again, the pain which Antony felt was the agony of a fever; and the visions which he saw, its delirium.

{44} Here is an instance of the original use of the word "monastery," viz. a cell in which a single person dwelt.

{45} An allusion to the heathen mysteries.

{49} A.D. 311. Galerius Valerius Maximinus (his real name was Daza) had been a shepherd-lad in Illyria, like his uncle Galerius Valerius Maximianus; and rose, like him, through the various grades of the army to be co-Emperor of Rome, over Syria, Egypt, and Asia Minor; a furious persecutor of the Christians, and a brutal and profligate tyrant. Such were the "kings of the world" from whom those old monks fled.

{52a} The lonely alluvial flats at the mouths of the Nile. "Below the cliffs, beside the sea," as one describes them.

{52b} Now the monastery of Deir Antonios, over the Wady el Arabah, between the Nile and the Red Sea, where Antony's monks endure to this day.

{60} This most famous monastery, i.e. collection of monks' cells, in Egypt is situate forty miles from Alexandria, on a hill where nitre was gathered. The hospitality and virtue of its inmates are much praised by Ruffinus and Palladius. They were, nevertheless, the chief agents in the fanatical murder of Hypatia.

{65} It appears from this and many other passages, that extempore prayer was usual among these monks, as it was afterwards among the Puritans (who have copied them in so many other things), whenever a godly man visited them.

{66a} Meletius, bishop of Lycopolis, was the author of an obscure schism calling itself the "Church of the Martyrs," which refused to communicate with the rest of the Eastern Church. See Smith's "Dictionary," on the word "Meletius."

{66b} Arius (whose most famous and successful opponent was Athanasius, the writer of this biography) maintained that the Son of God was not co-equal and co-eternal with the Father, but created by Him out of nothing, and before the world. His opinions were condemned in the famous Council of Nicaea, A.D. 325.

{67} If St. Antony could use so extreme an argument against the Arians, what would he have said to the Mariolatry which sprang up after his death?

{68a} I.e. those who were still heathens.

{68b} [Greek text]. The Christian priest is always called in this work simply [Greek text], or elder.

{72a} Probably that of A.D. 341, when Gregory of Cappadocia, nominated by the Arian Bishops, who had assembled at the Council of Antioch, expelled Athanasius from the see of Alexandria, and great violence was committed by his followers and by Philagrius the Prefect. Athanasius meanwhile fled to Rome.

{72b} I.e. celebrated there their own Communion.

{77} Evidently the primaeval custom of embalming the dead, and keeping mummies in the house, still lingered among the Egyptians.

{108} These sounds, like those which St. Guthlac heard in the English fens, are plainly those of wild-fowl.

{115} The Brucheion, with its palaces and museum, the residence of the kings and philosophers of Egypt, had been destroyed is the days of Claudius and Valerian, during the senseless civil wars which devastated Alexandria for twelve years; and monks had probably taken up their abode in the ruins. It was in this quarter, at the beginning of the next century, that Hypatia was murdered by the monks.

{116} Probably the Northern, or Lesser Oasis, Ouah el Baharieh, about eighty miles west of the Nile.

{117a} Jerome (who sailed that sea several times) uses the word here, as it is used in Acts xxvii. 27, for the sea about Malta, "driven up and down in Adria."

{117b} The southern point of Sicily, now Cape Passaro.

{118} In the Morea, near the modern Navarino.

{119a} At the mouth of the Bay of Cattaro.

{119b} This story—whatever belief we may give to its details—is one of many which make it tolerably certain that a large snake (Python) still lingered in Eastern Europe. Huge tame snakes were kept as sacred by the Macedonian women; and one of them (according to Lucian) Peregrinus Proteus, the Cagliostro of his time, fitted with a linen mask, and made it personate the god AEsculapius. In the "Historia Lausiaca," cap. lii. is an account by an eye-witness of a large snake in the Thebaid, whose track was "as if a beam had been dragged along the sand." It terrifies the Syrian monks: but the Egyptian monk sets to work to kill it, saying that he had seen much larger—even up to fifteen cubits.

{121} Now Capo St. Angelo and the island of Cerigo, at the southern point of Greece.

{123a} See p. 52. [Around footnote 52a in the text—DP.]

{123b} Probably dedicated to the Paphian Venus.

{130} The lives of these two hermits and that of St. Cuthbert will be given in a future number.

{131} Sihor, the black river, was the ancient name of the Nile, derived from the dark hue of its waters.

{159} Ammianus Marcellinus, Book xxv. cap. 9.

{160} By Dr. Burgess.

{163} History of Christianity, vol. iii. p. 109.

{203} An authentic fact.

{204} If any one doubts this, let him try the game called "Russian scandal," where a story, passed secretly from mouth to mouth, ends utterly transformed, the original point being lost, a new point substituted, original names and facts omitted, and utterly new ones inserted, &c. &c.; an experiment which is ludicrous, or saddening, according to the temper of the experimenter.

{209} Les Moines d'Occident, vol. ii. pp. 332-467.

{210} M. La Borderie, "Discours sur les Saints Bretons;" a work which I have unfortunately not been able to consult.

{212a} Vitae Patrum, p. 753.

{212b} Ibid. p. 893.

{212c} Ibid. p. 539.

{212d} Ibid. p. 540.

{212e} Ibid. p. 532.

{224} It has been handed down, in most crabbed Latin, by his disciple, Eugippius; it may be read at length in Pez, Scriptores Austriacarum Rerum.

{238} Scriptores Austriacarum Rerum.

{245} Haeften, quoted by Montalembert, vol. ii. p. 22, in note.

{256} Dr. Reeves supposes these to have been "crustacea:" but their stinging and clinging prove them surely to have been jelly-fish— medusae.

{257} I have followed the Latin prose version of it, which M. Achille Jubinal attributes to the eleventh century. Here and there I have taken the liberty of using the French prose version, which he attributes to the latter part of the twelfth. I have often condensed the story, where it was prolix or repeated itself: but I have tried to follow faithfully both matter and style, and to give, word for word, as nearly as I could, any notable passages. Those who wish to know more of St. Brendan should consult the learned brochure of M. Jubinal, "La Legende Latine de St. Brandaines," and the two English versions of the Legend, edited by Mr. Thomas Wright for the Percy Society, vol. xiv. One is in verse, and of the earlier part of the fourteenth century, and spirited enough: the other, a prose version, was printed by Wynkyn de Worde, in his edition of the "Golden Legend;" 1527.

{260a} In the Barony of Longford, County Galway.

{260b} 3,000, like 300, seems to be, I am informed, only an Irish expression for any large number.

{269} Some dim legend concerning icebergs, and caves therein.

{270} Probably from reports of the volcanic coast of Iceland.

{272} This part of the legend has been changed and humanized as time ran on. In the Latin and French versions it has little or no point or moral. In the English, Judas accounts for the presence of the cloth thus:—

"Here I may see what it is to give other men's (goods) with harm. As will many rich men with unright all day take, Of poor men here and there, and almisse (alms) sithhe (afterwards) make."

For the tongs and the stone he accounts by saying that, as he used them for "good ends, each thing should surely find him which he did for God's love."

But in "the prose version of Wynkyn de Worde, the tongs have been changed into "ox-tongues," "which I gave some tyme to two preestes to praye for me. I bought them with myne owne money, and therefore they ease me, bycause the fysshes of the sea gnaw on them, and spare me."

This latter story of the ox-tongues has been followed by Mr. Sebastian Evans, in his poem on St. Brendan. Both he and Mr. Matthew Arnold have rendered the moral of the English version very beautifully.

{274} Copied, surely, from the life of Paul the first hermit.

{283} The famous Cathach, now in the museum of the Royal Irish Academy, was long popularly believed to be the very Psalter in question. As a relic of St. Columba it was carried to battle by the O'Donnels, even as late as 1497, to insure victory for the clan.

{290} Bede, book iii. cap. 3.

{292} These details, and countless stories of St. Cuthbert's miracles, are to be found in Reginald of Durham, "De Admirandis Beati Cuthberti," published by the Surtees Society. This curious book is admirably edited by Mr. J. Raine; with an English synopsis at the end, which enables the reader for whom the Latin is too difficult to enjoy those pictures of life under Stephen and Henry II., whether moral, religious, or social, of which the book is a rich museum.

{299} "In this hole lie the bones of the Venerable Bede."

{303} An English translation of the Anglo-Saxon life has been published by Mr. Godwin, of Cambridge, and is well worth perusal.

{312} Vita S. Godrici, pp. 332, 333.

{316} The earlier one; that of the Harleian MSS. which (Mr. Stevenson thinks) was twice afterwards expanded and decorated by him.

{323} Reginald wants to make "a wonder incredible in our own times," of a very common form (thank God) of peaceful death. He makes miracles in the same way of the catching of salmon and of otters, simple enough to one who, like Godric, knew the river, and every wild thing which haunted it.

{330} That of the Salisbury Manual is published in the "Ecclesiologist" for August 1848, by the Rev. Sir W. H. Cope, to whom I am indebted for the greater number of these curious facts.

{331} I owe these facts to the courtesy of Mr. John Stuart, of the General Register Office, Edinburgh.

{333} "History of England," vol. iii. p. 256, note.

Lightning Source UK Ltd.
Milton Keynes UK
UKHW040038121122
412046UK00001B/105